"Poaching big game . . . check. A loveable yellow Lab . . . double check. Computer hackers from India . . . WHAT! That last item is the big checklist twist in outdoor writer Rob Phillips' latest novel, *Cascade Kidnapping*, the fourth in his Luke McCain series. As in all of Phillips' books, *Cascade Kidnapping* reinforces healthy respect for the outdoors and laws that protect it."
    –Bob Crider, retired editor and publisher, *Yakima Herald-Republic*

"*Cascade Kidnapping* has Washington State game warden Luke McCain and his yellow Lab, Jack, arresting salmon poachers, investigating a serial elk killer, and dealing with administrative duties. . . . Phillips' writing displays a real knowledge of the outdoors, as well as the duties and responsibilities of game wardens. A very enjoyable book!!"
    –Rich Phillips, book reviewer for the *International Game Warden Magazine*

"*Cascade Predator* is a well-blended stew of Northwest icons, a reflection of Rob's intimate knowledge of wildlife, outdoor realism, and page-turning curveballs that is just flat tough to put down. This latest edition to the Luke McCain series confirms Rob Phillips' standing as a skilled mystery writer. Already I want to read another."
    –Terry W. Sheely, northwest author and writer

"This is crime fiction at its finest–the perfect blend of a compelling mystery, a fabulous setting, the best dog ever, and a very likeable hero you won't forget."
    –Christine Carbo, award-winning author of the Glacier Mystery Series

"*Cascade Vengeance* takes readers on a thrill ride through the dual worlds of drug dealing and big-game hunting deep in Washington's Cascade mountains. Rob Phillips uses his extensive knowledge of the region to tell the fast-moving tale . . . on the way to the story's harrowing and heartbreaking conclusion."

–Scott Graham, National Outdoor Book Award-winning author of *Mesa Verde Victim*

"Rob Phillips delivers another page turner. *Cascade Vengeance* is full of murder, intrigue and suspense. And just when you think the case is solved, Phillips throws you a curveball. If you enjoyed *The Cascade Killer*, you'll love Phillips's latest in the Luke McCain series."

–Pat Hoglund, publisher of *Western Hunting Journal, Traveling Angler*, and *Salmon & Steelhead Journal*

"*Cascade Vengeance*, the second book in the Luke McCain series, is another hang-onto-your-hat, nonstop action episode with Luke, a Washington State Fish and Wildlife officer, his FBI girlfriend Sara, and Jack, his loyal yellow Lab. I felt like I was riding shotgun in Luke's Ford pickup, bouncing along forest service roads where very bad guys might be lurking."

–Susan Richmond, owner of Inklings Bookshop

"Another fast-paced, exciting chapter in the Luke McCain series that remains true to the Pacific Northwest. Phillips leaves readers with a splendid conclusion, helping us wonder when the next Luke McCain volume will be out. I am truly a fan of Luke and Jack!"

–Vikki J. Carter, host & producer of *Authors of the Pacific Northwest Podcast*

"If you're looking for an enjoyable read out in deer camp or for just sitting next to your fireplace, then *The Cascade Killer* is a definite winner."

–John McAdams, author of *The Big Game Hunting Blog* & host of *The Big Game Hunting Podcast*

"Real! Captivating! Once you start, you can't put it down! *The Cascade Killer* is VERY well done!"

–Scott Haugen, host and producer of *The Hunt* and author of numerous outdoor books

CASCADE MANHUNT

Book and cover design by Kevin Breen
Cover image derived from Adobe Stock photos

ISBN: 978-1-957607-21-4
Cataloging-in-Publication Data is available upon request

Manufactured in the United States of America

Published by
Latah Books, Spokane, Washington
www.latahbooks.com

The author may be contacted at yakimahunter@yahoo.com

CASCADE
MAN
HUNT

A LUKE MCCAIN NOVEL

ROB PHILLIPS

LATAH
BOOKS

DEDICATION

To Terri, Kyle, Kevin, Joi and Ayomi

CHAPTER 1

Claude Rakes was big for his age. From the time he started grade school in Havre, Montana, he was always the biggest kid in his class. He had a big square-shaped head covered in curly brown hair, big arms attached to wide shoulders, and big legs too. He was also slow—a slow walker and a slow talker. Unfortunately, he was judged by the way he looked and talked and acted. Early on, he was labeled as mentally retarded. Today, the experts, and anyone with a caring bone in their bodies, would call him "special."

Rakes' so-called friends called him "Dirt." As in dirt clod. All the other kids weren't so nice. They just called Rakes "the retard."

"There goes the retard. Where you going, retard?" they would say to his face.

When the adults heard the kids, they would scold them for calling Rakes names. Behind closed doors, however, they also called the slow-walking, slow-talking man-child retarded.

In reality, Claude Rakes was very intelligent. When he was a junior in high school, he was given an intelligence test, along with the rest of the students in his psychology class, and he scored higher than every other kid in the class, including three straight-A students who often made fun of him for being "dense" and "slow."

The teacher of the class had been confused by the results of the test. He'd wondered if Rakes might have cheated. If so, how had he done it? When he asked the boy about the test results, Rakes just smiled, and with a dead, cold look in his eyes, told the teacher he liked to read, saying, "I just know things."

On another test the psychology teacher gave his students that semester, he learned something else about Claude Rakes. The test answers showed the boy was most likely a sociopath and possibly a psychopath. As the teacher reviewed Rakes' test results, the hair on the back of his neck stood up. He remembered the look in the boy's eyes when he had asked about the intelligence test. A shiver as cold as a January Montana wind went down his spine.

A year later, after the boy (then the size of an NFL lineman) graduated from Havre High, the teacher was pleased to learn that Rakes had taken a job as a driver for an auto parts company in Great Falls. As far as he knew, Rakes was gone, never to be heard from again. That is, until a dozen years later when Rakes made the national news after he was arrested in Washington State and charged with the murder of a nineteen-year-old exotic dancer near Spokane.

When the high school teacher, now retired and living in Billings, learned that Claude Rakes had been arrested for that murder and was currently the prime suspect in several other cases of missing or murdered women in Washington, Idaho, Montana, and Wyoming, he started to shake uncontrollably. It was an 84-degree August day, but the January cold was again running down his spine.

The results from Rakes' psychology test immediately came to mind. Why hadn't he shared those with anyone? Maybe if he had, those women would be alive today.

He thought back to those years in Havre. The big, slow boy everyone thought of as mentally challenged had fooled everyone. Even though he looked and acted slow and stupid, Claude Rakes was anything but.

*

It hadn't taken Rakes long to get out of Havre after graduation that June. He was in a hurry. Not only did he want to get away from all the people who had bullied him, but he didn't want to be around when they found the body of a woman who had been especially vile toward him.

The woman, a divorcée who had blown into town the year before from who-knows-where, worked at one of the mini-marts in town. She was never vocal about her disdain for Rakes when he came into the store, but she would always treat him like an outcast when he stopped for food or a drink. On one particularly blustery day in late May, when he wasn't looking, she spit into his burrito before she sold it to him.

A few minutes later, she watched Rakes take a bite of the flour shell as he stood out by his truck near the gas pumps. As he chewed, he turned and gave her the evilest smile she had ever seen. In that instant, she knew he knew what she had done.

The mini-mart closed at eleven that evening, and as the woman went to her car, she noticed an old white Ford pickup drive by. She couldn't see the driver, but she had a feeling that whoever was behind the wheel was looking at her. She thought of the giant kid who gave her the creeps. But it wasn't the truck he was always in. He drove a blue Chevy.

Her gut was telling her not to go home. Maybe she should go to the tavern where she knew some of the regulars. There were a couple of guys there who she would hook up with every now and then. One of them would surely be up for taking her to his place.

But she was tired. Too tired for all that. So she headed straight for the pre-1990s double-wide manufactured home that she was renting out east of town. The place was a dump. It had cracks around the windows that let in the frigid temperatures in the winter. The ceiling over the kitchen leaked during heavy rains, but the place was cheap, and she didn't need much. The other nice thing about it was the landlord was a decent guy. When she was late with the rent, which occurred often, he would wait several days before he came asking her for a check.

When she pulled up to the small double-wide, which sat out in what could only be best described as a pasture, she saw nothing out of the ordinary. She parked her old Pontiac Fiero next to a big plastic garbage can and an antique push mower, turned off the lights, and climbed the three wooden steps to the front door.

The woman was of average height but very slim. She was a smoker. Whenever she got hungry, she would light up a cigarette and think about the shitty food they served at the mini-mart. That almost always took her mind off eating.

Tonight, though, even after what was probably her twentieth cigarette of the day, she was still hungry. She pulled a store-bought macaroni and cheese dinner out of the freezer and tossed it in the microwave.

As the small oven hummed away, she thought she heard a noise outside. She looked out the window over the sink but saw nothing. Sometimes racoons or stray dogs got into her trash can, so she went to the front door and stepped out to take a look.

Rakes was on her with unbelievable speed for a big "slow" man. He wrapped a muscled arm around her chest and covered her mouth with his large, gloved hand to muffle any scream. Then, with his hand still on her face, he pushed hard backwards and snapped her skinny neck.

Four minutes later, Rakes was walking through the black of night, across the pasture, to a little creek. He followed the creek a mile to where he had hidden his old man's pickup. Before Rakes left the house, he had stripped the woman naked, placed her into the bathtub, and turned the water on. He placed her wobbly neck over the side of the tub and then he spit in her face.

"That's for the burrito, bitch!" he said to her dead face, blank eyes staring up at him.

Rakes figured only a top-notch coroner would be able to tell the difference between a broken neck from a bathroom accident and homicide. The coroner in Havre was not top-notch. In fact, he was a tired old physician who had given up his license to practice medicine eleven years before, when the threat of a messy malpractice suit reared its ugly head. Still, the townsfolk believed he was the best man for the job—because heck, he wasn't going to kill anyone, they were already dead—so every four years they re-elected him.

Three days later, the landlord, coming to collect another late check, discovered the dead woman. He heard water running and saw the woman's Fiero in front of the house, so he decided to let himself in to see what was going on when she didn't answer his knock at the door.

When the coroner finished with his autopsy a week later, it was his belief that the woman, who very few people even knew, had slipped in the tub. Just another slip-and-fall in his medical opinion. A tragic death, for sure, but a good reminder to everyone to be careful getting into and out of the bathtub.

High school graduation was two days later, and when all the other seniors were headed out to an all-night party, Rakes went home, loaded his few worldly possessions into the back of his pickup, drove west out of town, and then south on Highway 87 toward Great Falls.

As he drove through the night, watching closely to avoid any deer or antelope that might be crossing the highway, he thought about killing the skinny mini-mart woman. He had no regrets. Nor did he find any real thrill in it. It was just something he'd needed to do.

To Rakes it was no different than the time his old man had told him to go round up the kittens their farm cat had birthed in the barn.

"We don't need no more cats around here," Rakes' father had said. "I don't care what you do with 'em, just get 'em gone."

Rakes had taken each of the small kittens and quickly and efficiently broken their necks and tossed them in the burn barrel. Again, he found no joy in it, and had no regrets. It was something that needed to be done, and he'd done it.

*

Four years after he'd killed the mini-mart woman in Havre, Rakes killed again. He had deliveries in Billings and was eating at an all-night diner near the interstate when a girl he had gone to high school with walked into the restaurant. Rakes had watched her, with another woman, drive up and park in a space across the parking lot. The girl's name was Gina Bender, and she spotted Rakes as soon as she walked through the door. When she did, she turned to the woman and whispered something. Then they started laughing.

The reaction was nothing new to Rakes. But it had been a while since he had seen it. When Rakes lived in Havre, he saw it all the time. But he had been able to blend in more in the much larger Great Falls. And, while he still didn't have any real friends, at least no one was calling him names. And they certainly weren't laughing at him.

At that moment, when the two women started laughing, he knew he was going to kill them.

The women walked to a booth on the other side of the dining area and sat down. Once in a while, they'd look at Rakes, and whisper, and laugh some more.

When he was done with his dinner, Rakes walked over to them. His huge frame dwarfed the two women sitting in the booth.

"Hi Gina," Rakes said. "I see you remember me."

"How could I forget," Bender said, looking up at him.

"You live around here now?" Rakes asked.

"Not that it's any of your business, but Jen and I are just passing through, headed to Wyoming."

Rakes just stood there and looked at them.

"Is there anything else?" Bender finally said. "We'd like to eat our meal in peace."

"Nice to see you, Gina," Rakes said as he turned to walk out.

"Uh-huh," Bender said. And then, under her breath but just loud enough for Rakes to hear, she said "retard." The two women laughed again.

They didn't see the smile on Rakes' face as he walked out of the restaurant. If they had, they would have been terrified.

*

The women were found four days later, their car stashed in some brush along a creek just off Highway 310 in Big Horn County, Wyoming. Officers who were called in to investigate the deaths quickly determined the women had been murdered. They'd discovered a small puncture in the gas line of the women's car, and they had run out of gas. The media release didn't say anything about how the women had been killed, but the investigators knew.

One woman, who was identified by her driver's license as Gina Bender of Havre, Montana, had such a severely broken neck that her head was turned 180 degrees and was facing upward while her body was frontside down across the back seat. The other woman, identified as Jennifer Morris of Fort Benton, Montana, had also died of a broken neck. Her face showed signs of being hit hard by something, and she was most likely unconscious when she died.

Most disturbing to the investigators was that the dead women had smiles on their faces when they were discovered. Closer examination showed that extremely thin monofilament fishing line had been rigged around the women's heads, tied to small fish hooks that had been buried inside the corners of their mouths. The line was hidden by the women's hair, and it was set perfectly, pulled tight to force their mouths into ugly, macabre smiles.

*

Rakes had never spent much time thinking about why people had been so cruel to him. He got it. He saw himself in the mirror when he shaved each morning. He wasn't someone who was easy to look at. But ridiculing him, or anyone for that matter, for how they looked or talked never sat right with him. Killing Gina and that other woman for laughing at him meant there were two fewer people in the world that would do it again. To him or anyone else.

After killing the two, as he drove farther into Wyoming, Rakes thought about the women. He'd rigged their mouths into a smile as a way of telling whoever saw them that it was the reason for their deaths. Whether anyone would get it or not, Rakes didn't care.

It was fascinating to him how quickly he could end someone's life. In less than five seconds, he could send someone into the afterlife. It didn't bother him, but it did interest him. Right or wrong, he had done what he did because he believed it needed to be done. Just like the kittens in the barn.

He knew there was a pretty good chance that one day he might end up in the electric chair for murdering the women, and when that day came, if it came, Rakes would deal with it.

CHAPTER 2

To those closest to him, Luke McCain still looked like Luke McCain. But to the rest of the world, including those who may have seen his face on TV or in a newspaper article, he would be hard to recognize. The beard he had grown was thick, dark, and somewhat unkempt, with just a sprinkling of gray here and there. His black hair was long, over his ears and collar. And he wore dark-rimmed glasses with lenses that had no prescription in them, giving him a look of someone right out of the 1960s.

The transformation into a new person did not include changing his imposing body size. Luke, now almost forty years old, still stood nearly six-foot-five inches tall and weighed 227 pounds. His weight was made up mostly of muscle and included a six-pack most men would kill for.

It had taken Luke five months to grow his beard and hair out to take on a new identity. When he arrived in Colville as Luke Haynes, he looked like just another dude who might be trying to get away from a former life, searching for a new start.

As he drove into town on that early April day, it was spitting snow. Spring sometimes took its time arriving in northeastern Washington. Luke parked his white 1994 Ford Bronco in front of the sawmill office and jumped out. The older rig looked just like the Bronco O.J. Simpson drove in the infamous slow police chase on the freeway in southern California.

Ever since the Covid pandemic, businesses around the state were hurting for good employees, and the Colville mill was no exception. Luke saw the "help wanted" sign in the front window and walked into the office. It smelled of sawdust, Christmas trees, and old lady perfume.

"How can we help you, young man?" a stern-looking, white-haired woman asked as she looked at Luke over glasses that had migrated almost to the tip of her nose.

"I'm new to town and looking for work," Luke said.

The lady, whose name was Agnes Huff according to a small name plate on her desk, looked Luke up and down and said, "You got any experience?"

"Yes, ma'am. I worked at Boise Cascade in Oregon a few years ago and did some work with the U.S. Forest Service during a couple of summers after high school."

"So, you're college educated?" Huff asked, picking up on the reference to the summer work.

"Some college, ma'am," Luke said. "But I never finished. Me and studying never got along."

"How long you been in town?"

"Just got here. I did some hunting up this way a few years back and really liked the area and the town. Don't even have a place to stay yet, but when I saw the sign in your window, I decided to come in."

Huff stared at Luke for a minute or so, like she was trying to figure him out. Then she reached into a desk drawer and pulled out some papers. "Fill these out. I'll need to check some references. You got a phone?"

"Yes, ma'am," Luke said and gave her his cell number.

*

As an enforcement officer with the Washington State Department of Fish and Wildlife, Luke had done a few other undercover assignments, but they were always short gigs. Once he had impersonated a hunter looking to buy a mountain goat hunt. In just two days, he had arrested the man who was illegally selling the hunts. Another time, he and another officer had worked a sting on two men who were illegally catching and retaining sturgeon on the Columbia River.

This new operation was going to be much more involved and time-consuming. In fact, it could take weeks, even months, to finally get everything needed to make arrests with enough evidence to convict the criminals.

Over the past year, the Department of Fish and Wildlife had received tips that a small group of men were poaching deer, elk, bear, cougars, wolves, and turkeys around northeastern Washington. Local wildlife officers had stopped a man identified as one of the poachers, but at that time the man was legal. He had a three-point white-tailed buck in his possession. The deer was taken during the late season hunt and was tagged legally. The man had a current Washington State license and everything checked out.

Still, the scuttlebutt was the man was one of those who had been involved in a month's long spree of killing wildlife out of season. There were also reports of them selling meat, hides, antlers, claws, gallbladders, and other animal parts.

At one point, after a reliable tip, WDFW officers obtained a warrant to search a house and garage of one of the suspected poachers. When they arrived, they found nothing but two suspiciously empty freezers. The man had no rifles or any other hunting equipment, and there was no sign that he had ever hunted a day in his life.

Still, the calls came in. Some of the local hunters were getting increasingly unhappy with the local game wardens because nothing was happening to try to stop this group from what was believed to be consistent poaching.

It was around that time that Luke was called into his captain's office.

"Olympia had a request for some assistance on a suspected poaching ring up around Colville," Bob Davis said. The captain had the physique of an aging college football player, which he was. He had brown hair going to gray and a big bushy gray mustache that made some folks think of Wilfred Brimley. "They want someone young and fit from outside the area to try to get in with these guys. The director has requested you."

"Gee, it's nice to be wanted," Luke said. "I'm surprised the director even knows who I am. But I'm not so sure Sara is going to be wild about me leaving. This sounds like it could take some time."

"I'm sure it will," Davis said. "We had a similar case back in the '90s, and the officer who went undercover was out-of-pocket for nearly four months. I'm not sure you can say no, being it comes from so high up."

"Okay, let me talk to Sara."

*

The discussion with his wife went smoother than Luke had anticipated. As it turned out, Sara, who was a special agent with the FBI working out of the Yakima office, had a big case she was going to be investigating and wouldn't be home much either.

"What about Jack?" Luke asked.

Jack was their hundred-pound yellow Labrador retriever. The big dog often went afield with Luke during his days patrolling the Cascade Mountains and other areas of central Washington.

"You can't take him with you?"

"I don't think so. I'd love to have him along, but I don't know what I'm getting into yet."

"Well, if we need to have someone feed him, I think Austin or Jessie could handle it if I'm working late."

Jessie Meyers and her son Austin were neighbors across the street from Luke and Sara. Jessie had divorced Austin's father eight years before, and Luke had taken Austin under his wing, taking him fishing and hunting. Luke had even helped Austin get his driver's license and buy his first truck.

"I'm sure they'd be happy to do that," Luke said.

Over the years, Jack had spent many hours at the Meyers' house. After Austin got a dog of his own, a yellow Lab named Bear, the two dogs had become great friends.

"So, when would you need to go?" Sara asked.

"Not for a while. I need to grow a beard and let my hair grow out a bit first. Captain Davis is worried that I might be recognizable after my photo was on the national news when we captured that alligator a while back."

"A beard? I'm not sure I'm going to like you in a beard."

"Well, it'll only last for a while, and who knows, you might just like it."

"I don't think so. Hide that handsome face under a bunch of whiskers? Beards have never done much for me."

Luke never thought of himself as handsome. Before he met Sara, he'd had a couple girlfriends and been on plenty of dates, but he always thought his best attribute, besides being in good physical shape, was his personality.

"Maybe there will be a lady or two in Colville that like a tall man with a beard?" Luke said with a grin.

"You do remember I carry a pistol, don't you?" Sara said, giving him a look through squinted eyes.

"You wouldn't shoot me, would you?"

"No, but I might come hunting anyone who comes after my man."

"I'll be sure to tell them that."

Sara walked over and put her arms around Luke, burying her head in his chest.

"You better," she said. "I'm going to miss you, for sure. And Jack, he's going to go crazy."

"I'm going to miss Jack too."

Sara waited for a few seconds and then stepped back and

looked up at Luke, again with the squinted eyes. He reached out and pulled her back in for another hug.

"And I am REALLY going to miss you," Luke said. "But we don't have to worry about any of that just yet. Lots of pieces have to fall into place before I go undercover."

*

Luke had just checked into one of the cheaper mom and pop motels in Colville when his phone rang. He didn't recognize the number, but since it was a 509 area code, he figured it must be the lady from the mill.

"Hi, this is Luke."

"This is Agnes Huff. Can you come in tomorrow morning at eight? We have a couple more questions for you, and the main boss wants to meet you."

"Sure thing," Luke said. "See you at eight. And thank you, Mizz Huff."

"You can call me Agnes. See you at eight."

The phone went dead, and Luke set it on the table. The computer wizards with the Department of Fish and Wildlife's Special Investigations Unit in Olympia had spent a great deal of time setting up the background for Luke Haynes, a 35-year-old single man from Roseburg, Oregon.

They had gotten Luke a current driver's license, a Social Security card, a debit card, and a credit card from US Bank, established a credit history and a criminal history, which consisted of a couple of speeding tickets, some unpaid parking tickets, and a night in jail for a bar fight. From where he went to grade school through high school and two years at a community college, they built Luke a new identity. One that would hold up.

The phone numbers Luke had listed all went to special cell phones at the Department of Fish and Wildlife and were answered accordingly based on which phone rang. The people answering the phones all gave Luke glowing recommendations.

"One of our best workers," the COO at Boise Cascade in Eugene told Agnes Huff.

"Hated to lose him," the owner of a local lumberyard in Medford had said.

*

At 7:55 the following morning, Luke walked through the front office door at the mill. He was dressed for work, just in case they hired him on the spot. The aroma of fresh coffee was now mixed with the smells of trees and cheap perfume.

"You're five minutes early," Agnes Huff said as Luke closed the door behind him.

"My father impressed on me that five minutes early is on time, and you need to be ready to start work when the bell rings."

Huff again looked at Luke like he might have just stepped off a spaceship.

"By the way, good morning, Agnes," Luke said with a grin as she stared at him.

In an instant, he saw the gruff office manager's attitude change just slightly. He even saw the tiniest of smiles appear on her round face.

"Mike should be in in just a couple minutes. Would you like some coffee?" she asked.

"No thanks. I'm fine. Mike is the main boss?"

"He is, yes. Mike Robertson. He runs a tight ship, but is fair, and everyone likes working for him."

Luke just nodded his head as if to say, good to know.

Huff was just about to ask a question, probably a personal one, Luke thought, when the back door to the main office opened and in walked a man of about fifty. He was average height and had a neatly trimmed light reddish-brown beard that wrapped around a small mouth under a large nose. The nose featured the telltale red spider veins of a man who had either done a lot of drinking in his days or had some other medical issue. A red baseball cap with a Stihl chainsaw and logo on the front covered the man's head. The red hat only accentuated the veins on his nose.

"You must be Luke," Robertson said as he walked toward Luke offering a hand to shake.

"Yes sir, Luke Haynes. Nice to meet you," Luke said as he shook the man's hand.

Robertson, like many men of his age, had let himself go. What was probably once a fit, slender body now featured a large belly perched on two skinny legs. And, as Sara would say, "the man had no ass." Robertson wore blue denim Wrangler jeans, a blue denim long-sleeve shirt, and red suspenders that, even at the start of the day, were already working overtime to hold his jeans in place.

Luke noticed that Robertson also wore a belt. Possibly the sign of a man who had trust issues. Or maybe he just really didn't want his britches falling off.

"Come on in," Robertson said as he pointed Luke to his office door at the back of the main office.

Luke followed the man into the next office and sat in a chair in front of an incredibly messy desk as Robertson moved around to the other side.

"So, tell me a little about yourself," Robertson said.

And Luke did. Some of what he told the boss man was real, and some of it was fabricated. Luckily, Luke actually had done some forest work during the summers in college, so he knew a bit about what went on in a logging operation. And, knowing he might end up at this place, he'd spent four days observing workers at a mill in Northern California. He didn't get much hands-on experience, but he was familiar with some of the jobs he might be asked to do.

After twenty minutes of talking, Robertson looked over the application and some other papers, which Luke assumed was the references report from Agnes Huff.

"When can you start?" Robertson asked.

"Right now, if you need me," Luke said.

"You'll need to get some more paperwork filled out. Get that done with Agnes, and you can start in the morning. We work seven to four-thirty with a half hour for lunch. Pay day is on Friday."

"Thank you, Mr. Robertson. You won't be sorry."

"Call me Mike," Robertson said and pointed Luke back to the door to the main office. "Agnes will have your papers for you."

CHAPTER 3

It had not been guaranteed that Luke would get hired on at the mill. In some undercover cases, the WDFW will work with an employer to get their person situated in a job. In this case, in a smaller town, everyone thought it would be best if no one other than the two WDFW officers working in the region knew Luke was an enforcement officer with the Department of Fish and Wildlife.

The local game wardens believed there was a leak somewhere in the sheriff's office because when they did try to catch one of the suspected poachers, they found no evidence of wrongdoing when they searched his house on a warrant. It was obvious the man had been tipped off to the search. So, neither the local city police department nor county sheriff's office was made aware of Luke's presence.

Luke had specifically tried to get hired at the mill because the men who were thought to be involved in the poaching ring worked there. Luke had their names and had seen their driver's license photos, so he would be able to recognize them when he saw them.

His plan was to stay clear of the three men to start. He didn't want to give them any hint that he was trying to get to know them or get close to them. It was kind of like playing it cool with a girl you liked in high school, Luke thought. Ignore her, and she'll come after you. Maybe.

Then he thought about the times he had tried that in high school—it had never worked. Still, he would wait and show no interest in the three men.

As it turned out, it was going to be a little more difficult than that. The first day of work, Luke was put on the green chain. It was a very physical job, pulling green lumber coming off the chain and placing it in the correct stack of lumber based on the size of the boards.

His supervisor on the green chain was a short, stout guy of about forty. His name was Brian Thomas, but Luke soon found out everyone called him "Buck." Thomas was one of the three men on the list he had received from the local WDFW officers.

Luke didn't know if Thomas was afflicted with "Little Man's Syndrome" or if he was just a jerk because Luke was the new guy, but from the time he started, Thomas was all over him.

"Move it faster, Rook," Thomas would scream over the noise of the equipment. "You're falling behind."

Actually, Luke was keeping up just fine. It was the two other guys he was rotating through with pulling lumber that were slowing everything down.

The job didn't take many brains but plenty of strength and stamina. About the fourth hour in, Luke was glad he had kept himself in good shape, working out every day. He was definitely looking forward to the lunch break.

Luke hadn't brought a lunch, so he walked down the street and got a burger, fries, and a shake at the local drive-in. He was just sitting down at a table to eat when two guys he recognized from the mill walked up to him.

"Hey, man, don't worry about Buck," one of the guys said. "He's an asshole to everyone."

"It doesn't help that you're about two feet taller than him," the younger man said. "But he'll get over it eventually."

Luke looked up at the two guys and said, "Thanks." Then he held out his hand and said, "I'm Luke Haynes."

"Jim Morris," the older of the two men said. "And this is Baldy Ames."

Luke shook both men's hands and looked at Ames, who had a full, thick head of brown hair. He didn't ask about the name, and neither man offered, so Luke let it go.

"Where you from?" Morris asked.

"Oh, here and there," Luke said. "Mostly from Oregon."

"Whatcha doing up here?" Ames asked.

"Getting away," Luke said.

"From the law?" Morris asked.

"Naw, away from people. And one female in particular."

Morris looked at Ames and smiled.

"We both been divorced," Ames said. "Damn women. Hard to please. At least my old lady was."

"How long you guys worked at the mill?" Luke asked, changing the subject.

"I've been there almost twenty years," Morris said before turning to Ames. "And you've been here what, ten?"

"Twelve," Ames said.

"Decent place to work then?" Luke asked.

"Yeah, actually it is," Morris said. "Mike takes care of the good workers. Not sure why Buck is still there though."

"He can be an asshole," Ames repeated.

About that time, someone called Morris's name from the pickup window, and the two men left to get their food. Luke finished eating quickly and headed back to the mill. As he walked back, he started thinking about the work. He could handle it for a while, but maybe his plan to sit back and wait would need altering slightly. He surely didn't want to be pulling lumber off the green chain three months from now.

*

After a week on the job, Luke had identified the other two men who were suspected to be in the poaching ring. Manny Hernandez was a forklift operator. The other man, Ricky Carter, was some kind of mechanic. Luke saw him moving around throughout the mill, working on saws, dryers, and other equipment.

He had yet to talk to either man, but did communicate with Buck Thomas. After four days of listening to the supervisor chastise him almost constantly, Luke walked up to the fireplug of a man during a break and quietly told him that he'd had just about enough of it.

Luke wasn't two feet taller than Thomas, but he had him by over a foot and he knew his size would mean something. His dad had once told him in grade school that the best way to deal with a bully is to call his bluff, and if you had to punch him in the nose, so be it.

"I'm working my ass off here, and you know it," Luke said quietly when he caught Thomas over by the vending machines. "So knock it off."

Thomas looked up at Luke with a slight grin and didn't say anything for a minute.

"Yeah, yeah," Thomas said. "I was wondering when you were going to say something."

"Well, I'm saying something now, and one way or the other, it is going to stop."

Luke was not smiling.

"Okay, tough guy," Thomas said. "It'll stop."

And it did. In fact, Thomas started coming around at breaks and lunch to chat with Luke. He asked the same questions as Morris and Ames had asked, although Luke was sure that Thomas already knew the answers to those questions from the grapevine that meandered around the plant floor.

Still, Luke stuck to the script. And tried to keep to himself. He ended up eating lunch with Morris and Ames a few times, but on other days he would find a spot to be by himself and read a book.

"That your Bronco out there?" Thomas asked Luke after coming up to him during lunch as he was reading a John Sandford novel.

"Yep," Luke said, looking up from the book. "Not great on gas mileage, but it gets me around."

"Looks like you're a hunter," Thomas said.

Luke had put an NRA sticker on the back window of the truck, along with decals for the Mule Deer Foundation and Rocky Mountain Elk Foundation.

"My favorite pastime," Luke said. "Haven't hunted much around here though."

It was early April, when nothing except turkey hunting is available to Washington hunters.

"Turkey season opens next Saturday," Thomas said. "You ever hunt turkeys before?"

"Yeah, down in Oregon. Killed a couple nice gobblers. Maybe I'll check around for some public land and give it a try."

"Well, good luck if you go," Thomas said and turned and walked away.

Luke went back to reading but kept an eye on Thomas who went over to where Hernandez and Carter were eating their lunch. The men talked and laughed as they ate.

*

Every third or fourth day, Luke would call his captain just to check in and let him know how things were going.

He called Sara every night. They would talk about their days at work and anything else that was happening in the world.

"So, it sounds like you're making a little progress," Sara said the night after Luke had talked with Buck Thomas during his lunch break. "You think they'll invite you hunting?"

"I'm not sure. But I'm not going to push it. It's still too early."

"Any more rumblings that they're doing anything illegal right now?"

"Not that we've heard. Maybe that raid on Carter's house scared them, and they've cooled it for a while."

Luke had also met with the two WDFW officers who covered the northern portion of Region One in eastern Washington. They'd met twice at a small, out-of-the-way restaurant in Spokane, an hour-and-a-half drive from Colville.

"From what I can tell, not much is happening," Luke said during the second meeting. "But I'm only around them during working hours, and even then, I'm not close enough to get a clue what they're discussing."

"We haven't had any more calls about them or any other poaching for that matter," Dave Whitson said.

Whitson was about Luke's age but was the polar opposite in appearance. While Luke was tall, dark haired, and muscular, Whitson stood five-foot-eight, weighed all of 150 pounds, and was a very fair-skinned blond.

The other officer was younger—Luke put him at about 30—slightly taller and heavier than his partner and had sandy brown hair. His name was Cody Stephens.

"Maybe we should try to put a tracking device on one of their rigs," Stephens said. "At least we would know where they're going when they're off work."

"We can do that with their phones," Whitson said. "At least generally we'd know where they are."

"I'd say let's hold off on all of that for the time being," Luke said. "Let me keep trying to earn their trust and see where that goes. I'm talking to Buck Thomas on a regular basis, and I think I might be getting close to getting him to take me turkey hunting."

The other two officers agreed.

"I'll keep you guys up to speed when and if anything happens," Luke said. "After all this effort, I want to get all three of these guys if we can."

That meant, in Luke's mind, there was the possibility he would have to break a law or two to gain the confidence of Thomas, who seemed to be the leader of the bunch.

That was the one big question all undercover officers had to face. Would they be willing to commit an illegal act to catch the bad guys? Some undercover wildlife officers purposely would miss shots at a bird or animal, and Luke thought about that as an option. But if he had to shoot an animal out-of-season to help make the case, well, he'd have to come to grips with that when and if the situation arose.

CHAPTER 4

Claude Rakes didn't have some innate need to kill. Not like most other mass murderers do. It wasn't a sexual thing. He didn't have a type. In fact, he really didn't want to kill them. There were just times when he believed the world would be a better place without the women he murdered. So, he did everyone a favor and killed them.

Rakes was very observant, and whenever he was in public, he watched people. To him, it was better than watching all the stupid so-called reality shows on television. In fact, he would go to a mall or a restaurant just to people-watch. That was true reality.

He quickly noticed that, no matter where he went, everyone was busy in their own little worlds, most with their faces in their cell phones. He saw an ever-increasing number of young parents whose children were begging for their mom or dad to pay attention to them. Something on the phone was way more important than what their child was doing.

That would make Rakes mad. His parents hadn't paid much attention to him as a child. Not that they'd been looking at cell phones back then. Mostly his parents had been working and trying to make ends meet. They didn't have time for their little boy. Then, when he was in the fifth grade, his mother took off one night to go get some groceries and never came back. That's when Rakes got the picture. No one loved him enough to care or cared enough to love him.

That, added with the way the kids at school and the people in town had treated him, molded Rakes into the man he had become. One who saw all the bad in bad people. And one who, when he watched people at the store or some other place where people gathered, occasionally spotted someone who, he believed, needed to die.

In a stopover near Boise one cool spring day, Rakes killed a woman who he watched continually berate a waitress at a restaurant. The young waitress was obviously new to the job, but the woman who criticized the waitress, usually loudly, was just not a good person. Any person who is mean to someone who is trying to serve them is not a good person, Rakes believed.

Three weeks later, a fisherman on the Boise River found the woman's body tucked into a pile of brush near the river. The angler had noticed some crows and magpies making a ruckus up off the riverbank and went over to take a look. When he discovered the body, the woman's head was turned in a gross and unnatural direction, and thanks to the birds, she had no eyes.

During the autopsy, the coroner found tiny amounts of skin under the woman's fingernails on her right hand. It was believed she had scratched her attacker just before her neck was broken. The skin cells were sent to the Idaho State crime lab, but after getting the DNA and checking the state database and then the records in the national database, no match was found.

Rakes had always been careful when he killed the other women. He wore gloves, and because he never raped them, he believed he left no DNA on the bodies. The restaurant woman had done something none of the others had done. As soon as he wrapped his massive arm around her chest, she reached up and scratched his face. Two seconds later, he pushed her head backward over his bicep and her neck popped.

The adrenaline was pumping, so Rakes never felt the scratch. He saw her hands flailing about near his face like they always did, but it wasn't until later that night, long after he had deposited her body well away from any civilization, that he noticed the scratch. He immediately thought about the possibility the police might get some of his skin. That wouldn't be good. He thought seriously about going back to where he'd dumped the body to try to deal with it but decided going back raised bigger risks. What if, by some crazy coincidence, someone had found the body. He didn't want to be seen anywhere near it.

No, he would take his chances. There should be no record of his DNA in any of the databanks. So, the authorities would have nothing to match it to. If they did get his DNA from the woman's fingernails, then it would be in the databanks going forward. Still, they had no clue as to who he was.

Rakes watched the news wherever he was to see if the bodies of the women he'd killed had been found. The two women he killed in Billings were found fairly quickly after he dumped them in Wyoming. The woman from Boise had yet to be found.

He was home when he read in a short article in the *Great Falls Tribune* a month after he had been to Boise that the woman's body had been found by a fisherman. He shouldn't have left the body so close to the river. There was nothing in the story about finding skin or DNA under the victim's fingernails. As of yet, no one was saying anything about a connection to the three other women who had been found dead with broken necks in Montana and Wyoming.

*

Killing the dancer in Washington four months later was the beginning of the end for Rakes. He had always been so careful. He was careful about where he killed the other women, and he was careful about not leaving any clues as to who he was. And he was very careful about where he dumped the bodies. He expected they would be discovered but hopefully weeks or months later, where potential clues to his identity might be eradicated by the weather, animals, and time.

She was an exotic dancer, but Rakes hadn't been to the strip club where she danced. He never had any desire to go into those places. If he did, because of his size and his looks, surely someone would remember he had been there. Plus, those places had security cameras everywhere.

The girl was hitchhiking from State Line into Spokane. Rakes often picked up hitchhikers, not to kill them, but for company. In fact, he had never killed a person he'd picked up and had no intention of doing so until the dancer started making rude remarks to him.

Rakes could tell she was high on something, so for a while he excused her rudeness. But after he made a comment about how she should be a little more grateful for the ride, she went off on him.

"You think I'm going to have sex with you just because you gave me a lift?"

"I don't want sex. I just want to hear a little appreciation from you. I didn't have to stop to pick you up."

"Here's your appreciation, you ugly retard," she said and threw the Big Gulp she had been carrying in his face, then started to climb out of the truck.

With unexpected speed and agility from such a large man, Rakes seized the girl by the back of the neck with his large right hand and jerked her toward him. In another quick move, he grabbed her chin with his left hand, and with strength enough to snap a two-by-four in half, he twisted her neck around and broke it.

He threw the dead girl's body on the floor in front of the passenger seat and started to drive.

Rakes drove around for a while, making sure he wasn't being followed. This was the first time he hadn't planned a kill, and he didn't know if anyone might have seen him. The girl had been walking along a siding road, next to the freeway. When he had stopped to pick her up, there were no cars on the road. But there were some businesses in the distance and some houses on a hill above the road.

So, he drove on, looking for the best place to get rid of the body.

He drove south of Spokane, past a golf course and out into the country. When he got far enough away from any homes or businesses, he took a side road that followed a creek. At one point, the road moved up a hill, while the creek dropped into a brushy canyon. He found a place to pull off, got out, and looked and listened for any vehicles that might be coming from either direction.

When Rakes lifted the girl out of the truck, he noticed blood coming from her mouth. None of the other women he had killed had bled. He must have ripped a vein with the violent twisting of her neck. The blood splattered across his shirt as he threw her over his shoulder to walk to the edge of the ravine. He put gloves on to carry the girl, but because it happened so quickly, in a moment of rage, Rakes had not had gloves on when he grabbed her neck and face.

He wasn't worried that somehow some of his DNA may have been transferred to her body at that time. He didn't think about the sweat from his neck and shoulders soaking into the girl's shirt. It was a hot night, and Rakes was sweating profusely.

The body dropped forty feet and landed with a thud in the brush near the stream. No one in their right mind would walk down there, and he hoped no one would ever find her body.

Rakes hustled back to his truck, listened again for any traffic, fired up the engine, and pulled out onto the road. He slowly worked his way back north and west to the interstate and soon was headed to Tacoma where he was to deliver a transmission.

As he drove, he replayed the events of the past hour. As was the case with the other women he had killed, Rakes felt no remorse. He didn't feel anything. She was not a good person, and the second she had called him a retard, he reacted. He reacted to the hundreds of times the kids had called him that in school. And he reacted to the times he heard the adults in town whispering about the retarded boy.

He looked down at the rubber floor mat where the girl had been lying. A small puddle of blood had collected there. He couldn't forget it. He would need to clean that up at his next stop for fuel.

Then Rakes remembered feeling the blood hitting him when he hoisted the dead body over his shoulder. He looked down at his shirt. There was a spot of blood. It was the one shirt from his company that he had brought on the delivery. A uniform supply company supplied shirts to the delivery drivers. Five shirts each week for each driver. They came with each driver's name stitched on them. The shirts had to be turned in each week when five freshly laundered shirts would be provided to the drivers. If Rakes didn't turn all of his shirts in, he would have to pay for the missing ones.

He would deal with the blood stain on his shirt when he returned to Great Falls.

About the time Rakes was driving west past Cheney, Spokane County deputies were receiving a call about a dead woman's body found next to Hangman Creek, five miles east of state route 195.

CHAPTER 5

"Hey, Rook. You want to go kill a turkey this weekend?" Buck Thomas asked as Luke sat at a table near the back of the lunchroom reading his book.

Thomas had called Luke "Rook" from the minute he'd started screaming at him on the green chain. Luke wondered if the man even remembered his name.

"I got nothing better to do," Luke said. "Just let me know what I need and where I need to be."

"Saturday morning," Thomas said. "I'll let you know what time later. You have a shotgun, I assume."

"Yep, but it's nothing fancy. Just an old Remington 870."

"That'll work. Wear camo from head to toe if you have it."

"Will do," Luke said as he watched Thomas wander off to talk to Hernandez and Carter.

Luke had said hello to the two other suspected poachers a time or two, but again, he had purposefully kept his distance. He wondered if they would be hunting with him and Thomas come Saturday morning.

Turkey season had been underway for ten days. Luke had gone hunting on his own a couple of times but had no luck. There were plenty of turkeys in the region, but most of the birds were still in the valleys because colder-than-normal temperatures kept the snowline low. The majority of those lands were privately owned, so access was limited to hunters who had permission to trespass.

Washington turkey hunters can take up to three turkeys in the spring, but they must be taken in certain regions, and they all must be birds with a visible beard, signifying that they are toms, or male turkeys. Occasionally, hens will have a beard, which made them legal as well.

Luke had purchased two turkey tags but fully intended to use only one. He figured if he did kill a bird, that was plenty enough for him to eat. He would tell Thomas he only had one tag to see what kind of response, or possible pressure, he would get if he filled the tag and the opportunity to take a second or third bird popped up.

Thomas picked Luke up at his apartment at 4:45, the prearranged time. Thomas was alone in his Ford F-150 four-by-four pickup.

"Morning, Rook," Thomas said as Luke climbed into the passenger side. "You ready to shoot a turkey?"

"That would be nice for a change," Luke said. He went on to tell Thomas about the other two times he had gone without having any success. And he told Thomas what he had discovered about the birds not yet migrating up into the National Forest, where Luke was hunting.

"We don't need to worry about that," Thomas said. "I have some private spots. Coupla dairy farmers. They hate the turkeys. Pests they call them. Want us to shoot every one we can."

"So, you've probably already filled your tags then?" Luke asked.

"Oh yeah, and then some. Some of my buddies have filled theirs too."

"Nice. So, you set up and call them in?"

"Sometimes, but if that don't work, we have spots where I put grain out, and the birds just come in."

"I thought that was against the rules," Luke said.

"Nah, not on private land. The farmers want 'em gone, so we do what we need to do to get 'em close."

They had driven three miles south of town and had turned onto a road that led into farm country. A mile down the road, they pulled into a two-track dirt road and hit a locked gate. Big signs on each side of the gate read "NO TRESPASSING."

"This is old man Ferguson's place," Thomas said. "I deliver a couple bottles of Jack Daniel's before the season, and that gets me a key to the gate."

Thomas got out and unlocked the chain holding the gate to a post. He swung the gate open, came back, climbed in the truck, and they drove through.

"Jump out and close the gate," Thomas said. "No need to lock it."

Luke did as Thomas told him, jumped back in the truck, and soon they were bouncing down the two-track through some pines and fir trees.

It was still dark, and Luke knew the turkeys would be on the roost. He was interested to see how Thomas was going to handle the hunt. When he had gotten in the truck, he noticed that Thomas had brought a shotgun. But there was also a rifle in a gun rack in the back window. If Thomas had filled his turkey tags, as he had said earlier, what was he going to do with the shotgun, or the rifle for that matter. It didn't take long to find out.

"Right there!" Thomas said as he hit the brakes hard.

Luke looked out the left side of the windshield and saw a coyote standing only forty yards away.

Thomas rolled down the window, and without loading the shotgun, pulled it up, stuck it out the window, and shot the coyote.

"Good shot!" Luke said, wanting Thomas to think he was all for what he just had done. Shooting out of a vehicle on a county road was illegal, but on a private road like this, it was just very unsportsmanlike. Thomas did have a loaded shotgun in the truck coming from town, so that was a violation for sure.

As Thomas continued driving down the road, Luke asked, "Aren't you going to get it and sell the hide?"

"Naw, too much trouble. We just let 'em lay. The only good coyote is a dead coyote."

Again, shooting a coyote without retrieving it is not against the law in Washington. Luke understood why people hunted the predators. Coyotes killed plenty of game birds and fawns, not to mention who-knows-how-many cats and small dogs around the country. Still, he felt it was a waste to just shoot something and let it lay.

Since Thomas' shotgun had been loaded the whole time, Luke had to believe the man's rifle was also loaded. He would keep an eye on that. Getting accidentally shot while undercover was not high on his list of things to do.

They drove another five minutes through scattered trees until they hit a small creek.

"We'll get out and hike down the creek a ways," Thomas said. "There's a roost tree just up the hill, and the birds like to work down to the creek for water. We'll set up there."

The two men grabbed their shotguns and hiked down the creek quietly for about four hundred yards and stopped.

"Sit with your back up against that big fir tree," Thomas whispered to Luke, pointing at the tree. "I'll go over to that tree over there and make some calls once it gets light. Stay very still and don't make a sound."

Luke had hunted turkeys several times over the years and enjoyed it immensely. Turkeys have incredible hearing and eyesight and, because they are being pursued by predators pretty much from the time they hatch, they are incredibly wary. They can be very tough to fool.

On the other hand, during the spring mating season, sometimes the toms can be coerced easily into shotgun range. With only mating on their mind, they will, at times, run right into calls made by hunters who mimic the sounds of a hen turkey looking for love.

As he sat, watching nighttime slowly turn to dawn, Luke listened.

In the distance, he heard the purr of a hen turkey somewhere in a roost tree. Then there was a gobble, and then another. Pretty soon, it sounded like there were gobbles coming from every direction.

A short time later, Thomas made a few quiet clucks and purrs. His calls were immediately answered by a gobble. Then there was another gobble and a third. Every time the tom gobbled, it sounded closer. Luke listened and got his shotgun in position, ready to shoot.

He heard the turkey walking before he saw it. The rustle of leaves under the trees up the hill told him the bird was nearly in range. Then Luke saw the bright blue head and the tail feathers of the big tom strutting slowly along. The mature tom had a long, thick beard. There were other birds behind the tom, but Luke concentrated on the first bird that was all puffed up in full strut.

When the turkeys were twenty yards out, Luke heard Thomas growl, "shoot him." And as soon as the big tom was clear of the other birds, Luke did just that.

At the shot, the other birds scattered. Some flew, others ran. The tom Luke was targeting had folded at the shot, but now it was fluttering and kicking, already dead, but its body didn't know it. The downed bird's commotion caught the attention of some of the turkeys that had scurried off, and three mature toms came back and started attacking the turkey Luke had shot.

"Shoot 'em," Thomas growled again.

Luke didn't hesitate. He knew he had the second turkey tag. It was all legal. He didn't need another turkey to eat. But to keep up his cover, he shot. One of the three toms went down next to the first bird.

At the second shot, the two remaining toms took off running down the creek past Thomas. There was a shot, and one of the birds rolled. Then there was a second shot, and the third bird started flopping around.

"Who-hooo! Four birds in, four birds down!" Thomas yelled as he stood and started to run to the two turkeys he had shot.

Luke wondered how many turkeys Thomas had killed so far this year.

As Thomas walked back to Luke, who had gone to where his two turkeys lay, he said, "That was some good shooting there, Rook. Kinda fun, huh?"

"It was the wild west there for a few seconds," Luke said. Then he pulled out his wallet to dig out his turkey tags.

"What are you doing?" Thomas asked.

"Getting my tags out to tag these birds."

"You don't need no turkey tags around here," Thomas said. "No one's gunna check us in here, and you might need 'em later."

"I don't know," Luke said. "I'm one of those nervous kinda guys that worries about the law. I can't afford a ticket."

"Don't you worry about nothin'. I've never been checked. You'll be fine."

Luke acted like he was thinking about it for a minute.

"Okay, if you say so."

"Listen," Thomas said as he picked up the two toms he had shot and started walking to the truck. "These two right here are my eighth and ninth of the year. We're good."

"What do you do with all those birds?" Luke asked as he grabbed his turkeys and followed Thomas.

"I eat some and give the rest away to friends. We're doing the farmers a favor, remember."

When they got back to the truck, Luke said, "That was fun. I'd be happy to buy you breakfast if you're up for it."

"We're not done hunting yet," Thomas said. "I got another place I want to check."

When they finally left old man Ferguson's place, Luke had killed one more tom turkey, missed another on purpose, and Thomas had killed two more.

"That was a pretty good day, huh Rook?" Thomas said once they hit the paved road and were headed back to town.

"Yeah, a great day. Thanks a bunch!"

Luke had Thomas take a photo of him with two of his turkeys, and while Thomas wasn't looking, he took photos of the pile of birds in the back of the pickup.

"Do you think we should cover those birds so no one sees how many we have back there?" Luke asked as they drove along.

"Boy, you are a worrier, ain't ya. We'll be fine. Now, do you still want to buy me breakfast?"

CHAPTER 6

Obviously, whoever dumped the woman's body off the road near Hangman Creek didn't see the dark green tent sitting on the bank some seventy yards upstream. Three 15-year-old boys were in the tent having a campout. Yes, one of the boys had stolen a six-pack of Bud Lights from his dad's beer refrigerator in the garage. But they weren't drunk. The beer had given them a little buzz, and with the eight hot dogs they'd consumed between them, they were ready for bed by midnight. They climbed into their sleeping bags and were quickly sound asleep.

Sterling Cook didn't look at his phone when he woke up with an urgent need to pee. All he knew was he had to go. Bad. His bladder was about to bust from the beer and three Mountain Dews he had drunk, so he climbed out of the tent and was relieving himself when he heard a commotion up on the bluff. He looked up just in time to see a big guy toss something over into the brush next to the creek.

Whatever the dude had thrown over the bank was fairly large, and it made kind of a sickening thud when it landed. So, Cook grabbed his flashlight and walked down the creek on a game trail to see what it might be.

He started freaking out when, in the bright beam of the light, he saw a woman all contorted weirdly, her face pointed up into the starry night, dead eyes wide open.

"You guys!" Cook yelled. "Come see this!"

The guys didn't answer, so he ran back to the tent and shook them awake. He grabbed his phone too, and with his two buddies following him, Cook ran back to the body.

"Oh man," Devin Barrett said after seeing the dead woman's face. "I'm going to be sick."

Then he turned and puked. Twice.

Cook dialed 911 and told the operator what he had seen and where they were located.

"Do we need to send an ambulance?" the operator asked.

"No ma'am," Cook said. "This poor lady is really dead."

It took seventeen minutes for the first sheriff's deputy to locate the boys and another seven to figure out a way down into the ravine. While they waited, the boys talked about the woman and how she might have been killed.

"Did you get a good look at the guy who threw her down here?" Barrett asked Cook as he sipped on a bottle of water to get the puke taste of regurgitated beer and hot dogs out of his mouth.

"Not really," Cook said. "He was big, but I didn't see much of his face."

"That's good," Devin's twin brother James said. "Cause if you can identify him and he finds out, he might just come do the same thing to you."

All three boys shivered.

Cook and James Barrett took a photo of the dead woman with their phones. Devin Barrett couldn't look at her again. Then they sat and waited until a deputy walked down the creek to them. The deputy took the boys' statements and radioed back and forth with other deputies who arrived in ones and twos. After Cook had pointed out exactly where he had seen the man throw the woman off the bluff, the area was taped off to preserve any possible footprints, tire tracks, or other evidence.

The Spokane County coroner and a Washington State Patrol officer showed up fifty minutes after the first deputy arrived, and they asked the boys the same questions the deputy had. No, they hadn't touched the body. Yes, it was exactly as they had found it. No, Cook, who was the only one up at that time, didn't get a good look at the man who threw the body down here. All he knew for sure was the man was "a big white dude." Yes, he heard a vehicle drive off, but no he didn't see it so he didn't know what kind of vehicle it was. The engine sounded loud and powerful. Based on the sound, he thought it was traveling west when it took off, but he couldn't be sure. No, he didn't know exactly what time the body was dumped because he hadn't had his phone on him, but based on his call to 911 it must have been around 2:15, give or take a minute or two.

The state patrol officer took the boys' contact information and then told them they could go home.

"And boys," the officer said. "I'm going to overlook the beer drinking. I should call your parents, but since you were here and helped with this, I'm not. Just know that drinking at your age can get you into all kinds of trouble."

"Yes sir," the three boys said in unison.

As they walked away, Cook said to the twins, "How'd he know we were drinking beer? I didn't say a word about that. Did you?"

"Maybe he smelled it coming from Devin's pile of puke," James said.

*

Rakes stopped just off I-90 in Ellensburg to fuel his truck and to grab a couple of McDonald's breakfast sandwiches. As he was getting gas, he cleaned out the cab of the truck. He grabbed the girl's Big Gulp cup and tossed it into a nearby trash can. Then he pulled the floor mat out and took the window squeegee from a bucket of soapy water by the pumps and worked at washing the blood away. As he was putting the floormat back in, he spotted a small gold purse with a long gold chain on it just under the seat. He didn't remember seeing the purse when the girl had climbed into the cab, but it had to be hers.

Before he touched the purse, he put gloves on. He opened it and found a wad of one-dollar bills, along with the girl's driver's license, some breath mints, and a small ring with two keys attached. The license showed a bad photo of the girl, looking either drunk or stoned, kind of like she had when she'd climbed into his truck. Her name was Desiree Murphy. Rakes quickly did the math based on her birth date and figured she was nineteen. Another month and she would have been twenty.

Too bad, Rakes thought. She shouldn't have called him names.

He had never taken anything from the previous women he had killed. He wasn't a thief. He didn't kill them for their money. But since the girl wasn't going to need it anymore, Rakes stuck the wad of cash in his pocket. He decided not to throw the purse in the trash. Someone might find it and get the cops involved. He would throw it out the window somewhere on the road ahead.

Rakes looked at the floormat again. The thing was still dirty, but he couldn't see any blood. He would power wash it at a carwash after he made his delivery. That should take care of any remaining blood spots.

*

The coroner determined that a broken neck had caused the woman's death. He believed, based on the slight bruising around the back of her neck and what the Cook boy had told him about seeing the man throw her off the bluff, that she was dead well before she'd landed in the brush. Possibly by an hour or more. His test of her liver temperature confirmed it.

Deputies found a fresh tire track coming out of a small mud puddle near where the boy had seen the man on the bluff. The forensics folks made a plaster mold of the tracks, but by the width of the tire and the depth of the impression, it was thought to have been made by a heavy vehicle, probably a truck.

Other officers followed the road, both west and east, looking for any potential video or security cameras, either on private homes or on businesses. Almost all the homes were well off the main road, and most didn't have cameras. But they did get some footage from a gas station just south of the interstate and discovered two different trucks had passed by between 2:30 and 3:00 a.m.

One of the trucks was an 18-wheeler with Walmart plastered all over it. The other was a light-colored—maybe white, maybe silver—Ford F-650 box truck with a large metal van on the back. On the side was printed Big Sky Auto Parts.

The discovery of the trucks was made at 9:00 a.m. Where the trucks had gone from there was anyone's guess, but the State Patrol put out a "be on the lookout" for these rigs whose drivers were persons of interest.

*

At about that same time, Claude Rakes was turning off I-90 onto Highway 18 on his way to Tacoma where he was to drop off a transmission for a 1966 Corvette at an auto repair house.

Most of the time as he drove, Rakes would just think about things. He would think about the terrible kids in Havre. He would think about his crappy teachers, none of whom would stand up for him. And he would think about his poor excuse for a father. What a shitty life he had had.

Occasionally, he would think about his mother. He really didn't care, but sometimes he wondered where she was. He thought he'd seen her once in Portland, Oregon. But he was driving and couldn't stop in time.

What would he do, what would he say if he did ever see her again? Then he would think about killing her. He knew he could, but would he?

As he wound his way over Tiger Pass, through a bunch of turns, he decided to turn on the radio. A talk radio station came up first. As he listened, he started thinking about the dancer. As if he had magically made it so, the announcer on the radio said, "And in regional news, this morning police discovered the dead body of a woman near Spokane. The body was discovered next to Hangman Creek just south of the city. Police are saying the woman was murdered and dumped in the area."

What? How could that be? He had been careful. Not careful enough evidently.

Rakes concentrated on the road. He would make his delivery and then he would find a motel. He had been driving for seventeen hours. He needed some rest.

*

From nine o'clock on, State Patrol officers and Spokane sheriff's deputies had stopped fourteen Walmart trucks. The things were everywhere. Only two of the trucks had been in the area south of Spokane, and after determining which truck it was, they eliminated the driver because he was short, slender, and of Mexican heritage.

No one had spotted a Big Sky Auto Parts truck, but one of the officers went online on his phone, did a little searching on the internet, and found that there were three auto parts stores and distributors with that name in Montana. On the second call, to Big Sky Auto Parts in Great Falls, he hit paydirt.

"Yeah, we have a truck headed to Tacoma with a transmission for a Vet," the manager of the auto parts place said. "The car, not a soldier. Driver's name is Claude Rakes. Why you looking for him?"

"We have an interest in talking to him," is all the officer would say.

"Ah, geez," the manager said.

"You said that like you might have some information about Mr. Rakes."

"Naw, nothing specific. He's just a little strange. Smart as a whip, but kind of slow acting and funny looking."

"Is he a big guy?"

"Boy howdy," the manager said. "You know those guys you'd

like to have standing next to you in a bar fight. Rakes is that guy. But I've never seen him get mad, or even raise his voice to anyone. Don't tell him I told you this, but he looks kind of special. You know, like a little retarded."

"I see," said the officer.

"But like I said, he's really smart and a great delivery guy. Does what's supposed to be done, when it's supposed to be done, with never a gripe or complaint."

"You have a phone number for Mr. Rakes?"

"I do. I tried to call him an hour or so ago, just to see where he was and how he was doing, and there was no answer. That usually means he's sleeping somewhere and doesn't want to be woke up by his phone. Probably is turned off."

"How about an address of the place he was to deliver the transmission?"

The manager took a minute to look up the repair shop in Tacoma and gave the address to the officer.

"I hope he's not involved in anything," the manager said. "He's my best delivery guy."

The officer thanked the manager, clicked off, and immediately called his supervisor.

"I may have identified our killer," the officer said. "A big guy. The driver of the delivery truck we found on the security footage at the gas station, not far from where the body was dumped. I have an address for where he is headed in Tacoma. We should get Tacoma PD to check on that, and we need to get a track on his phone right away. It's probably turned off now, but we should be able to ping it, if it was on, and see where he was throughout the night."

*

After making his delivery with no problems, Rakes headed back toward Seattle. He found a cheap motel near SeaTac International Airport and paid cash for a room for one day. He had to slip the lady behind the counter an extra twenty to coax her into letting him check in early.

He had turned his phone off right after he'd killed the girl, and he'd kept it off. He had seen on the TV news where the police in Moscow, Idaho had tracked the guy who allegedly killed four University of Idaho students just by pinging his phone. Rakes didn't need that.

When he finally got to bed and fell asleep, he had no idea law enforcement officers throughout King and Pierce Counties were looking for his truck, and for him.

CHAPTER 7

When Luke got home after the turkey hunt with Thomas, he quickly showered and changed clothes, then hopped on his computer and wrote out a detailed report of everything that had transpired that morning. He attached the photos he had taken, including a photo of his two turkeys with the tags affixed to their legs. He tagged the birds as soon as he got them inside his apartment.

Next, he dialed the cell number he had for Captain Davis in Yakima.

"Hey, Cap," Luke said after the man answered. "Sorry to bother you on the weekend, but I wanted to let you know that I got in on a turkey hunt with Buck Thomas today."

"How'd that go?"

"He only broke about six laws. I wanted to arrest him so badly, but I want those other guys too."

"You're learning why going undercover can be so difficult."

"Yep. I won't bore you with the details. I've written a report and emailed it to you. I plan on meeting with the local officers tomorrow in Spokane to fill them in."

"Sounds good. Keep after them. Hopefully, we can wrap this up soon."

"I hope so too. My wife misses me, I think. I know my dog does."

The two chatted for another minute, and Luke said, "Gotta run. I have turkeys to clean."

*

During morning break at work on Monday, Luke sat down with Thomas, Carter, and Hernandez.

"I ate some of that turkey," Luke said as he opened a granola bar. "It was pretty good. Did you find a home for any of those other birds?"

"Shhhh!" Thomas hissed. "We don't talk about that stuff at work."

Carter and Hernandez gave Luke looks that could kill.

"Sorry," Luke said, holding his hands up. "Won't happen again."

"Damn right it won't, Rook," Carter said as he stood up to leave.

Luke almost laughed. Carter had the lean body of a long-distance runner, or a meth head. He stood five foot ten or eleven, and Luke swore he could wrap his hand fully around Carter's bicep. And the man walked funny. He leaned back just past vertical and took long, high steps, like he was going uphill all the time. Luke was reminded of the Keep On Truckin' guy whenever he saw Carter moving through the plant.

"Yeah, I'm not sure you're the man to make me," Luke said, standing up quickly, ducking his head down to get right in Carter's face. "And no one calls me Rook but Buck. Do it again, and I'll tie a half-hitch around your ass with those skinny arms of yours."

Carter's face went beet red, and he was visibly shaking.

"Got it?" Luke asked, still in his face.

Carter started nodding, but Luke could tell the man was beyond pissed. He would have to keep an eye on him. Especially if they ended up hunting together.

"Okay, okay," Thomas said. "You made your point. Let's get back to work."

Luke looked over at Hernandez and saw he was smiling. He had enjoyed the little altercation immensely. As soon as Hernandez saw Luke looking at him, the smile disappeared, and he walked away.

"Sorry about that," Luke said to Thomas as they walked back to the green chain a couple minutes later. "I was bullied in school, and I don't take crap off of anyone."

"I see that," Thomas said with a smile. "You sure got Carter's attention, along with all the other guys in the break room."

"Confidentially," Luke said. "I did a little time for beating up a guy pretty bad a few years ago. I wouldn't want it to get around though."

"Your secret is safe with me," Thomas said.

Of course, it was all a lie, but Luke figured by afternoon break, most of the guys in the plant, and possibly even Agnes Huff and Mike Robertson, would know all about his fake checkered past.

*

It had been over a week since his little blow up on Carter, but no one in management had said a word to Luke. He caught Carter giving him the evil eye a couple of times, but every time he did, Luke would just stare at him and chuckle.

"The boys and I are going to go out and see if we can find a coyote on Saturday," Thomas said to Luke at lunch. "You want to join us?"

Luke acted like he was thinking about it for a minute and then asked, "The boys?"

"Yeah. Me, Manny, and Ricky."

"Yeah, I don't know. I'd like to go, but I'm a little concerned Carter might shoot me in the back if he has the chance."

"Oh, don't worry about him. He's harmless."

"No one's harmless when they have a loaded weapon in their hands."

"It'll be fine," Thomas said. "We'll pick you up Saturday morning at five."

"Okay. So, I just need my rifle?"

"Bring your shotgun. We might see some turkeys too."

Luke wanted to say, "I've already filled my turkey tags, plus one, you poaching idiot," but he just nodded.

*

Saturday morning rolled around, and an older Ford Excursion pulled up in front of the apartment complex where Luke was living. Luke came out with his rifle and a small cooler with some drinks and snacks.

"Where's your shotgun?" Thomas asked out the passenger window. Carter was driving, which was okay with Luke. That way he could keep his eyes on the scrawny creep.

"Eh, I've had my fill of turkey," Luke said. "You guys can have 'em."

"Your call," Thomas said.

Luke jumped into the backseat. Hernandez sat on the other side. Luke glanced in the back, and it looked like someone had robbed a gun shop. There were four different rifles, not counting his, and at least three shotguns.

"Looks like we could take on the fourth division with all the weaponry in the back," Luke said with a laugh.

Evidently, the other guys didn't find any humor in the statement.

"We like to be prepared," Carter said.

Luke thought the man almost called him Rook again, but caught himself. He was looking at Luke in the rearview mirror. Again, Luke just smiled at him until Carter put his eyes back on the road.

This time, instead of heading south out of town, Carter turned the vehicle north. They drove for a good twenty minutes and then turned east into some hills covered with trees. Luke had been up this way when he went turkey hunting on his own, so he knew it was National Forest land. Back then, it was covered in ten inches of snow, but now the snow was mostly gone.

"We know where there are a couple winter kills," Thomas said. "The coyotes should be working on them good."

"Coyotes can clean up a deer in a day or less," Luke said. "I shot a buck that I couldn't find in the dark one time. Came back the next day, and it was mostly just bones and hide thanks to the coyotes."

"These haven't been dead long," Hernandez said with a chuckle. Carter laughed too.

When they stopped the rig on the Forest Service road, Thomas said to Luke, "You and I will get out here. Ricky and Manny will drive up the road a piece and sneak over the hill. They'll be ready to ambush any coyotes leaving the kill after we move in on it."

Luke grabbed his rifle and got out of the Excursion. Thomas walked around to the back and pulled a rifle out of the pile of long guns. Luke loaded his. Thomas did not, telling Luke the gun was already loaded. He figured every gun in the back was most likely loaded and ready to fire.

"We'll give them a few minutes to get into place," Thomas said. "You ever shoot coyotes before?"

"I've killed my share," Luke said.

Luke had killed a few coyotes in his day. Pretty much all of them in the line of duty. Many he'd had to shoot to put out of their misery after being struck by cars. A couple other times, he'd come upon a pack of coyotes about to attack deer. He would shoot one and watch the others run off. He'd also gone in to help ranchers protect their calves and sheep against coyotes that were killing the stock. But just to kill them for the fun of killing, that never appealed to Luke.

"You should get a chance here in a few," Thomas said. "Come on."

The two men walked slowly and quietly up a game trail, side-hilling around a forested hillside. Luke could feel a slight breeze in his face, so he knew any coyotes wouldn't smell them. But, like just about every creature in the wild, coyotes seemed to have a sixth sense when danger was coming, so Luke knew the canines wouldn't just be standing around.

They snuck along for another sixty yards, and Thomas froze in his tracks.

"There they are," he hissed. "Get on one, and I'll take another."

Luke looked around Thomas and saw a group of seven coyotes. But they weren't coyotes. They were wolves. One of the most protected species in the state.

About that time, the wolves sensed the men, and they were off and running. Luke jumped at the sound of Thomas's rifle going off so close to him. The stocky little man fired twice before the wolves disappeared into the trees.

Twenty seconds later, they heard four more shots. Hernandez and Carter were shooting at the wolves.

"Did you shoot?" Thomas asked.

"I couldn't get on them," Luke lied. "Those were the biggest coyotes I've ever seen."

"They weren't coyotes," Thomas said as he was looking through his scope at the area where the big canines had run. "Those were wolves. We can get some good money for their hides. Damnit! I think I missed. Hopefully, those guys got one or two."

"Well, we better go check for blood," Luke said. "Just in case you didn't miss."

They first walked to where the wolves had been feeding. The remains of two white-tailed deer were there, pretty torn up. Without looking too hard, Luke could see that one of the deer had a bullet hole in its head. He didn't say anything. He would come back later to get a better look and take some photos. Obviously, one of these guys had killed the deer and left them there as bait. Bait for coyotes, or maybe they were after the wolves all along.

Luke was an excellent tracker, even without Jack along to assist.

"Here's some tracks," he said to Thomas. "But I don't see any blood."

"We'll follow them for a bit, but I'm pretty sure I missed. They'll lead us to where them other guys shot."

After following the tracks for a couple hundred yards, Luke could hear Hernandez and Carter talking.

"They're just ahead," Luke said quietly to Thomas.

Thomas whistled, and one of the men whistled back. As they got closer, Luke could see two wolves lying in the dirt. Hernandez and Carter were all smiles.

"Good shooting, you guys," Thomas said. "We missed."

"That's a thousand bucks laying there," Carter said, looking at Luke. "You guys should shoot better."

"A thousand bucks!" Luke exclaimed and whistled. "I guess so. I could use some extra money."

"Yep, we get five hundred dollars a hide," Hernandez said. "No questions asked."

"That's good," Luke said. "Because the tree-huggers and animal lovers will send you away for life for shooting one of these poor little creatures, if they had their way."

"What do you know about it?" Hernandez asked.

"Just what I read," Luke said. "Never should have introduced the damn things back into the state. They'll just end up killing all of our elk and deer and whatever else they can find. Like you said about the coyotes, the only good wolf is a dead wolf."

All three men just looked at Luke.

"Wish I could've got on one," Luke said and kneeled to get a closer look at one of the animals. "I've always wanted to shoot a wolf."

"Stick with us," Hernandez said. "You'll get another chance, I'm sure."

Unfortunately, the boys weren't done with their poaching. After they had skinned the wolves and packed the hides to the Excursion, they drove farther into the forest.

"We know where some elk are," Thomas said. "I never filled

my elk tag during the season, and I have a hankerin' for some elk steaks."

"Me too," said Carter. "You like elk, Roo—er, Luke?"

Luke just stared at him. Carter started to shake a bit.

"Yeah, I love elk. Never had one taken in the spring though. Should still be good eating, huh?"

"Oh, spring elk are the best," Hernandez said with a smile. "Almost as good as roasted bald eagle."

All three men laughed.

"Yeah, real funny," Luke said. "You think you'd be in deep shit for shooting those wolves. Just shoot an eagle."

"There you go worrying again," Thomas said. "We're just joshing ya."

But by the look Carter gave Thomas after he'd said that, Luke was pretty sure somewhere along the line one or more of the men had killed an eagle.

Fortunately, the elk were nowhere to be found. The big animals are not plentiful in the northeast corner of Washington, but there are some around. They are not standing around every bush, however, and they are not normally milling around next to Forest Service roads. None of the men seemed very interested in actually getting out and hunting.

After they dropped Luke off at his apartment, he went in and again typed a detailed report into his laptop. He hadn't been able to take any photos of the wolves, as he didn't want to push it. But he planned to run back up to where the remains of the dead deer and the skinned carcasses of the wolves were. He would take some photos and tissue samples as evidence.

CHAPTER 8

Claude Rakes heard the pounding on his door, but he was so dead tired he worked the noise into his dream. He was dreaming about his mother. It was a nightmare really. She was in his face, screaming at him, calling him names, and then she was pounding on a counter.

Bang, bang, bang! "Claude Rakes, open the door. King County sheriff! We need to talk to you."

Shit. He sat up, scratched his head, and went quickly through his options. He could try to go out the bathroom window. He had looked at it when he first got into the room. It was not very big, and he could get stuck, so that wasn't going to work. He could open the door and bull rush the cops. That could get him beat up, or worse yet, shot.

"Coming!" Rakes said and got up to grab his pants. He looked at the small digital clock next to the bed. It was 4:22 in the afternoon. How had they found him?

*

The coroner had identified Desiree Murphy by her fingerprints. She was in the system in Spokane County after being arrested for drug and prostitution charges more than once. When officers got her name, they went to her last known address at an apartment complex in east Spokane and talked to another known drug user and hooker who said she was Murphy's roommate.

The police officers went through all the standard questions. When did you last see her? What kind of car does she drive? Where does she work? Does she have any relatives in the area? Any boyfriends?

"She's a dancer at Girls, Girls, Girls in Stateline," the roommate said. "She danced there last night as far as I know, but she never came home. She don't always come home. Sometimes she ends up going home with someone from the club. You know, to make a few more bucks. Her old lady lives in town here somewhere. Her old man is dead. And she's never been with a guy for more than a day or two as far as I know."

"What about her car?" one of the officers asked.

"It's a Jeep. Blue. No idea how old it is, but it is a POS."

"POS?" the officer asked.

"A piece of shit. Always giving her trouble. Won't start. Won't shift into reverse. She needs to get rid of the thing. Why you looking for her anyway? More drug stuff?"

"No. We found Miss Murphy's body on the other side of town. She's been murdered."

The roommate got a sick look on her face, but she didn't start crying.

"Jesus, God and Mary," she finally said. "I always knew this was going to happen to one of us. Maybe I should be thinking about another line of work."

"Probably so, ma'am," the officer said and handed her his card. "If you can think of anything else, give us a call."

The police found Murphy's Jeep Wrangler in the parking lot

of the Girls, Girls, Girls club. After looking through the Jeep, they called for a tow truck to impound it so the crime techs could go through it. Then they talked to the manager and a few of the girls at the club. No one knew anything, and all were sorry to hear about Desiree, but none seemed too surprised that she had been killed.

"When that POS of hers doesn't run, she will hitch a ride with most anyone who comes along," a girl named Cherokee said. "Who knows what kind of freak might pick you up. I bet that's what happened. Is that what happened?"

The officers said they were still collecting evidence and trying to figure out exactly what happened. They asked any of the girls to call the Spokane police department if they remembered seeing anything or thought of anything else that might help.

*

Rakes pulled on his pants and went to the door. Two deputies were there. Both had a hand on their sidearms, but they hadn't pulled them. Again, Rakes thought about taking them on, but he still wasn't sure why they wanted to talk to him.

"Are you Claude Rakes?" the first officer asked, looking up at the big man.

"Yessir," Rakes said in his slow cadence. "Is there a problem?"

Rakes had read enough books about the law and how crimes were solved to know that these officers were most likely fishing. There hadn't been enough time to get any real evidence that he had killed the girl in Spokane. He was still amazed someone had found her so quickly, but he was pretty sure no one had seen him kill her in the dark of his cab.

"We need to ask you a few questions," the second officer said.

"Sure, what do ya need to know?"

"Were you driving through the Spokane area early this morning, around two thirty?"

"Yes, I was."

"Do you mind telling us what you were doing there?"

"Just driving through. I got sleepy, late as it was, so I got off the interstate to find a place to park and catch a nap."

He knew they must have had a photo or video or description of his truck, and that's how they had run him down. No sense lying about where he was. He would confirm that. Again, they couldn't have any real evidence that it was him who killed the girl.

"Where exactly off the interstate?" the first deputy asked.

Rakes didn't tell them he pulled off where he'd dumped the girl. Instead, he said that he found a pull off, and that's where he slept for a couple hours. He made up a story about how, as he was sleeping, someone went driving by and started blaring their horn about two forty-five or so. That woke him up, so he got back on the road. He told them where and when he'd made his delivery, and that he had been at the room, sleeping since about ten o'clock that morning.

"I must have been tired," Rakes said slowly. "I didn't realize it was this late in the afternoon."

"Did you happen to stop at a topless dancing place near the Idaho border?"

"No, sir. I never go to those places," Rakes said. That answer wasn't a lie.

"Pick up any hitchhikers?"

"No, sir. I do sometimes, just for the company, but I didn't last night."

"How long are you here in western Washington?"

"I'm picking up some parts in Renton tomorrow morning, and then I'm headed back to Montana."

"Could you give us your phone number in case we need to reach you?"

The officers already had the number, but they figured they would ask to see how cooperative Rakes would be. They also knew the phone had been off since early that morning, right around the time the girl had been killed.

Rakes gave them his phone number and then said, as if he'd just remembered the phone was turned off, "Aw, man, my phone's been off. I bet my boss has been trying to reach me. He likes to check in to make sure everything goes okay with the deliveries."

He grabbed his phone and turned it on.

"Yep, I have three messages from my boss. Hope he's not pissed."

"You mind if we look around in your truck?" the first deputy asked.

"No, sir," Rakes said. "Whatcha looking for?"

"Nothing in particular," the other deputy said.

"I don't drink or do drugs," Rakes said, thinking about the floor mat. He hoped he'd done a good job getting rid of the girl's blood. "You won't find anything illegal in there."

The deputies didn't find any drugs, but they did find a long blonde hair on the headrest of the passenger seat. They removed it and put it in an evidence bag.

Then one deputy noticed a small, red-brown spot on the door jamb that looked like it could be blood. He pulled a Q-tip out of a kit and swabbed the spot with phenolphthalein. The reaction indicated the dark spot was indeed blood. The test didn't distinguish between human blood or animal blood, but it was enough to do a more detailed test.

"Mr. Rakes, we need to ask you to come to the sheriff's office with us," the first deputy said. "You aren't under arrest, but we do want to ask you a few more questions."

This was it, Rakes thought. They had something. He had not been careful enough.

*

The Boise County sheriff had seen the news about a woman found dead in Spokane near a creek with a broken neck. It sounded too much like the case his investigators were working on to be a coincidence. He called the Spokane County sheriff to see what other information they might have.

"We don't have a lot of evidence, frankly," the Spokane sheriff said. "A kid camping nearby saw the guy dump the body. That's how we got on it so quickly. But he didn't get a very good look at him. Said the man looked big. And the kid heard the vehicle the man was driving pull away. Sounded loud or big, like a truck."

"Anything that might have DNA?"

"Possibly. There were some dried spots on the back of the dead girl's shirt that could be sweat from the person who tossed her. We're still checking it."

The Boise County sheriff filled him in on what they had, which was not much.

"We do have DNA though," the Boise sheriff said. "We think the woman scratched the guy, and we got enough skin from under her nails to do the test. Couldn't find a match anywhere though."

"I just heard from the sheriff in King County. They found a panel truck that had driven by a mini-mart close to where the body was dumped right after the kid says it happened. They are questioning the driver now. They say he's a big guy. Found blood in his truck, but they don't know if it's human or not. They're trying to get a voluntary swab of his mouth for DNA testing now."

"Okay," the Boise sheriff said. "Sounds promising. Let me know as soon as you have anything."

"Will do," the Spokane sheriff said. "By the way, did you happen to check to see if there were any other women mysteriously dumped with broken necks?"

"Actually, we did. Wyoming state patrol found two women dumped off a highway near the Montana border a few years back. Both with broken necks. Not raped. Just killed. No DNA or any other evidence around them."

"Hmmm, we might just have a mass murderer on our hands. Maybe we should check with Montana to see if they have any unsolved cases with similar circumstances."

"That was going to be my next call," the Boise sheriff said. "I'll let you know if we find anything."

"We'll do the same," the Spokane sheriff said.

*

Again, Rakes thought about taking out the two deputies who were now ushering him to their SUV. They hadn't placed him in handcuffs, so he could do it no problem. Even though he walked and talked slowly, he knew he was fast enough to take them both down. He could even kill them. But he didn't.

When they got to the King County Sheriff's Office, they walked Rakes back to a small room and asked him to sit down.

"You've still not told me what this is all about," Rakes said. "Do I need to call a lawyer?"

"That's your right, Mr. Rakes, but we just want to ask you a few more questions."

"So, what's this about?"

"We just want to know a little more about your stopover in Spokane. Did you know we found a dead woman not far from where you say you slept for a while?"

"I heard on the radio they found a dead woman in Spokane, but I didn't know it was close to where I parked my truck. Just because you saw my truck there doesn't mean I did anything."

"A person saw someone who looked a lot like you throw the dead girl's body over a bluff."

Rakes didn't say anything. How had he not seen someone close enough to see him do that? Maybe they were lying to him. Then again, how had they found the body so quickly?

"There's a thousand people out there that look like me," Rakes said.

The deputy asking the questions thought to himself that there weren't twenty people out there that looked anything like this guy. "Would you mind letting us swab your mouth?" he asked.

A mouth swab meant they wanted his DNA. Where would they find any of his DNA on the woman he'd killed in Spokane? He had been very careful. They wouldn't find any of his DNA on her.

"Sure. I haven't done anything. Swab away."

While the deputies were talking with Rakes, the crime lab people were getting a better sample of the blood found in his truck. And they were working on getting DNA from the blonde hair found on the passenger seat.

They swabbed Rakes' mouth and left him sitting in the little room. As he sat there, he thought more about the DNA. He rubbed his face. He hadn't shaved in two days. The stubble of his beard was scratchy. In that second, he remembered the scratch that had long since healed on his face from where that bitch in Boise got him. His face went flush. His heart started pounding. They had him. Maybe not for the girl in Spokane. But they had him.

CHAPTER 9

"One more outing with these guys, and I think I'll have enough to get them all," Luke said to Captain Davis the night after the men killed the wolves. "I need to wrap this up. I've never worked so hard in my life."

Luke had actually been promoted at the mill. Mike Robertson had called him into his office during an afternoon break and had complimented him on his work ethic.

"You're doing a great job, Luke," Robertson said. "How would you like to get off of the green chain?"

"I'll do whatever you need me to do, boss. As long as I get a paycheck each Friday, I'm happy."

They moved him over to the dryer. Not easy work, but a little easier than pulling heavy green lumber off the chain. It also moved him away from Thomas. He didn't like being out of touch with the leader of the ring, but on most days he would join Thomas, and sometimes the other guys, for lunch or on break.

"I think you've got enough now," Davis said over the phone.

"But if you can get another nail or two for their coffins, I'd say go for it."

"They were talking about killing an elk, so I think they'll be going again. Whether I'll get an invite or not, I don't know. And they said they'd take me along the next time they go for wolves, but who knows when that might be."

"Why don't we start tracking their cell phones," Davis said. "I know service is sketchy up in that area, but even if they go without you, maybe we'll have an idea where they are. You could just happen onto them, or would that be too obvious?"

"Let me think on that. I believe they'll invite me along sometime soon. And if I have enough to arrest them, I'll want Whitson and Stephens standing by. Three against one would be enough for them to try to come after me. I can handle a couple of them, but not all three."

"What about the local deputies? You could call them in."

"The Spokane guys are pretty sure there's a leak in that department. How else did Hernandez know to clear his house right before that raid last year?"

"That's right. You told me that. Okay. I'll call the enforcement captain in Spokane and let him know what's happening. He can pass it on to Whitson and Stephens."

✳

A few days after Carter and Hernandez killed the wolves, Thomas stopped by a table where Luke was reading another Sandford novel during afternoon break.

"Hey, Rook. You up for something this weekend?"

Thomas and the others made it a point to never say anything about going hunting or what they might be going after.

"I guess it depends on what's on the menu."

"We'll chat later. Stop by the tavern after work. The boys and I will be there making some plans."

"See ya there," Luke said and went back to his book.

Luke would have liked to have been wired up to record the

conversation at the tavern, but there wasn't enough time to make that happen. If he got the opportunity, he would try to record the meeting with his cell phone. He would play that by ear. He certainly didn't want to create any suspicion by doing something stupid now.

Ricky Carter gave Luke the evil eye anytime he was around. Luke didn't trust him, and he knew the feeling was mutual. Thomas and Hernandez seemed more at ease with Luke. They treated him like a friend and gave no sign that they thought he was anything more than just another down-on-his-luck dude who had stumbled into town and found a job at the mill.

Still, Luke was not fully in their circle. He knew they did things together at other times when he wasn't included. One or all of them had gone out and killed the two white-tailed deer they had used for the coyote bait. He might end up in their inner circle at some point, but that was going to take more time. Time he didn't have.

Luke was tiring of all this. He had been undercover for almost two months. He missed Sara. He missed Jack. And he missed his job patrolling the Cascades in central Washington.

One way or another, this was going to end soon. He hoped this next outing would be it.

*

Luke walked out of daylight into the hazy darkness of the Pastime Tavern, a favorite watering hole for many of the workers at the mill. Smoking was not allowed in the establishment, but there was always a smoky fog in the place. It smelled of beer and fried food. He had been in the tavern a couple of times before, but didn't make a habit of stopping after work. Luke wasn't a big beer drinker, but he would have one now and again to keep up appearances.

Two guys Luke recognized from the mill were playing pool at the lone pool table in the back of the place. Luke spotted Thomas, Hernandez, and Carter sitting in a booth, not far from the pool table. George Strait's "Amarillo by Morning" was playing from a jukebox somewhere in the building, and there was the normal tavern din of people talking, glasses clinking, and pool balls clattering.

Luke had his cell phone in a chest pocket, turned on to record the conversation. With all the ambient noise, he wasn't sure it would work, but it was worth a try.

"What's up, fellas?" Luke asked as he sat down next to Hernandez. Carter didn't even look at him.

"You still want to check ol' White Fang off your bucket list?" Hernandez asked.

"I wouldn't turn down the chance," Luke said.

"The fur buyer is screaming for pelts," Thomas said. "He's now paying seven hundred and fifty bucks a piece for them. Would be a quick way to make a little extra money."

"If I got one, I'd want to tan the hide and keep it," Luke said.

"That's your choice," Hernandez said. "Me, I like having the money."

"Me too," Carter mumbled.

"We need to do a little prep work," Thomas said. "We gotta get some bait out and keep replenishing it until we see the right canines working it."

"Happy to help," Luke said. "Just let me know when and where."

"We'll all go out on Friday after work and see if we can get some bait," Hernandez said. "Then, on Saturday, we'll put it out."

"We'll pick you and your bait up at daybreak on Saturday," Thomas said.

The four men sat for a while longer, drinking their beers and chatting about work. Carter was watching a couple of young women who had come in and sat at the bar, and Hernandez noticed it.

"There you go, Ricky," Hernandez said. "You said you were needing some female companionship. One of them pretty ladies should work. Go talk to 'em."

"Shut up, Manny," Carter said. "They're not my type."

"You mean, they are real living, breathing women, not blow-up dolls," Thomas said. He and Hernandez laughed. Luke did not.

"Screw all of you," Carter said and got up and left.

"We're just teasing," Thomas said to Carter as he was leaving. "Take it easy."

"You sure Ricky is mentally stable?" Luke asked after Carter was gone. "He looks at me like he wants to kill me."

"Oh, he's just sore about that comment you made to him in front of everybody about not calling you a rookie," Hernandez said. "I wouldn't put too much into it."

"He got knocked around some by his old man when he was growing up," Thomas said. "But he's always been good with us. He's dependable and doesn't mind doing some of the nasty jobs."

Luke wondered what that meant.

"Yeah, you can count on Ricky showing up with some bait on Saturday morning," Hernandez said. "He's been hunting all his life, living off the land most of it."

"I gotta run," Thomas said.

"Me too," Hernandez said.

They both stood and left Luke sitting at the table. When they were gone, he also got up and walked to the front door. As he did, the two gals at the bar turned and gave him a good, long look. Then one, a tall woman of about thirty, with long reddish-brown hair, got up and followed him out.

"Hey there," she said as Luke was reaching for the door handle on his Bronco. "Do I know you from somewhere?"

Luke looked at the woman. He didn't recognize her and hoped she didn't know him as the real Luke, a clean-shaven enforcement officer with the Department of Fish and Wildlife.

"Not unless you work at the mill," Luke said. "That's where I spend most of my life."

"You look like someone I saw on TV once," she said. "You ever been on TV?"

"No, ma'am," Luke said. "Not that I know of."

Could someone really remember seeing him with the alligator almost two years ago?

"Hmmm, it'll come to me. Why you leaving so soon. I'd be glad to buy you a beer."

"That's awful nice of you, but I have all kinds of things I gotta get done before work in the morning. And sleep is right at the top of the list."

"Okay then," she said as she turned back toward the bar. "Hope I see you around."

Luke climbed into the rig, fired it up, and headed for home. When he got there, he pulled his phone out and listened to the audio recording. He hadn't remembered the exact conversation, but most of it was audible when he listened again. It wasn't totally incriminating, but there was enough there to add to the stack of evidence he was collecting.

Like Captain Davis had said. One more nail for their coffins.

He listened to his discussion with the woman too. He would have to somehow erase that. If Sara heard it, she would be driving to Colville to drag him home.

*

Luke could only assume the other three men were going out Friday night to spotlight some deer. That would be the easiest and quickest way to get some fresh meat for a bait pile. Drive out into a field where deer were feeding, shine a powerful light in their eyes to make them stop and stare—á la a deer in the headlights—and blam, you had deer meat.

Luke disliked poachers, and he was always happy when he or the other enforcement officers were able to catch them. Game animals belong to all citizens, and when someone killed them illegally, they were stealing from the public.

In his career, Luke had seen all kinds of poachers. Some just got so excited in the moment they couldn't resist taking a buck deer or bull elk with too many or too few antler points. Other poachers were those who liked to kill for the thrill of killing. And many were into poaching primarily for the money. There are black markets for all kinds of meats and body parts from game animals, including antlers, gallbladders, and hides. The three men Luke worked with at the mill were probably a combination of those who enjoyed killing and wanted to profit from it.

The final kind of poacher was the person who was killing simply to feed themselves or their family. Luke always had a soft spot for those poachers. He could empathize with them to some extent and figured if his family were starving, he would shoot a deer or elk out of season to feed them. Unbeknownst to his superiors, Luke had, after checking out their stories, let some people go who had killed an animal illegally to feed their family.

Luke would need to acquire some animals for bait by Saturday, and after the men mentioned it, he had come up with an idea that would not require taking any animals illegally.

Across America, it is estimated that there are close to two million animals killed by vehicles each year. Of those killed, deer are the animals most likely to be involved in a collision. In Washington and many other western states, citizens can salvage a dead deer or other game animal simply by contacting the state wildlife department to get approval and a salvage number. In the two months of driving around northeastern Washington, Luke had seen dozens of dead deer along the road. Instead of going out and poaching a couple of deer to add to the bait pile, his plan was to drive the highway to Spokane and back on Friday night. Surely, he would find a couple of fresh roadkill deer to salvage.

CHAPTER 10

It had taken Luke until almost midnight to get two road-killed white-tailed deer. They were lying on a blue tarp in the back of his Bronco when Buck Thomas pulled up in front of his apartment.

As he was driving Highway 395 south the night before, Luke wondered if having everyone go get some deer for the bait pile was a test. Besides the one turkey, the men had not seen Luke take an animal illegally. So, as a simple precaution, to keep gaining cred with the trio, Luke had taken both road kills up into the National Forest and shot each in the head to make it appear as if they'd been killed by a rifle.

One of the deer had an obvious broken leg from being struck by a vehicle, so Luke also shot it at the break to make it look like he had made a poor first shot. A trained eye would see other evidence of a collision with a car, including scuffs in the hide and broken ribs, but Luke hoped the men wouldn't look past the bullet holes.

"How'd you do?" Thomas asked.

"Two deer," Luke said.

Thomas almost looked surprised.

"What?" Luke asked. "Isn't that what we were supposed to do?"

"No, yeah," Thomas stuttered as he helped Luke load one of the deer into the back of his truck. "These are perfect. Good job."

Luke noticed Thomas also had two deer in the bed of the truck—a doe that had been shot in the head and a young buck with small velvet-covered antlers that had been shot in the side.

"Manny heard some wolves howling up near Mount Rogers last night, so that's where we are headed."

"Sounds good," Luke said. "I assume this will take some time to get them to come in?"

"It usually does, but who knows. We might just get lucky and spot them without having to bait them."

Luke had not communicated with officers Whitson and Stephens in the past week, but now he wished he had. If the men ended up killing some wolves, he would want to make arrests right away. He would somehow have to deal with it if that is what happened.

Thomas drove to the north edge of town where Hernandez and Carter were waiting in a pullout in Hernandez's Chevy pickup. As Thomas parked behind the Chevy, both men got out.

"You get any bait, Hayes?" Carter asked with a tone in his voice that barely disguised his distaste for Luke.

"It's Haynes," Luke said, staring at Carter.

He didn't answer Carter's question. Thomas did though.

"He sure did. Two deer. And I got two more. How about you boys?"

"I got three," Carter said proudly. "And Manny got two."

"Nice," Thomas said. "That'll give us enough for four bait piles. One of them should attract something."

Seven poached deer in one night. Luke wondered just how many deer these men had killed illegally over the years.

"Oh, I'm sure they will," Hernandez said. "Let's get them placed."

With that, Hernandez turned and jumped back into his truck with Carter trailing.

Luke climbed into Thomas's rig, and they followed Hernandez north out of town toward Mount Rogers.

"We stake the deer down, so the coyotes or cougars can't drag them away," Thomas explained. Luke had noticed the deer the men had used for bait earlier were staked down with heavy limbs, sharpened to a point.

"And we like to put game cameras up so we can see what's coming in."

"Don't you need phone service for that?" Luke asked naively, although he knew the answer already.

"Yes, but where we don't get good service, we check the cameras every night. Once we see the wolves are feeding on the bait, we move in right away."

"What if it's on a weekday?"

"One or two of us might just get the flu and call in sick at work."

"I've heard the animal lovers and Feds get real possessive of their wolves here in Washington. Aren't you worried they might figure out what's happening to some of their precious babies?"

Thomas laughed. "We only take five or six a year, and we move around. And we never shoot a collared one. They've never suspected a thing. Besides, no one seems to really know how many wolves there are. The game department has estimates, but from what we can see, they are way off. There are lots more wolves than they think, so we take one here and one there, and they are none the wiser."

"Good to know," Luke said. "I guess I better get one soon or you guys will be done for the year."

"We'll get you one," Thomas said. "But it might take a bit."

The four men spent most of the rest of the day staking out the dead deer and placing the game cameras. Luke paid special attention to where the cameras were placed, as he planned to come back out and take photos of the deer baits. He certainly didn't want to get caught on one of their cameras.

The bait piles were positioned on four sides of the mountain. Hernandez, who seemed to be the expert at baiting, believed that by doing so, the wolves, which can travel many miles a day, would smell the deer and get on one of the baits within twenty-four hours.

"If they don't, we may have to do this again," Hernandez said. "Damn coyotes will gobble the deer up in no time if the wolves don't get there first."

"I don't mind," Carter said with a sly smile. "I like shooting deer."

"We have phone service on two of the cameras," Hernandez said. "Buck will keep an eye on those with his computer. I'll come out early tomorrow morning and see what else is on the other two cameras. You need to be ready to get up here if we got a pack working one of the baits," he said to Luke.

"I'll be ready," Luke said. "But won't you guys be coming along too?"

"Yep, but we're always ready," Carter said. "You ain't the only one that wants a wolf. I need the cash."

*

Driving out of the mountains, Luke spotted four elk just up the hill in some trees. He was still in Thomas's truck, and they were leading the way down the road. He almost said something to Thomas about the elk but thought better of it.

Unfortunately, Carter saw them too. Luke looked back just in time to see Hernandez's Chevy slam to a stop, and Carter bailing out of the cab with a rifle.

Thomas noticed the truck had stopped and said, "Grab your rifle. They may have spotted some wolves."

Luke knew that even if he really hustled, Carter and maybe Hernandez would have already taken a shot at the elk. He looked up, and the elk were running through the trees.

Boom! Boom! Boom!

Luke was out of the truck with his rifle in seconds, but the elk were gone.

"Did you hit anything?" Thomas asked.

"I hit the last one," Carter said.

"I'm pretty sure I missed," Hernandez said.

"Well, we better go find the one Ricky hit," Thomas said. "We'll park the trucks off the road back there, and we'll go butcher it up."

"Good thing Luke is here," Hernandez said. "He looks like he could pack half an elk all by himself."

It was dark when the men finally found the dead cow elk. When they cleaned her, they discovered she was pregnant. The dead calf was near term. It really pissed Luke off. It was a senseless waste of an animal. He was going to really enjoy taking these guys down.

"I've never seen an unborn calf before," Luke said in awe, as if he were really interested in the fetus. He took out his phone and snapped some photos.

The men looked at him like he was stupid. Little did they know it was another nail in the coffin.

When the elk was skinned and cut up, each man took a quarter and threw it over their shoulder. Luke also carried one of the backstraps. Hernandez carried the other.

Carter struggled with his load. Maybe because he always looked like he was walking uphill, and with the weight of the elk meat on his back, he fell backwards three times. And he had to stop to rest frequently.

"Come on, man," Luke finally said when Carter stopped to rest again. "Why'd you shoot this thing if you can't even get it out to the truck."

It was another chance to get under Carter's skin. And it worked. Carter, who had already dropped the front quarter he was carrying, pulled the knife he had used to butcher the deer.

"I've had it with you!" Carter said, walking toward Luke. "I'm gunna cut you into little pieces."

Luke quickly dropped the hind quarter he was carrying, and then he started to laugh. That made Carter stop.

Thomas and Hernandez just stood there and watched.

"You better think twice about what you are going to do here, Ricky," Luke said to Carter. He said "Ricky" like he was talking to a five-year-old child. "It will only end one of two ways. You'll either get the shit beat outta you, or you'll be dead."

"Is that right?" Carter hissed. "I'm the one with the knife."

Luke was glad Carter had left his rifle in the truck because he was pretty sure if the scrawny man had had his gun, he would have shot Luke.

"That's what the last guy said to me," Luke said. "He ended up in the hospital, and I went to jail. I don't want to go to jail again, and I'm pretty sure you don't want to go to the hospital, or to the morgue."

Finally, Thomas weighed in.

"Okay, okay. Put the knife away, Ricky. I've never seen Luke fight, but my guess is he'd have you eating dirt in no time, knife or no knife."

Hernandez laughed.

"Your choice," Luke said. "But whatever it is, let's get on with it. I'm hungry and tired."

Luke could see Carter thinking very hard. There was rage in his eyes, but he was coming to quickly realize that Luke wasn't scared and was ready for a fight. Finally, Carter slid the knife back in its sheath on his hip and picked up the elk quarter.

As he walked by Luke, Carter said under his breath, "Just you wait."

Luke chuckled and said, "Keep on truckin'." Then he picked up the elk meat and followed the group down the trail. He would never let Carter stand or walk behind him again. The last thing he needed was a knife in the back.

CHAPTER 11

The first test on the blood found in Rakes' truck confirmed it was from a human. The DNA part of the test on the blood, and on the long blonde hair found in the cab, would take a little longer. The King County Sheriff's Office believed it had the right person, but the county prosecuting attorney was of the opinion they didn't have enough to hold Rakes.

"Mr. Rakes," the arresting deputy said as he came back into the room where they were holding the big man. "We're going to release you. But we may need you to come back in for more questions. You'll need to stay in the Seattle area for another day or two."

"Yessir," Rakes said and stood up to leave.

"Please keep your phone on so we can reach you if necessary."

"Yessir," Rakes said again. "I need to go pick up those parts in Renton in the morning. Is that okay?"

"That's fine. But don't leave the Seattle area."

The forensic team had gone through Rakes' truck with black

lights, tweezers, and vacuum cleaners and had dusted for prints. They'd found two different usable prints on the passenger side door handle where someone would pull the door closed. There were other prints that were smudged and unidentifiable.

Neither of the usable prints matched Desiree Murphy. The prints were sent on to Boise and Wyoming. They were not a match to the dead women there either.

Rakes was surprised they had let him go. He knew it took some time to get DNA from saliva, so maybe that's what the cops were waiting for. And maybe they didn't know about the woman in Boise. But he couldn't count on that.

They allowed him to take the truck, which he also thought was strange. If they really did have something on him, would they do that? He needed to think about it.

Rakes called his boss, who seemed to be very concerned about him and the truck and the parts in Renton that needed to be picked up.

"Don't worry," Rakes said. "The police brought me in for some questions, but they released me. I think it's all a misunderstanding because I parked to take a nap near where some woman was found dead."

His boss gasped. He said he had read about the murdered woman near Spokane.

Rakes reassured him he would be picking up the parts first thing in the morning and then would be headed back to Great Falls.

"Okay," his boss said. "Let me know when you are on the road back."

"Will do," Rakes said and hung up.

Rakes drove the truck back to the motel near SeaTac. He took a hot shower and lay down on the bed. Within seconds, he was asleep.

In his dreams, the skinny woman he had killed in Havre came to him. She was alive, except her head was not right. He was looking at her from behind, but her head was facing him. Her face was as white as snow. Her eyes were wide open, unblinking. She was mouthing words, but no sound was coming out. Repeatedly, she mouthed three words. You. Are. Dead. You. Are. Dead. You. Are. Dead.

Rakes fought to wake up. He hadn't thought about the woman in years. Now, here she was haunting his dreams. Or was she? No, he decided it was just his subconscious telling him what he already knew. He was about to go down for murdering the woman in Spokane, and possibly for the woman in Boise as well.

He had never regretted killing those two women, or any of the others. But he would just as soon not spend the rest of his life in prison. As he lay there, thinking about the woman ghost, he decided it was time to disappear. There were four million people living in and around the city of Seattle. Even he could become invisible in a mass of humanity like that.

*

The first test that definitively tied Rakes to the murder of Desiree Murphy came back early the next morning. The blood found on the door jamb of the truck was a match to the woman. It was enough to arrest Rakes, and as soon as the sheriff's department received word, two deputies were sent to the motel where he was staying.

When the deputies arrived, the Big Sky Auto Parts truck was there in the parking lot. But Rakes was gone.

A quick run-through of the motel's security camera footage showed Rakes leaving his room at 3:04 a.m. He walked out of the room, past the truck, and the last they saw of the big man was him walking up a sidewalk, headed east.

The King County Sheriff's Office immediately put out an APB on one Claude Rakes.

*

It was three days later that the DNA match was made on the blonde hair found in Rakes' truck. It just confirmed what the law enforcement people already knew. Desiree Murphy was in his truck, and Rakes was probably the killer.

They were even more certain when Rakes' DNA was then matched to the skin samples taken from under the fingernails of the murdered woman in Boise. That confirmed he had most likely killed her as well. There was still no actual evidence connecting Rakes to the two women who were found murdered in Wyoming, but officials there were of the belief he had killed them too.

Soon Rakes' photo was being shown on newscasts and on the internet all around the Northwest. How could such a large, strange-looking man go unnoticed, people wondered. Yet, no one had seen Rakes since he'd walked away from the motel in SeaTac.

*

On any given day, there are an estimated twelve thousand homeless people in Seattle. Fewer than half are in shelters. Most of the others live in tents, cardboard boxes, make-shift lean-tos, or they just huddle in doorways or under bridges and overpasses covered in sleeping bags, blankets, and coats.

It had only taken Rakes about twenty minutes of walking before he hit the first homeless encampment. The overcast, moonless night made it darker than the inside of an old boot, but he was able to still find some items that seemed to be unclaimed. Or at least they were unclaimed enough that he could make them his. Next to a half-torn tent was a blanket. The thing was dirty and stunk like urine, but he didn't care. He pulled the blanket up over his head and shoulders. He didn't need it for warmth—he needed it to cover his face and to blend in.

Rakes walked on. Twice, people came up to him and asked him for money, but as soon as they saw how big he was, and his face, they walked away.

At a second camp, Rakes secured a sleeping bag and found a Safeway shopping cart that was empty and just sitting there. By the time it was light enough to see, Rakes had transformed himself into just another homeless street person, pushing a cart full of items, blanket over his head, sleeping bag wrapped around his shoulders. To add to the disguise, Rakes had taken a piece of burnt wood from a fire ring in one of the camps and had wiped the black ashes all over his face. When he was done, it looked like he hadn't bathed in weeks.

*

In Great Falls, people were also on the lookout for Rakes. Police believed he would return there, so they put an officer at his small house south of town, watching it twenty-four hours a day.

The local TV stations had interviewed Rakes' boss at the Auto Parts Company.

"He's a little different, but very smart," the manager said. "Talks slow. Moves slow. But don't let that fool you, Claude is very intelligent."

"Yet, he was just a delivery man," the twenty-six-year-old anchorwoman of the morning news said very seriously, wrapping up the story after the interview played on the NBC affiliate in Great Falls.

Rakes' photo was all over the media in Montana. A waitress at an all-night diner in Billings believed she had seen Rakes in the restaurant the night before the women were found with broken necks in Wyoming. Montana State police obtained records from the Auto Parts Company and found that Rakes had made deliveries in Billings that afternoon, and in Cody, Wyoming the next day.

Not that they were needed, but the records also showed he had picked up some parts in Meridian, Idaho just outside of Boise on the day the woman who was killed there went missing.

As one TV reporter put it, "It seems Claude Rakes has been a very bad boy."

*

Rakes hadn't seen any news reports, but he had to assume his photo was being shown around if they had matched his DNA to the woman he'd killed in Boise. He still didn't think they could tie him to the girl in Spokane.

Counting the money he had taken from the girl's little gold purse, Rakes had a hundred and seventy-six dollars in his pocket when he'd walked away from the motel. By only spending a few dollars each day on cheap McDonald's or Burger King food, he had enough to last for a couple of weeks. He worried about going into those places, that someone might recognize his face, but he would always time it so he followed another homeless person or two into the restaurant. To the seventeen-year-old kid behind the cash register, the homeless people all looked, and smelled, the same.

He had even gone into a McDonald's where two Seattle city police officers were enjoying a Big Mac. He walked right by them, and they never even looked up. Maybe he could stay incognito like this for a while. At least until the news cycle moved on to the next big story, and they started to forget about Claude Rakes.

When he left the motel and the truck, he had also left his phone. And he had not used any credit cards. He knew they could track him with those. Not that any respectable business would accept a card from a person who was homeless and looked like he did.

He moved around a lot but spent most nights under an overpass not far from where the Mariners played their home games. When it rained, he would stay holed up under the overpass until it cleared.

On two different occasions, homeless men tried to harass him, but when they got close enough to size him up, and looked past the grime on his face, they moved on. If he had to, Rakes would kill anyone who gave him any problems. And he wouldn't give it a second thought.

*

Three days after the news came out about four women in the Northwest found dead from a broken neck, Dr. Johnny Jim Lawrence, a retired forensic dentist from Washington and the new coroner in Havre, Montana, started searching through old autopsy files, specifically looking for women who had died from a broken neck. The coroner had discovered several errors on past cases made by the former coroner, who evidently was bad at his job and might have been under the influence of alcohol for much of his tenure.

Interestingly, Dr. Lawrence came upon a case of a woman who had, according to his predecessor, succumbed from a broken neck sustained during a fall in her bathtub.

About that same time, Meagan Lockhart, a reporter for the Havre Daily News, started doing some digging after she heard that Claude Rakes had been born and raised in Havre. A search through past Havre High School yearbooks showed that Rakes had graduated thirteen years before. Lockhart tracked down some of Rakes' classmates who still lived in the area and asked about him. To a person, they said they remembered Rakes as a big kid, a little slow, but none remembered seeing him after high school.

"It's like he just disappeared after graduation," a former classmate, who wanted to remain anonymous, said. "He didn't seem to have any friends. I can see why he left. Some people called him names and thought he was mentally challenged."

The anonymous classmate didn't happen to mention that she was one of the people who made fun of Rakes.

Lockhart also talked to some teachers from back then. They remembered Rakes as being quiet but intelligent.

"Claude always did well in my class," said a former biology teacher. "Several of us teachers wondered if he might be cheating on tests, but we watched him, and he didn't cheat. He was just very smart. He talked slowly, and moved around slowly, but I wouldn't call him mentally slow."

After seeing the newspaper story reminding readers that now-suspected murderer Claude Rakes grew up in Havre, Dr. Lawrence reached out to Lockhart and told her he was reviewing the autopsy of Addy Dawson, a thirty-six-year-old woman who had died from a broken neck thirteen years earlier. Lawrence had looked at the x-rays and the photos taken at the scene, and he was of the opinion there was no way Dawson could have broken her neck in a fall like that.

While not coming right out and accusing him of the murder, Lockhart's next story in the daily newspaper pointed several fingers at Rakes as Addy Dawson's killer. The woman had been murdered thirteen years ago, shortly before Havre High School graduation, and her death, according to the new medical examiner, couldn't have been an accident. It appeared Claude Rakes had left town just before the woman's body was discovered.

In the article, Lockhart wrote: "Although just a young man of eighteen, Claude Rakes had incredible size and strength. Addy Dawson, recently divorced and new to Havre, was seemingly trying to get her life back together. Could she have been the first victim of this now suspected mass murderer? Local police would certainly like to talk to Mr. Rakes about that."

The story went on to quote several other local people, who now seemed to remember Claude Rakes vividly. Most believed at the time that the teen could have been a killer just by the way he acted, talked, and looked. They also remembered Addy Dawson as being a cheerful, friendly, pretty woman, who certainly didn't deserve to die, although truth be told, no one really remembered her at all.

CHAPTER 12

Sixteen days after Rakes walked away from the motel in SeaTac, he was arrested for the murder of Desiree Murphy. Who knows how long he might have lived among the homeless if a University of Washington college professor hadn't identified him. The professor was living with the homeless as part of a study to determine where the people who were suffering from "housing insecurities" came from.

Dressed as if he, too, were homeless, the professor spent most of every day in the camps and around other places where the homeless congregated. Then, in the evenings he would catch the light rail to his posh, two-bedroom apartment not far from the Space Needle. It seemed the professor wanted to learn as much about the homeless as he could, but he was unwilling to give up a warm, dry, soft bed, a hot shower, and his morning cup of fresh-ground Seattle's Best coffee to do so.

At home, the professor read *The Seattle Times* and watched the evening news, so he was quite aware authorities were looking for Claude Rakes in connection with at least one woman's death. Not that he was out searching for Rakes, but since the man just magically seemed to have disappeared, the professor believed there was a chance Rakes could be living among the thousands of faceless junkies, mentally ill, and others who were living on the streets of the Emerald City.

The professor spotted Rakes one day walking out from under an overpass and watched as the man walked across a freeway, jumped a jersey barrier, and crossed some railroad tracks on his way somewhere. The man, the professor thought, looked homeless, but he didn't fit the type. He moved slowly, but not from years of alcohol or drug abuse. The big man was constantly looking around, watching for something or someone.

Instead of calling authorities right away, the professor kept an eye on Rakes for two more days. Once, he worked his way around so that he would pass Rakes coming at him on a sidewalk. Rakes kept his head down, but the professor got a good glimpse of his face. Even through the dirt and grime, he knew the man he had just seen was Claude Rakes.

The next morning at dawn, before the professor had finished his first cup of gourmet coffee, six Seattle police officers arrived in three patrol cars at the overpass where Rakes had taken up residence and arrested the big man without incident.

*

When the cops finally showed up, Rakes was almost relieved. He was running low on money, and his back hurt from sleeping on concrete. Seeing there were six officers there, some pointing pistols at him, others holding Tasers, Rakes gave up without a struggle. They handcuffed him, walked him to one of the police cruisers, shoved him in the back seat, and drove away.

As they drove off, Rakes looked up at his spot under the overpass. Two men were already gathering up his blankets and coats and sleeping bags. No one was paying any attention to the police cars. It was something they saw frequently, and they had no interest in who they had just picked up or why they'd taken him.

The Seattle city police had arrested Rakes on a warrant issued by the Spokane County district attorney. He was wanted for the death of Desiree Murphy. When they officially read him his rights, they told Rakes why they were arresting him. It surprised him a little because he thought there just couldn't be enough evidence there. Obviously, he had fouled up.

The Seattle police put him in a room like the one he had been in when the King County deputies had brought him in for questioning days before. They kept him handcuffed and waiting in the room for almost an hour.

When the door finally opened, a nicely dressed detective entered. "Mr. Rakes," she said. "My name is Alicia Royer. I know the arresting officer read you your rights, but I want to make sure you are clear on just what they are."

She spoke to him slowly, like he might have trouble with the English language. He could never get away from it. This woman, just as many other people had throughout his life, judged him only by his looks. She thought he was slow. Stupid.

Rakes just looked at her.

"You know you don't have to answer any questions without an attorney present, and we can provide an attorney for you if you can't afford one?"

Again, Rakes just looked at her.

"Do you understand, Mr. Rakes?"

Still no answer. He would not be giving her, or anyone else, any answers.

Rakes had read dozens of books and seen plenty of TV shows that showed police procedures. He knew that if the Spokane County DA had issued the arrest warrant, he wouldn't be staying in Seattle long. They would be transferring him to Spokane at some point soon. There was no sense in talking to these people. So he didn't.

The Seattle police moved Rakes to the King County Jail in downtown Seattle where he sat for three days waiting for an arraignment. Because they needed to keep him apprised of his rights, the court appointed a public defender to communicate with, and for, Rakes.

The public defender was a young black man named Jamal Jordan who looked like he might be all of nineteen years old. Rakes, of all people, didn't judge the lawyer by his looks and didn't ask about his age or credentials.

"Spokane County is requesting that you be transferred as soon as possible," Jordan said during a brief meeting with Rakes at the jail. "Is there any reason to try to delay that?"

"There is no reason to stay here, is there?" Rakes said.

"Not that I know of. It sounds like Idaho wants to file charges against you as well. But since you were arrested under the warrant in Spokane, they need to have you there first."

"A jail's a jail, whether in Spokane or Boise. Doesn't mean much difference to me."

"You don't seem to be very upset about all this, Mr. Rakes."

"They must have enough evidence to convict me. As my lawyer, I can tell you that I did kill those women, and a few others too, without you telling anyone else, right?"

"That's correct."

"I did it because they were bad people. I've dealt with bad, mean, nasty people my whole life. The world is better without those women in it."

Jordan thought about that for a minute.

"You are most likely right, Mr. Rakes. But our society doesn't abide by people just killing someone because they are mean or nasty. The courts don't take kindly to folks taking the law into their own hands."

"I did what I had to do," Rakes said.

Again, Jordan hesitated as he thought about it.

"They will be sending you by van to Spokane tomorrow morning. Best of luck to you, Mr. Rakes."

Rakes looked Jordan in the eyes and just nodded.

*

The transfer of Rakes from Seattle to Spokane would have happened a day earlier, but the authorities delayed it so another prisoner could go along. Travel budgets and all that. Might as well take two birds in one bus and save the good taxpayers of Washington a few bucks.

Rakes was dressed in an orange jumpsuit and shackled with handcuffs and ankle restraints that were connected by a chain that ran down his front. When the officers loaded him into the transport van, there was already another orange-clad prisoner in the back seat. The man was shackled just like Rakes, but whoever had done the shackling made it a bit more uncomfortable on the man. The chain between the handcuffs and ankle restraints was much shorter than Rakes was, and it forced the man to hunch over all the time.

Even before he got into the van, Rakes could hear the other prisoner yelling about something.

"You dirty son-of-a-bitch, you did this on purpose," he yelled at the officers in the front seats.

"Yeah, yeah, just shut up and enjoy the ride," the officer in the passenger seat said. "We'll be there in six or seven hours."

Rakes' arrival quieted the other man down, but only for a minute.

After the officers got Rakes situated, they locked the door on the steel cage that surrounded the prisoners on three sides in the back of the van. On the fourth side, the front side of the cage, a heavy Plexiglass barrier was set up between the back and the front of the van. Small holes had been drilled into the Plexiglass so the officers could communicate with the prisoners.

"Well, what do we have here," the man already in the cage said to Rakes. "My, aren't you an ugly one."

"Shut up, Jenkins," the officer in the passenger seat yelled.

"What's your name, boy?" Jenkins asked.

"Rakes."

"Like the lawn tool?"

"Yep."

"Well, Rakes, my name is James Earl Jenkins. I guess we're gunna be travel buddies."

Jenkins was smaller than Rakes, and younger. He had a pockmarked face like he'd had bad acne as a kid, along with greasy, shoulder-length blond hair, and a tattoo of a spider crawling up his neck.

"Whatcha in for?" Jenkins asked.

"I killed some women," Rakes said.

"Yeah, well, we got something in common then, because so did I."

Rakes didn't say anything to that. He just watched the buildings and people on the sidewalks go by as the van motored through downtown Seattle, headed east to the interstate.

"How'd you kill 'em?" Jenkins whispered.

Rakes said nothing.

"I shot my old lady in the face and then killed her mother too. Both of them was A-number-one bitches. I was tired of listenin' to them, all the time ragging on me to get a job."

Rakes continued to watch the world go by through the metal bars on the side window. The bars made him think about prison. Until the police arrested him under the overpass, he had never given much thought to being locked up. He believed he had been so careful when he killed the women, he would never do jail time. But now, it was looking like he might just end up spending the rest of his life behind bars.

He knew Washington no longer had the death penalty, but he wasn't sure about Idaho. If they did have the evidence to convict him on the killing of the woman in Boise, would he end up there on death row?

Montana did have capital punishment. But he thought there might be a statute of limitations on the woman he had killed in Havre. That was what, fourteen years ago, so maybe the clock had run out on that one. Besides, the police surely had no evidence to convict him for killing her. If they did, they would have come after him a long time ago.

He thought about it some more. If he had the choice, maybe he would just go ahead and take the electric chair. Quick and easy, without having to stare at concrete walls and bars for the next fifty years. And he wouldn't have to listen to people like this idiot Jenkins who had been talking non-stop for the past hour.

"Could you please shut up?" yelled the officer in the passenger seat.

"I can talk if I want to," Jenkins said. "I know my rights."

Rakes shut it all out and watched the cars, the buildings, and the trees go by.

CHAPTER 13

Luke was awakened out of a dead sleep by his phone ringing. It was 5:15. He looked at the screen and saw the caller was Buck Thomas.

"Hey, Buck. What's up?"

"We got wolves on one of the baits. We need to get up there right away. We'll pick you up in fifteen minutes."

"Okay," Luke said, but Thomas was already gone.

"You guys awake?" Luke asked after he clicked off the phone.

Dave Whitson and Cody Stephens were climbing out of sleeping bags in Luke's apartment. Whitson had slept on the couch, and Stephens on an air mattress on the floor.

"We're up," Stephens said. "What's the word?"

Luke had contacted Whitson the day before. He told him there was a chance that they might be needed in the morning, and that he and Stephens needed to be ready to roll at a moment's notice.

"We need to stay someplace in Colville," Whitson said. "A motel isn't going to work."

"How about rolling out at my place?" Luke proposed. "If I get a call to go, you can be right on our heels. And if not, I'll make you breakfast."

After discussing the possibilities the previous evening when Whitson and Stephens arrived at Luke's, they decided that Luke would carry a small GPS device that the officers could track.

When Luke received the call, he put the tracking device in his hip pocket and buttoned the flap. All three officers put Kevlar vests on. If Thomas, Hernandez, or Carter shot a wolf, the plan was to take all three of them down. The men would be armed, so the situation called for vests.

Luke had shown the officers where the baits were set via a GPS map of the area, and because the call came so early in the morning, he assumed they had seen the wolves on one of the two cameras that were sending photos to Thomas.

"Just in case you lose the tracker, that is where we'll be," Luke said, pointing at the map as he was getting ready to go. "Either here or here."

He hadn't worn a pistol during any of the past hunts with the men, but this time he did. Luke hoped they wouldn't notice it under his jacket, but if they did, he would figure out a reason for having it. And, for the first time, he carried his badge, which he put in his other back pocket. And he put some zip ties in his coat pocket. He preferred handcuffs, but this was a situation for less obvious restraints.

Luke grabbed his rifle, put his jacket on, and said, "Good luck, you guys. I hope this goes smoothly, but prepare for the worst. No one needs to get hurt. We'll get these guys at some point if we don't get them today."

When he stepped out his door, Thomas, Hernandez, and Carter were waiting for him in Carter's Excursion.

"Morning, Luke," Thomas said after Luke climbed in the back seat and closed the door. "If that is your name."

Luke looked at Thomas and said, "Of course, it's my name."

"You know those two women we was teasin' Ricky about at

the Pastime the other day?" Hernandez said. "I had an interesting conversation with one of them last night. Seems she thinks she seen you on TV."

"Yeah, if it's the tall one with reddish hair, she said the same thing to me after you guys left the other night. I've never been on TV in my life."

"She thinks you look like some game warden who caught an alligator down Yakima way a while back, and they put it on the news. She thought the game warden was very cute and says you look just like him."

Luke was thinking as fast as he could while trying to remain cool.

"I look like lots of people. I had a guy the other day that thought I had graduated from Colville High with his brother. I didn't graduate from Colville High, I've never spent any time in Yakima, and I don't know nothing about any alligators."

Carter was giving Luke the evil eye in the rearview mirror.

"What, you think I'm some kind of spy or something?" Luke asked.

"Stranger things have happened," Hernandez said.

"If I was a cop, wouldn't I have tried to arrest you when you shot those wolves the other day? And I sure as hell wouldn't be working at the mill."

Luke could see Thomas thinking about it.

Finally, Luke said, "Let me out. You don't trust me, I don't want to be where I'm not wanted. I'll walk back to the apartment and see you at work tomorrow."

Carter started to slow the truck down.

"No, no, keep driving, Ricky," Thomas said. "We need to figure this out."

"There's nothing to figure out, Buck," Luke said. "I worked my ass off for you on the green chain. Call Agnes. She checked all my references. Unless you think she's a cop too?"

After a moment of silence, Luke said, "I thought we were friends. Let me out."

He could see Thomas relaxing a little.

"No, you're right," Thomas said. "No one would work that hard at a shitty job if they didn't have to. That chick put a scare into us though."

"You put a scare into me," Luke said. "All I want to do is shoot a wolf. But I don't have to if you don't want me around."

Luke looked at Carter staring at him in the mirror. The guy was paranoid and slightly deranged. Luke would keep his eyes on him and take him down first when the time came.

*

Whitson and Stephens were in Whitson's personal truck, a newer GMC Sierra four-wheel-drive pickup. They took off from Luke's apartment three minutes after Luke had climbed into the older Ford Excursion.

"I've got a good signal," Stephens said as he looked at the laptop sitting in his lap. "Looks like they're headed right where Luke said they would."

They followed the signal out of town and into the National Forest to the northeast. They didn't push it, staying three miles behind the Excursion, marked on the map as a red dot moving along a Forest Service road.

Their plan was to wait until they saw the tracking unit stop. That would tell them Luke and the poachers had parked and were on their way into one of the baits.

"They've stopped," Stephens said.

Whitson stopped the truck, and they waited.

After two minutes, the red dot was moving off the road. Luke was out of the truck and walking to the bait.

"Okay, let's get up there," Stephens said. "Luke's out of the truck."

*

The plan, according to Thomas, was to move into the bait the same way they had the last time. He and Luke would move in one way, and Hernandez and Carter would come in from another to try to ambush any wolves that were moving away from the bait.

"You lead the way," Thomas said to Luke. "I want you to have first crack at them if they're still there."

It made Luke more than a little nervous that Thomas was going to be behind him, given the conversation they'd had earlier. But he had to take the lead to make sure this whole thing was going to work out like he and the other two WDFW officers had planned.

Luke was a skilled woodsman and hunter. He had learned at an early age how to walk through the woods quietly, and had been successful many times stalking to within easy gun range of deer and elk. He went into stalking mode and paid attention to all his senses. He used his eyes to search for the wolves while listening to every step that Thomas was taking behind him. If there were such a thing as a sixth sense, Luke was concentrating on it too. Any quick movement or the sound of a rifle coming off Thomas's shoulder, Luke would be ready to move.

"We're getting close," Thomas whispered to Luke when they stopped for a minute. "You ready?"

"Yessir," Luke whispered back. "Can't wait."

He had already decided he would not shoot a wolf. He would fire and miss if the animals were still at the bait. That might bring more suspicion from Thomas, but it didn't matter. If everything went as planned, they would be arresting the three men, and this would finally be over.

Luke didn't have to be told they were getting close. He knew precisely where the dead deer had been staked. He inched along, placing one foot in front of the other, making sure not to break a twig or crunch a leaf.

He could hear some magpies squawking just ahead. And he could hear Thomas breathing behind him. The short, stocky man wasn't in the greatest shape, and even this gradual uphill hike had him breathing harder. Luke slowed and crouched as he moved forward. He was listening for any sound that might tell him the wolves were feeding on the deer when BOOM, a rifle went off.

*

Whitson had dropped Stephens off at the spot on the GPS map where Luke had walked toward the wolf bait and then moved up the road to where the Excursion was parked. Stephens got out, grabbed his rifle—the same exact Springfield Armory .223 rifle that Whitson had taken—and moved into the trees, headed to the mark Luke had pinned on the GPS map.

Stephens and Whitson wore blue jackets with State Police boldly printed on the back. They had their badges affixed to their shirts, and caps with Washington State Department of Fish and Wildlife on the front. Both were wearing utility belts that held their state-issued pistols in a holster, pepper spray, a Taser, a flashlight, handcuffs and an ASP collapsible baton. They also carried radios that allowed them to stay in touch with each other and the regional dispatcher to call in for backup or medical assistance if that was needed. The men agreed they wouldn't talk on the radios until absolutely necessary.

Neither man knew how close they were to Luke or the others until the gun blast shook the woods. At the crack of the rifle, both men moved ahead quickly.

*

Luke jumped at the sound of the rifle. He certainly wasn't expecting it. In the first millisecond, he thought Thomas had fired the shot, but in the next, he realized the shot came from up the hill and through the trees. It was close, but not as close as Thomas was.

"What the hell?" Thomas hissed.

"Let's get up there," Luke said and took one step forward. As he did, he looked ahead and saw two wolves—one almost black, the other brown and gray—charging at them down the trail. They were close and getting closer.

"Look out," Luke yelled, as much to warn Thomas as to try to scare the wolves off the game trail they were on.

It worked. The two big canines made a right turn so quickly it was almost imperceptible.

"Shoot!" Thomas yelled.

And Luke did. He had brought his rifle up the second he saw the wolves headed their way and tracked them after they turned. They were flying through a patch of young pine trees. Luke caught movement in his scope and knew that if he actually tried to hit one, he would most likely miss. Intent on missing, he didn't lead the running wolves but shot right at them, knowing he would either hit a tree or hit a foot behind the last wolf.

Boom! Boom!

Thomas was firing as well. Luke could see his shots were missing too.

In an instant, the wolves were gone.

As he was tracking the wolves for his shot, Luke was aware there were other shots being fired from up the hill. The pack had split up, and Hernandez and Carter must have been firing at the other wolves.

Thomas's last shot was still echoing through the trees when he turned to Luke and said, "Well, hell, that wasn't how we planned it."

"Those things were moving so fast through the trees, I couldn't get a good shot," Luke said.

"Me either," Thomas said. "Let's go see what those guys got."

*

At the sound of the first shot, Whitson was moving quickly toward it. He hadn't gone fifteen yards and there were more rifle shots. Some sounded like they were coming from straight ahead of him and some down to his left. He ducked behind a tree just in case the shots were coming his way. He hadn't heard any bullets whirring by, so he didn't think someone was shooting at him, but it was better to be safe than sorry. He stayed there until the shooting seemed to be over.

Stephens' response was the same. He jumped behind a tree immediately.

Whitson figured the men must be shooting at the wolves, and

so, after waiting for a few minutes to make sure no more shots were fired, he moved ahead slowly. He crested a small rise in the hill and saw two men holding rifles, standing over a dead wolf.

"Got 'em," he whispered to himself.

But he didn't make his move just yet. There had been other shots fired. He wanted to wait until he heard Luke whistle.

CHAPTER 14

Luke knew this is where things could get dicey. The plan was that when Whitson and Stephens heard shots fired, they were to move in close enough to take the men, but to wait until Luke whistled for them to come in and identify themselves.

Since they weren't that far from where the other shots were fired, Luke decided to stay undercover for just a few more minutes. If he and Thomas could get over to Hernandez and Carter, it would be the best-case scenario. He would whistle for the officers, who hopefully were very close, and as soon as they appeared, Luke would draw his sidearm and tell the men to drop their rifles and lay face down on the ground.

So much for best laid plans.

*

"Good shot," Carter said as he and Hernandez walked up on the downed wolf. "Seven hundred and fifty dollars, baby!"

"I think you hit that light-colored one," Hernandez said after the men stood and admired his prize.

"I do too," Carter said. "I'm gunna see if I can find any blood."

"I'll start skinning this one. I wonder if Buck and Luke scored."

"I hope that sumbitch missed," Carter said. "But we'll know soon enough. Here they come. I'm gunna see if I hit that one."

Luke saw the two men standing and talking over a dead wolf, but as soon as they crested the hill, Carter turned and headed down a little draw.

"Wonder where Carter's going," Luke said.

"Maybe checking to see if they hit any others," Thomas said. "Looks like one of them scored."

That's when Luke's plan went sideways.

*

As he walked into the draw, Carter found some blood in the leaves from the wolf he had been shooting at. When he spotted the bright red blood, he whistled back to Hernandez to let him know he had hit the wolf. He whistled loudly.

Hearing the whistle, Whitson and Stephens came over the hill with their rifles at the ready.

"STATE POLICE!" Whitson yelled. "EVERYONE ON THE GROUND!"

As soon as they saw the game wardens coming over the hill, both Thomas and Hernandez started bringing their rifles up.

In the instant they were doing that, Luke pulled his pistol, pointed it at the two men, and said, "I wouldn't do that."

Hernandez and Thomas looked at Luke. It took a half second, but then it dawned on them. The woman from the bar had been right. They slowly lowered their rifles.

"You are under arrest," Luke said. "Drop the rifles and get face down."

"You son of a bitch," Hernandez said. "We trusted you."

Thomas was just smiling, like he knew something that no one else did.

Whitson and Stephens were almost to Luke when Stephens took a bullet to the chest. A nanosecond later, they heard the gunshot. It came from down the draw.

"Shit," Luke said as he quickly ducked behind Thomas and searched for Carter.

Whitson dropped down and crawled to Stephens. Luke kept his pistol on Thomas and Hernandez while trying to see Carter in the draw. They were sitting ducks where they were.

"Can you drag him over to those trees?" Luke asked Whitson. "I'll cover you."

"Don't you guys move," Luke said to the other two men. "I WILL shoot you if I have to."

He looked for any motion down where the shot had come from but saw nothing. Whitson dragged Stephens to some trees and got him behind a large log.

"Now, hands behind your backs," Luke barked at the two men, all the while watching for Carter.

The men complied, and Luke quickly pulled the zip ties out of his pocket and secured the men's wrists behind their backs. He helped both men to their feet and kept them between him and where he thought Carter was. Luke knew if the scrawny man had a shot at him, he would take it.

As Luke was moving the men into the trees, he heard Whitson on his radio. "Wildlife 127 requesting an ambulance and backup. We have an officer down with a GSW and two men in custody."

Luke pulled out his GPS, looked at the location, and gave Whitson the coordinates, who then relayed them to the radio operator.

"10-4, Wildlife 127. Ambulance and county deputies are on the way."

Stephens was groaning but not moving.

"I don't see any blood," Whitson said to Luke. "I think the vest stopped the bullet, but I don't know."

"I can't believe you're a cop," Thomas said, shaking his head. "We shoulda listened to that woman."

"What you should've done is obeyed the laws," Luke said. "Then you wouldn't be in this mess."

"Why didn't Alf warn us?" Hernandez asked Thomas, who turned and gave him a stern look.

"Alf, huh?" Luke said. "That's your man in the sheriff's office? We'll be having a visit with him as soon as I get Carter rounded up."

"Good luck with that," Hernandez said. "This is his backyard. If Ricky doesn't want to get found, you ain't gunna find him."

Luke wanted to get after Carter right away, but with two men in custody, and one officer injured, plus a crime scene to oversee, he had to stay put.

"I just can't believe it," Thomas said again.

*

It took twenty-four minutes for the EMTs and two Stevens County deputies to arrive. The EMTs, both young, one man and one woman, went to work on Stephens, who was now more alert but in obvious pain.

The older of the two deputies was slightly overweight, with a gray mustache over a thin upper lip. The other deputy was a younger man in his late 20s, average height but way above-average muscles. His shirt sleeves could barely contain his biceps, and the buttons on his uniform shirt were straining to hold the shirt together.

The deputies looked around to assess the situation. They looked at the downed officer, Stephens, and at Thomas and Hernandez in zip ties. Then they looked at the dead wolf lying a short way away.

"One of you guys Alf?" Luke asked, checking to see if one of the two deputies was the snitch.

He looked at the older deputy, thinking Alf, or Alfred, would likely be an older man's name, but the deputy shook his head and pointed at the bodybuilder.

"Great," Luke said as he again pulled his pistol and pointed it at the young deputy.

"What the hell?" Alf asked.

"Put your hands behind your back," Luke said. "Whitson, handcuff the deputy please. And take his sidearm."

Whitson looked at Luke like he didn't understand, but did as Luke said.

Luke watched to make sure the deputy didn't do anything.

"Those linked or hinged cuffs?" Luke asked.

"Linked."

"Put these zip ties around his wrists too, just to be safe."

Luke had seen more than one man break the linked handcuffs by twisting them just right. Alf had the strength to do it, and he wanted to make sure he kept the deputy under control until they got it all cyphered out.

"What the hell?" the young deputy asked again. Then he looked at Thomas. Thomas dipped his head at Hernandez as if to say, "He screwed up and dropped your name." He didn't say it, but Alf got the message.

"I'm going to call the sheriff," the older deputy, named Franks, said.

"You do that, deputy. I'd like to talk to him as well," Luke said.

The EMTs had brought a stretcher in with them, and after looking at Stephens, they worked to get him on the device to transport him back to the ambulance.

"The bullet didn't penetrate the vest," the woman EMT said. "But he may have a broken rib or two, and he's going to have a heckuva contusion. We need to get him checked out at the hospital, for sure. Good thing he was wearing his vest."

"I think I can walk," Stephens groaned as they placed him on the stretcher.

"Take the ride," Whitson said.

"Can you walk with them, Deputy Franks?" Luke asked. "The guy who shot Officer Stephens is still out there somewhere, armed and dangerous."

The deputy put his hand on his service revolver and said, "Ah, geez. It's not that goofy Ricky Carter, is it?"

"The one and only," Luke said. "How'd you know?"

"He runs with these two," Franks said, motioning a hitchhiker's thumb at Thomas and Hernandez. "So, it only makes sense."

"Well, keep your eyes open. He's shot one officer. He may be willing to do it again."

"Will do," Franks said and walked up the hill behind the EMTs carrying Whitson on the stretcher.

CHAPTER 15

Road construction on I-90 over Snoqualmie Pass had closed the freeway to all eastbound traffic for six hours. Instead of sitting and waiting for the freeway to open, the detention officers who were transporting Rakes and James Earl Jenkins decided to go north on I-5 out of Seattle and over Stevens Pass via Highway 2. Unfortunately, when they tried to get on Highway 2, the pass was closed due to rockslides.

"What the hell?" the officer in the passenger seat said. "We're never going to get there."

"We'll go up to Highway 20," the driver said. "That will get us there. Better than driving back down south through that godawful traffic again and waiting on Snoqualmie."

It was a longer route to Spokane, but with the delay on I-90 and Stevens Pass closed, they would still arrive much sooner at the Spokane County Jail. That was a necessity to everyone involved, especially the officers, who were of a mind to shoot Jenkins because the man would not shut up.

"Would you please stop talking!" the driver shouted back at Jenkins.

"Am I bothering you?" Jenkins asked. "I don't think I am bothering mister yard tool here. Am I?"

Jenkins looked at Rakes who didn't look back. Rakes had never done any yoga, but he had read about Buddhism and was now in what might be described as a Zen-like state. He had learned how to do this as a teenager, when things were not going well at home, or when the kids at school were calling him names and making fun of him. He would just close everything out of his mind and go to one of his favorite places.

Back in Havre, he had spent many days and plenty of nights in the outdoors. He'd traveled the creeks and the coulees in the eastern Montana landscapes and learned many skills about surviving in the wilderness.

His father didn't have time for him, so Rakes learned everything he needed to know from reading books. He was an avid reader and he retained most of what he read. He didn't have a photographic or eidetic memory, but he was good at remembering things. That's how he had done so well on the IQ test in high school.

From books, Rakes learned how to build a fire with no matches. He learned how to set snares to catch small animals and birds. And he learned how to field dress and butcher bigger animals such as deer and antelope. He could even build a sturdy lean-to that would keep him dry and out of the wind in less than twenty minutes. During one cold Montana winter, he built an igloo of sorts. He spent half of his Christmas vacation in the structure he had constructed out of snow and ice.

That was the year his mother left. His father was too busy to really care what Rakes was up to and seemed only too happy to have the boy out of his hair.

Rakes knew there would be no Christmas tree or gifts that year. Not that any of their Christmases had been much, but at least his parents usually got him a small gift. One year, it was a knife. Another year, it was a sleeping bag.

His father had an old Remington pump action .22 caliber rifle, a 12-gauge double-barreled shotgun, and a .30-06 Winchester rifle that Rakes used during hunting seasons and other times of the year when the family was low on meat. His father never told Rakes to go poach an animal, but he didn't tell him not to either. And his father seemed quite happy to sit down to a fresh deer steak or an antelope roast, whether it was taken in October or March.

It took a while for Rakes to learn how to stalk animals. He was big and somewhat clumsy as a kid, but he soon learned that his propensity to move slowly helped when trying to get close to a deer. He usually had nothing but time, so he would slow his normal unhurried pace down to that of a snail. By moving only when an animal had its head down or was looking away, he could inch close enough to take a deer with a well-placed shot to the head with the .22 rifle. Ammunition for the little rifle was far less expensive than the ammo for the large caliber .30-06.

The local game warden knew that someone was taking game out of season but never suspected Rakes because, well, everyone knew the kid was slow, maybe even mentally handicapped. He couldn't be the poacher.

Rakes was thinking back to those days as a teenager on the plains of northeastern Montana while Jenkins prattled on about something. Occasionally, one of the corrections officers would holler back at the man to be quiet, but that only seemed to spur him on.

"You know what I mean, shovel?" Jenkins, who was still all humped up from his shortened shackles, said to Rakes as he kicked his seat with his bound feet.

It was too bad Washington had done away with capital punishment, Rakes thought. For two reasons. One, the world would be rid of this piece of crap. If Jenkins was convicted of killing those women, he would spend the rest of his days in the penitentiary, costing the tax-paying citizens of the state hundreds of thousands of dollars. And two, maybe Rakes would have also gotten the electric chair, saving him from dealing with idiots like Jenkins for the rest of his life.

Rakes had only killed women, but if he were to kill a man at some point, Jenkins was quickly climbing to the top of the list. He was not a good man. And frankly, Rakes figured not a soul would miss Jenkins if he died.

He started thinking about that. There were plenty of bad men who had passed through Rakes' life. Some of them were worse than the women he had killed. Why had he only picked out women?

A psychiatrist wandering around in Rakes' head would most likely tell him it was because of his relationship, or lack thereof, with his mother. Rakes thought about that for a while and then decided that wasn't it. He'd had a terrible relationship with his father too.

No, it went deeper than that. Maybe clear back to the first grade when a girl he had a secret crush on called him retarded and spit on him. When the boys called him dirt or other names, it didn't seem to bother him that much. Boys being boys and all. But when the girls did it, it just seemed cruel and malicious, and it hurt.

Twelve years of girls being mean and doing cruel things to him had been building up to the point where the nasty woman at the mini-mart, a lady that always looked at Rakes as a second-class citizen and treated him like he had a disease, spit in his burrito. It was the proverbial straw on the camel's back. He could take it no more.

"You know what I mean, pitchfork?" Jenkins said, again kicking Rakes' seat and bringing him out of his daze.

Rakes didn't acknowledge his fellow prisoner but did start looking around. He didn't know how much time had gone by, but now they were in the mountains. Trees lined the highway, and they were gaining elevation as the van sped along.

"You sure ain't very talkative," Jenkins said. "Something wrong with you or something?"

Rakes ignored the man and watched the world go by through the one window he could see out of. This country was nothing like eastern Montana, but it was similar to the Rocky Mountains. He hadn't spent much time in the Rockies, mostly just driving through them, but he'd always enjoyed the scenery.

He was watching the trees fly by when the officer in the passenger seat yelled, "Oh shit!"

Rakes looked ahead through the windshield and saw the back end of a semi-truck trailer swinging into their lane on the highway. Smoke rolled from the big truck's trailer tires as the driver applied the brakes. The officer driving the van jerked the steering wheel to the right to avoid the trailer, and then the whole world was spinning and rolling.

The second Rakes saw the trailer in their lane, he grabbed the bar next to his seat with his handcuffed hands and tucked his manacled feet under the seat ahead of him. With all his strength, he tried to hold himself in place.

The officers had fastened seatbelts around Rakes and Jenkins, which helped some to hold them in their seats. But as the van started to spin, and then roll, all the occupants were shaken like rag dolls.

People say that in traumatic events such as a car accident, everything seems to slow down, and that's how Rakes viewed the wreck. He watched everything as if it were in slow motion on a television screen. He watched the world outside turn over once, twice, and on the third time, a large evergreen tree seemed to jump in front of the van and stopped everything. Rakes was aware of the sounds of metal crunching and glass breaking. Dirt and broken glass flew around inside the van like the white stuff in a snow globe. And then, just like that, it was over.

Rakes felt a burning on the top of his head, and his shoulder muscles were barking at him. But after looking himself over, he saw nothing that would indicate he was seriously injured. He looked over at Jenkins and saw that he, too, was awake, though he seemed to be in a daze. The two officers in the front of the van both looked to be either unconscious or dead.

Rakes unbuckled his seatbelt and looked around. He and Jenkins were still locked inside the cage. He grabbed at the door, and even though it was bent at the top where the roof of the van was crushed in, the door held fast.

"What happened?" Jenkins asked, finally cognizant enough to know they weren't moving down the road.

"We were in a wreck. Come help me," Rakes said and unbuckled Jenkins' seatbelt.

"You're bleeding," Jenkins said, pointing to the top of Rakes' head.

"I'm fine," Rakes said. "Let's see if we can kick this Plexiglass out."

Rakes helped Jenkins up, and they moved to the Plexiglass barrier that cut the van in half. It was secured in brackets at the top and bottom of the van, but like the door to the cage, the bracket that held the Plexiglass in place was bent.

Rakes lay down on his back, lifted his legs, bent his knees to his chest, and kicked out at the plastic wall. Jenkins did the same thing, although his shortened manacles made it difficult.

"Kick together," Rakes said. "On three."

They timed their kicks, and on the fourth try, the Plexiglass cracked. On the fifth kick, it broke out. Both men scrambled to their feet and hobbled to the front.

"We gotta get the key for the cuffs," Jenkins said and moved to the officer in the passenger seat.

Rakes moved forward behind Jenkins and checked on the driver. The officer had blood all over his face, and Rakes could see white stuff—possibly brain matter—coming out of a big crack in the left side of his head. The man was not breathing.

The officer in the passenger seat was alive and moaning. He, too, was bleeding from his head.

Jenkins dug into the officer's breast pocket and fished out the long device that would unlock the cuffs and foot manacles. They called it a key, but it looked more like a ballpoint pen.

"Here, unlock me," Jenkins said.

"You unlock me first," Rakes said. He didn't want this idiot to be unlocked first and take off with the key.

Jenkins looked at the big man for a second, then unlocked Rakes' handcuffs. He handed Rakes the key, and Rakes unlocked his own ankle manacles. Then he unlocked the restraints on Jenkins.

As soon as Jenkins was free from the handcuffs and the ankle devices, he unbuckled the officer in the passenger seat and took the safety belt and wrapped it around the officer's neck.

"This is for being an asshole," Jenkins said as he pulled the belt tight.

Rakes thought about it for a second. The officer had been a jerk, but he didn't need to die. He grabbed Jenkins by the greasy long hair in the back of his head and wrenched him back. In the next instance, he put his big left hand over Jenkins' chin and his right hand on the back of Jenkins' head, then with a quick twisting jerk, Rakes snapped his neck. Jenkins flopped to the ground and made some gurgling sounds, but he was already on his way to hell.

As was the case with the women he had killed, Rakes felt no remorse. He felt nothing. Jenkins needed to die, and Rakes was the right man in the right place for the job. No more court proceedings. No more lifelong prison sentences. No more tax payers' dollars being tossed down a shit hole. It was totally justified in Rakes' mind.

There wasn't much he could do for the guard who was still alive, but Rakes did grab the officer's cell phone, stepped out of the van, and dialed 911. While he was talking to the emergency operator, Rakes looked around. There were no cars stopped up on the highway, and he couldn't see the truck or trailer that had forced them off the road.

Rakes could feel blood running down the back of his neck. And his head burned like crazy. He walked over to the mirror on the passenger side of the van and jerked it off the door. He held it up over his head and saw a piece of glass protruding out of his scalp in hair that was matted with blood.

He wanted to get out of there before someone came along, but he took two minutes to search the van for a first aid kit. He found it under the passenger seat, opened it, pulled some gauze out, and reached up and removed the shard of glass from his head. That made the wound bleed more, but he placed a big gauze pad on it and held it tightly against his head. In the kit, Rakes found some white tape, and he wrapped it around the gauze on the top of his head and under his chin several times. He looked like someone who was trying to secure his jaw shut.

Rakes then stepped back and looked around. He had no idea where he was, but with woods and mountains for as far as he could see, he decided he would head uphill to get a better view. He was wearing a jacket over his orange jumpsuit but figured he could use more clothing, so he took Jenkins' jacket and the dead officer's coat. Neither man was as big as Rakes, but anything might help if he was going to be in the mountains for a while. He tucked the first aid kit under his arm and headed up the hill, across the highway and into the trees.

Rakes was a free man again. For how long, he had no idea.

CHAPTER 16

Ricky Carter's heart was going about two hundred beats a minute. He hadn't thought about the repercussions of shooting a police officer. That was one of his problems. He often acted before he thought. But as soon as he had heard someone yelling state police back where Thomas, Hernandez, and that douchebag Haynes were, he knew he had to do something. He had moved quickly back up the draw, and when he'd seen the two officers coming down the hill, he had raised his rifle and shot.

Carter hadn't seen Luke pulling his pistol on Thomas and Hernandez, or he might have put two and two together. If he had, he would have surely shot Luke before trying for one of the other officers.

At the shot, the officer had gone down, and Carter took off down the draw. He was a good enough shot to know he'd hit the man in the chest, and it was likely the officer was dead. He believed he was now wanted for murdering a police officer. He needed to get as far away as possible.

*

Luke was itching to get after Carter, but he had more pressing things on his hands. Three men were in custody and needed to be transported to the county jail. Whitson was there, but walking three handcuffed men back to the road was more than one man could handle. Even with their hands restrained, there was a risk that they might jump the officer or just take off running in three different directions. Plus, Carter could be waiting someplace to shoot someone else.

"Okay, let's get going," Luke said to Thomas and Hernandez as he helped them up.

Whitson was standing with a hand on Alf and moved to grab Thomas by the arm when Hernandez spun in Luke's grasp and was coming with a roundhouse kick. Luke saw it coming and blocked it with his arm, then swept Hernandez's other leg with his leg, sending the man face down in the dirt, hard.

Simultaneously, Alf gave a twist and was out of Whitson's grasp, kicking him in the knee. Whitson yelled and went to the ground, but he pulled his revolver and aimed it at the deputy just as he was about to kick him again.

"I'll shoot," Whitson said. "You know it, Alf."

"And if he doesn't, I will," Luke, who also had drawn his pistol, said. "I'm a pretty bad shot with these things, but I believe I could hit a big fella like you at five yards."

Alf dropped his head.

During all this, Thomas had just stood still and watched.

"We'll just add that to your charges," Luke said. "You okay, Dave?"

Whitson was sitting on the ground rubbing his right knee. "Yeah, I'll be okay. It's a bad knee in the first place. Old football injury."

Luke looked at the short, thin officer and wondered where he might have played football, but let it go.

Whitson stood up, but he was having trouble putting weight on his right leg.

"Do I need to get the EMTs back here?"

"Naw, I can make it. I'm going to keep my pistol drawn though. If one of these guys makes one wrong step, I'm going to shoot them."

Luke read all three men their rights. Alf looked like he was going to cry. Thomas just kept shaking his head. Hernandez was moving his face into his shoulder, trying to wipe the dirt and pine duff out of the scratches in his face that he'd incurred while skidding in the dirt.

They slowly made it back to where Whitson had parked his truck. The ambulance was gone, taking Stephens to the hospital, but Deputy Franks was there. He had pulled a rifle from his county patrol SUV and was watching the men walk down to the trucks.

A quick thought went through Luke's mind. What if Franks was in on this too? If that was the case, he had the drop on the two game wardens and could release the men if he were so inclined.

But Franks eased the rifle down as the five men approached the truck.

"I was watching for Ricky," Franks said. "I've known him since he was a kid, but I wouldn't put it past him to shoot me too."

"Did you call the sheriff?" Luke asked.

"I sure did. He should be here in a few."

"Good. We'll need some help transporting these guys and booking them."

"I can't believe you're involved in all of this," Franks said to Alf.

The big man didn't look at the older deputy and didn't say a thing. He still looked like he was on the brink of tears.

"I think we're good here now until the sheriff shows up," Luke said to Whitson. "If you want to drive to the hospital to get that knee looked at, go ahead."

"No, I'm going to stay and have a word with the sheriff myself," Whitson said. "We've been trying to work with him, and he didn't believe there was a leak in his department. I want to see his face when he finds out we've arrested one of his men."

Luke sat the three men in handcuffs on the ground next to the road as they waited for the sheriff to arrive. Thomas just kept staring at Luke and shaking his head.

"I thought we were friends," Thomas finally said.

"Yeah, well, I would have liked to be friends, Buck. I liked all you guys. Well, maybe not Ricky so much. But it's hard to be friends with guys who think the hunting laws don't pertain to them."

"So, was that you the gal at the bar saw on TV?"

"I guess so."

"We really shouda listened to her," Hernandez said.

"You sure worked hard to catch us," Thomas said. "All for what, a few fines. You know we won't do any real time."

"Like I tried to tell you the other day, killing wolves is a whole different set of circumstances," Luke said. "Shooting animals on the Endangered Species list is serious stuff. My guess is you'll do several years. Manny and Ricky might do more than that."

Hernandez looked at Luke to see if he was telling the truth and could see he was dead serious.

Sheriff Bill Miller arrived a few minutes later and parked behind Franks' SUV. Miller was a short, slender man of about fifty who wore a big white cowboy hat that made his smallish head look even smaller. A full, dark Fu Manchu mustache sat on his upper lip and curved down around his small mouth like Tom Selleck's character in the movie *Quigley Down Under*. Miller carried a .357 caliber revolver in a black leather holster tied to his leg with leather straps coming from the bottom of the holster. The handgun and holster took up most of his upper right leg.

Luke had once heard someone say, "All hat, no cattle." That seemed to fit this situation. Everything about the man said he was trying desperately to make up for some major insecurities.

"What in the hell is going on here?" Miller barked as he marched up to the men.

Luke introduced himself to Miller and gave him a brief recap of his undercover work.

"One of our officers was shot by Ricky Carter. Luckily,

he should be okay because he was wearing a vest, but Carter is running."

"Why wasn't my office made aware of what was going on here?" Miller asked gruffly. He was gesturing with his hands and kicking dirt as he talked.

"Because we were told there was a leak in your department regarding fish and game investigations. Your deputy here was the leak."

"That's bullshit," Miller said, kicking some more dirt. "Alf wouldn't do that. None of my deputies would."

"Not only was he the leak, he assaulted Officer Whitson," Luke said. "That will be added to the other charges we'll be filing."

"Well, hell," Miller said, kicking some more dirt and putting his hands on his hips. Then he turned to Franks and asked, "Did you see Alf assault the game warden?"

"No, sir. I wasn't there," Franks said. "I was escorting the wounded warden to the ambulance in case Ricky was out there bent on shooting someone else. But Officer McCain did hear Hernandez mention Alf's name as their insider."

"I just can't believe it," Miller said.

"And I seen it in Alf's eyes and face," Franks said. "He done it, no doubt."

"So, what do you want from me?" Miller asked Luke.

"The suspects have already been placed under arrest and had their rights read to them. Can you and Deputy Franks take them to your jail and hold them? Officer Whitson will go along with you to fill out the paperwork."

"Where are you going?" Miller asked.

"I'm headed after Carter," Luke said.

"Good luck with that," Miller said. "That boy knows this country like the inside of his own house. Best just let him be. He'll show up back in town in a week or two, and we can grab him then."

"If he thinks he killed a police officer, and my guess is he does, then he's not coming back. The sooner I get after him, the better."

Luke had his rifle and sidearm but nothing else he really needed to track Carter through the mountains.

"I'm going to run back to town and get my gear," Luke said after thinking about it a minute.

"Do you want us to round up a posse?" Miller asked. "My deputies are much more familiar with this area than you are."

"That would be helpful," Luke said. "Can you have everyone back here in an hour?"

"I'll do my best," Miller said and turned to help walk Thomas, Hernandez, and Alf to the SUVs.

"I can drop you at your place before I go to the jail," Whitson said.

✳

After pushing hard away from where the game wardens were, Carter slowed down to take a breather. He was regretting shooting the officer now and he knew he would be doing some serious time for killing the man. He might even go to prison for the rest of his life.

They had to catch him first though. Canada wasn't that far to the north, and he could make it in three days by staying in the mountains. If he could get to a highway and hitch a ride, it would only take him a couple hours to get out of the country.

Carter knew he would need ID to get through the border crossing, and he did have his driver's license, but the sheriff probably already had him tagged. They would be looking for him at the border.

His other option would be to head west and try to get to Seattle where he could get lost in the big city. He had a brother there who could help him.

Carter thought about what he should do. Head north through nasty country without any provisions? Or try to get to the highway and hitch a ride west? He could make the journey north, even without his gear. He had spent many a night in the woods with little to no food, water, or warm clothes.

But the idea of catching a ride and getting to his brother's place was more appealing. That's what he was going to do. He turned west and headed toward the Columbia River and Highway 25.

CHAPTER 17

Sheriff Miller, along with three uniformed deputies and two civilians, met Luke where Ricky Carter had parked his Excursion. Luke looked at the four men and one woman with some trepidation. Two of the men were at least thirty pounds overweight, and none of the deputies looked like they were in shape enough to be hiking very far, for very long, in the mountains.

Luke had loaded his pack with his normal overnight gear, including a small tent, sleeping bag and pad, water, and energy bars. He still was carrying his personal hunting rifle, a .257 Weatherby. He had his state-issued .45 caliber pistol in a holster on his utility belt that also carried handcuffs, a Taser, and some other items.

From underneath his big hat, Miller said, "My deputies know this area well, so I'd like to take the lead on this."

"Fine with me," Luke said.

He wasn't in the mood to get in a pissing match with the sheriff. The deputies worked for Miller and would follow his orders. Luke figured they would all poop out in a couple of hours, and he would be on his own, which is what he preferred.

Miller pulled out a map of Stevens County and spread it over the hood of his patrol rig. The deputies and the two other guys all gathered around. Luke, who was taller than all of them by three inches or more, and almost a foot taller than the sheriff, looked in over the top of the group.

"Here we are," Miller said, pointing to the map. "Can you point out where you last saw Ricky, Officer McCain?"

Luke found it interesting that everyone called Carter by his first name. They obviously knew him well.

"Call me Luke," he said as he elbowed his way into the group to point to the draw where Carter had shot Stephens. "Right here. You all seem to know Carter fairly well. Any idea where he might want to go?"

"Canada," said one of the civilians, whose name was Lee something.

"I think Lee is right," Miller said, pointing again at the map. "We should concentrate our efforts to the north, here and here."

Luke looked at the map and noticed the narrowness of the topography lines. Those indicated that the country Miller was pointing at would be very steep.

"That looks like rough country," Luke said. "You think Carter would purposely go into it?"

As he asked the question, Luke was thinking about how scrawny Carter was, and how he walked like he was going uphill on flat ground. Walking like that had to work against him climbing hills.

"Ricky's hunted in this country all his life," Lee something said. "He don't need no supplies or nothin'. That's where he'll go so the law can't follow him."

The other people in the posse nodded their heads in agreement.

Miller tipped his big hat back and started pairing off people and directing them where to start the search.

"You all have radios," Miller barked. "Check in with me every thirty minutes."

The sheriff had directed one of the deputies, a man about Luke's age who stood five-foot-ten and easily weighed two hundred and forty pounds, to be Luke's partner. Some big guys can hike all day, but by the look of the deputy's belly drooping over and almost covering his belt buckle, Luke quickly concluded that this guy wasn't one of them.

"Excuse me, sheriff," Luke said. "I'd prefer to go alone. I'm going to find Carter's tracks and follow them."

The overweight deputy stifled a laugh.

"You aren't going to be able to track Ricky," he said. "He's probably miles from here by now. That's why the sheriff is placing us where he is."

"You can come with me if you want, deputy," Luke said. "But I'm going to get on his tracks and go where he goes."

"Why don't you go with Lee," the sheriff said to the deputy after thinking about it for a minute. "We'll let officer, er, Luke, do his own thing. Anything else?"

"He's already shot a police officer," Luke said. "I would be extra careful if you do catch up with him. My guess is he believes he killed Stephens and is wanted for murder. That changes how a person thinks. You might know Carter, and maybe even consider him a friend, but I wouldn't trust him at all."

Luke could see his words were falling on deaf ears. They knew Ricky Carter better than he did. And, as was the case in other places he had been, they didn't even really think of Luke as law enforcement. He was just a game warden.

"Check in every thirty minutes," Miller reminded the crew. "And be safe."

The small group disbanded and headed to their vehicles. Luke shouldered his pack, grabbed his rifle, and headed back to where Carter had disappeared after shooting Stephens.

*

Carter figured the whole Stevens County sheriff's department was out searching for him. The one thing he had going for him was that all the deputies were out of shape. Some were overweight too. They couldn't keep up with him on their best day. Still, whenever he stopped to rest, he would watch his back trail closely.

He figured the Columbia River was ten miles from where he had shot the officer. But that was as the crow flies. He would need to snake around the steepest terrain and cross some ravines. It would be ten hours anyway before he saw the big river, and by then it would be dark. Carter was okay with that. He had spent plenty of time in the dark woods.

Poaching was a way of life for Carter and his family. His father worked odd jobs here and there, but his temper got in the way of keeping steady work. When he lost a job for arguing with the boss or fighting with a co-worker, it was always the other person's fault. The only skill Carter's mother had was birthing babies. When Ricky had left home at seventeen, there were six little brothers and sisters running around in their tiny two-bedroom house. Shooting a deer or the occasional elk in season or out wasn't for sport, it was so the family could eat.

Carter had grown up with half the deputies in the department. They knew his situation, so they would look the other way when someone reported Carter for spotlighting a deer. Ricky was just feeding himself and his family.

The law-abiding hunters didn't quite view it the same way and called the regional game department office to complain. The enforcement officers tried to catch Carter, and later Thomas and Hernandez, but the group always seemed to know when the game wardens were in the area and when they weren't.

Alf Potter had gone to high school with Carter, and they'd become good friends. When Potter ended up in the sheriff's department, Carter told Thomas that he thought his good buddy might offer up information, for a price.

Selling wolf hides, bear skulls, and gallbladders, along with some antlers and venison, had become a lucrative side hustle for the men, so whenever Potter would tip them off to something, Thomas would send a little thank you note to the muscular deputy. The note was affixed to a couple hundred-dollar bills.

It was all going good until those game wardens showed up.

Carter thought about that. How the hell had they known when to come in on him and Hernandez? Thomas wouldn't have tipped them off. And what the hell happened to Alf? He should have known they were coming and told them.

Then he thought about what Hernandez had said that morning about the tall woman with the reddish hair thinking she had seen that asshole Haynes on TV. What had she said? She thought he looked like the game warden carrying an alligator down in Yakima.

"Shit," Carter mumbled to himself.

It had to be him. That's how they knew. The more he thought about it, the madder Carter got. If he had the chance, he would shoot that son-of-a-bitch too.

*

It didn't take Luke long to get on Carter's tracks. They were the only human tracks in the draw, and although there was grass in some areas, the dry dirt here and there would reveal footprints which Luke followed for almost a mile. Carter was not headed north like Lee and the other posse members thought. He was headed in a westerly direction. Luke pulled the GPS unit out of his pack and, after acquiring the satellites necessary to triangulate his location, he studied the map on the screen.

"Where are you going, Ricky?" Luke said to himself.

He traced his finger along the map in the direction Carter was walking. Eventually, it took him to Highway 25, running north and south on the east side of the Columbia River.

Luke thought about it a minute. If he were on the run, that's what he would do too. Get to a well-traveled road where he could hitch a ride. Then he could go north to try to get into Canada, or south or west.

Just to make sure Carter was staying on that same course, Luke followed the tracks for another half mile. When he was convinced that was what Carter was doing, Luke turned around and headed back to his truck. It was going to take Carter several hours to get to the highway, and Luke planned to be there waiting for him.

In all the excitement of the shooting of Stephens and the arrest of the three men, nothing had been done with the dead wolf Hernandez and Carter had shot. Luke figured he had plenty of time to get around to where Carter might pop out on the highway, so he stopped where the wolf lay and took some photos. He then went down to where he'd found Carter's tracks earlier and looked around more closely. Carter was headed down the draw for a reason, and Luke thought he must have hit another wolf.

It took five minutes of searching before Luke spotted blood in some leaves. He picked up the trail of blood drops every four or five feet and followed them down the draw. Within seventy-five yards, Luke found a second dead wolf. After taking more photos, Luke grabbed the wolf by the hind legs and dragged it back to the first wolf. Then, taking each wolf by a back leg, he dragged them out to his Bronco. He laid the animals on the same blue tarp that had been under the roadkilled deer two days earlier, closed the back tailgate, climbed into the driver's seat, took a big drink of water, started the truck, and headed for town.

As he was walking back with the wolves, Luke decided he wouldn't tell Sheriff Miller about his plan to ambush Carter. In the first place, he didn't know if he was right about where ol' Ricky was headed. And secondly, he didn't want the sheriff or his minions stepping into it and messing things up.

Instead, Luke called Whitson to let him know he was bringing the poached wolves to town.

"Hey, Luke," Whitson said when he answered his phone. "Did you catch him?"

"No, but I think I know where he is headed."

"That's good. You need some help?"

"Actually, I do. Can you meet me at my place? I have the poached wolves in my rig and want you to get them to a cooler."

"Wolves. As in more than one?"

"Yep. There are two. That's where Carter was headed when you guys came over the hill. He had hit one and was going to find it."

"Huh," Whitson said. "Sure, I'll meet you there."

"I'll be there in twenty," Luke said and hung up.

Whitson was waiting in his GMC pickup when Luke pulled in.

"How's that knee doing?" Luke asked as Whitson climbed out of the truck and started walking toward Luke with a noticeable limp.

"Sore," Whitson said. "The ER doc said I'm probably going to need to go under the knife to fix it. I'll schedule that when I get back to Spokane."

"And Stephens? How's he doing?"

"He's sore too. But he should be fine. Very lucky, that's for sure. He wants to get back out here, so that's a good sign. His wife is forcing him to stay at the hospital for another day. Scared her half to death when she got the call."

Before they transferred the wolves into Whitson's pickup, Luke asked if he could borrow it. He had been thinking that if he was in a vehicle Carter hadn't seen before, he might be able to get close enough to him to grab him.

"Sure, if you need it," Whitson said.

"Take my rig. The wolves are in the back," Luke said. "I'll have yours back to you later tonight or tomorrow morning at the latest."

The men exchanged keys, then they loaded up and headed in different directions.

Since he had some time before he needed to be on Highway 25, Luke drove to the little drive-in where he had eaten lunch the first day of work at the mill. It had been just two months, but it seemed like it was a year ago. He had eaten at the hamburger place several times since that first day and liked the food.

When he walked into the place, Mike Robertson, the mill boss, was sitting at a table with a teenaged girl. The young lady had long strawberry blonde hair, bright blue eyes, and a smaller version of the bulbous nose of her father—minus the red spider veins.

"Hey, Luke!" Robertson said. "If that is your name."

Of course. Robertson, and probably most of the town, already knew what had happened earlier.

"That's my name," Luke said with a smile. "Sorry about that. I would have let you know what was happening, but I was under strict orders."

"Hey, no problem," Robertson said. "You were a damn good worker. I'm going to hate to lose you."

Robertson introduced Luke to his daughter, Sadie, who smiled and blushed when Luke smiled at her. Robertson offered to buy Luke lunch.

"Thanks, Mike," Luke said. "I'm just going to grab a burger and go."

"Where should we send your last paycheck?" Robertson asked.

"I'll get you an address," Luke said. "The state will end up with it, just like all the others."

CHAPTER 18

It was just starting to get dark when Luke pulled off onto a wide shoulder on Highway 25. He had looked at the map on his GPS and tried to figure out where Carter might hit the highway based on the direction he had been walking and the topography of the surrounding area. It was likely Carter would take the easiest path, and Luke thought he had found it.

As he was driving, Luke called his captain to give him a recap of the events of the day.

"Yeah, I heard from Jerry Hill, the Region One captain," Bob Davis said. "I guess Cody Stephens was a lucky man."

"Very lucky. We have everyone in custody, except the guy who shot Stephens. I'm trying to track him down now."

"Sounds like there's enough evidence to put the poachers away for a while," Davis said.

"I think so. I'll be glad to get back to Yakima," Luke said. "Sara says she has been looking at singles dating sites."

Davis laughed. "And that dog of yours might not even know you anymore."

"Sara says he's been moping around the place, so I think he misses me as much or more than she does."

"Well, get this Carter guy and head home."

"That's the plan."

After finishing his call with Captain Davis, Luke called Sara to update her on things.

"Are you coming home?" she asked.

"Probably not tonight, but tomorrow hopefully."

He told her what had happened that morning, and Sara gasped when Luke told her about Stephens being shot. Luke left out the part about Hernandez trying to take him down. No need to worry her any more than she already was.

"Would you like to have Jack with you?" Sara asked.

"Yeah, I might have tried to track this guy down with Jack. But I think I have it figured out where he is headed."

"I sure hope so. We really miss you."

"I miss you too. I'll let you know when I catch him."

After they'd hung up, Luke started thinking about Sara. He really did miss her. They had been married for four years, and to Luke she was still the perfect match for him. Sara was smart, funny, and incredibly beautiful. Way out of his league. He still didn't know how he had gotten so lucky.

*

Carter walked steadily around steep inclines, down through brushy ravines, over hundreds of downfalls, and through creeks. He had cut across several Forest Service roads and at one point saw a Stevens County Sheriff's SUV parked on one of the roads by a big meadow. From what he could see through his rifle scope, the rig was empty. The deputy was most likely out looking for him.

Carter watched the sun and kept on a westerly course. He had never walked this way before, but he knew that sooner or later he would end up on the highway that would take him out of the forest. His legs were sore and felt like they were going to start cramping, so he slowed down but kept moving. Part of the issue was he hadn't had anything to drink all day. He had crossed a few creeks, but he knew that if he drank from one of them, he might end up sick from beaver fever. He had seen the effects of giardia on a couple of friends who had drunk unfiltered water from the local streams, and the last thing he wanted or needed was a horrible gut ache and fire hose diarrhea. He told himself he would get a drink after he made the highway and could catch a ride.

When the sun slipped behind a hill in the distance, Carter figured he had walked nine miles, give or take. Another mile, and he would be very close.

When it was completely dark, Carter slowed his pace even more. He couldn't see well enough in the trees and didn't want to step into a badger hole or trip on something. At one point, he stopped to rest, and he thought he could hear cars moving on a road in the distance somewhere in front of him. He pushed on another quarter mile and stopped again. He listened and could definitely hear highway traffic. He was almost there.

✱

Luke didn't know if Carter knew for sure he was an undercover officer, but after the takedown this morning, he would most likely figure it out. Ricky Carter wasn't the shiniest penny in the change jar, but he wasn't totally stupid either.

The white Ford Bronco Luke had been driving to the mill was unique enough that you didn't see one every day. If Carter had figured out Luke was an officer of the law and saw the Bronco, there was a good probability he would turn and run. Luke was glad he had made the trade with Whitson.

He kept the GMC running as he sat in the pullout and watched. The chances of Carter walking off the hill right where he was parked were slim, but he kept his eyes open. His plan was to drive a two-mile stretch of the highway, up and back as soon as it was dark. If Carter came out and was hitchhiking, Luke would try to grab him.

*

As soon as he could see the highway and the river beyond, Carter stopped and rested. Highway 25 wasn't the busiest highway in the county, but there was enough traffic that he should be able to thumb a ride in fairly short order. This was the country, and people weren't so stuck up about giving folks a ride.

Carter thought about the rifle slung over his shoulder. What should he do with it? Yes, folks were friendly enough to help a person out, but they might not be so eager to pick up a hitchhiker if he was armed. During hunting season, there was the occasional hunter carrying a rifle along the backroads, so it wasn't an uncommon sight. But this was a highway, and it wasn't hunting season. Plus, there was the chance that the sheriff had contacted the local radio station, and it was out on the airwaves to be on the lookout for one Ricky Carter, armed and dangerous, wanted for killing a police officer. Carter mulled that over as he watched a car, and then a pickup, drive up the highway.

He really wanted to hang onto the rifle, but he decided it would be easier to get a ride if he ditched it. There was a lone pine tree thirty yards up the hill above him, so Carter climbed up there and hung the rifle by the sling, upside down, on a broken branch right up against the tree trunk. The rifle wouldn't totally be out of the weather, but it would be fairly protected. If someone stumbled along and found it, so be it, but Carter figured he would find it right there when he returned, whenever that might be.

After securing the rifle in the tree, Carter slowly made his way down to the highway. He stood in some tall brush just short of the road's shoulder. He listened for any vehicles coming, and hearing none, he jumped across the bar ditch onto the shoulder and hustled across the asphalt. He needed to go south before he could connect with the highway to Seattle.

*

Luke had first traveled north on Highway 25. He drove just below the speed limit so as not to look like he was searching for something, or someone. As he drove, a blue sedan came up from behind, passed him on a short straightaway, and sped off into the darkness.

If Carter wanted to head for Canada, he would be hitchhiking in this direction. Luke believed that was what he would be doing, but he wasn't putting all his butter on that one biscuit. So, after driving north for five minutes, Luke turned around and went back the other way.

He was headed south, just past where the blue sedan had passed him on the straight stretch of road, when Luke spotted someone in his headlights walking on the shoulder, three hundred yards ahead. He recognized the walk immediately. Leaned back, high-stepping it uphill on flat ground, it looked just like the Keep On Trucking guy. Ricky Carter was trying to hitch a ride.

*

Carter couldn't believe his luck. He had only been on the highway a couple minutes, and here came a car. He turned and saw the thin, white headlights of a newer vehicle. He held out his arm, stuck a thumb up, and waved it up and down. It worked. The car, no, it was a pickup, was slowing down. Bingo. He would be on his way to Seattle in no time.

As the truck approached, it slowed more and came right at him. The driver still had his bright lights on, and Carter was having trouble seeing. He put his arm up to shield his eyes from the lights.

"Turn your brights off, dumb shit," Carter said as the truck slowed some more and stopped just ten yards from him. He tried to see the driver, but it was impossible in the lights.

He started to walk toward the truck, and the driver's door opened.

"Howdy," Carter said. "Thanks for stopping."

*

Luke only had a few seconds to think. How was he going to handle this? He could let Carter walk up to his window and then try to grab him. Or better yet, he could stick a pistol in Carter's face. But if the man bolted, Luke would still be stuck in the truck.

No, the better plan would be to keep the bright headlights on Carter for as long as he could, effectively blinding him, until he could climb out of the truck and point his pistol at him.

Or he could just run the man over. If Carter spotted Luke before he was able to exit the truck, that would be plan C.

Luke saw Carter hold his arm up to try to block the blinding lights of the pickup. He didn't want to get too close because if he did, the lights would stop hitting Carter in the face, and he might be able to see Luke. So, he stopped ten yards short.

His pistol was already drawn, and as Luke opened the door and stepped out, he leaned through the opening between the door and the door jamb, raised the pistol, and pointed it at Carter. Luke watched Carter continue moving forward, eyes squinting, face lowered, trying to get out of the lights. He still couldn't see Luke or the pistol.

"That's far enough, Ricky," Luke said. "Move, and I'll send you into another life."

A look of puzzlement came over Carter's squinting face. Luke didn't know if he was trying to figure out who was attached to the voice or if he didn't get the part about another life.

"Stop! And turn around slowly," Luke said as he moved out around the open driver's door.

Carter stopped and started to turn around, but instead he yelled, "You son-of-a-bitch!" and sprinted at Luke.

*

Carter couldn't figure out why the driver of the pickup wouldn't dim his lights. He decided to get closer, out of the lights. He could see the shape of the door open, but that was about it. He closed his eyes, and all he saw were bright spots burned into his retina from the high beams.

Then a voice said, "That's far enough." Carter recognized the voice, but from where? The voice said something about another life, but he was concentrating too hard, searching his memory, to catch it. Whose voice was that?

As soon as the voice said, "Stop," it came to Carter. It was that asshole, Haynes. He was obviously a cop of some kind, and he probably had a gun on him, but Carter had been wanting to take it to this guy ever since he had called him out in front of the whole crew in the lunchroom at work.

In an instant, the rage exploded inside of him. He might get shot, but this was his chance. He screamed and ran at the open truck door.

CHAPTER 19

The human brain is an amazing organ. When confronted with a dangerous situation, it can take in and process all the parameters faster than the most advanced computer. The instant Carter started for him, Luke's brain started computing. He could shoot. Even as bad a shot as Luke was with a pistol, he would almost assuredly hit the fugitive at that close range. It might even kill him. Or he could holster his pistol and take the man on bare-handed.

Luke weighed a good eighty pounds more than Carter, but he'd seen wiry guys fight before and knew they could be tough to handle. He had watched a short, slender guy take on a much bigger man in a fight over a dead deer once. The smaller guy was all over the big dude like a spider monkey. The big guy eventually won the brawl, but it was no cake walk.

He braced himself for Carter's arrival, but just as the man arrived, Luke shifted to his left and used Carter's forward motion against him. As Carter was stumbling by, Luke gave the man a healthy shove, and he went face first into the open door of Whitson's truck.

Unfazed by the crash into the truck, which caused an instant bloody nose, Carter was up and coming at Luke again.

If Carter's nose wasn't broken from the collision with the door, it was after Luke hit him dead center in the face with his fist. Luke's much longer arms allowed him to hit Carter before he could even touch Luke.

The punch put Carter down, but he was not out. He worked his way to his feet and stood there on unsteady legs.

"Had enough?" Luke asked.

Carter didn't say a word. He wobbled a little more and wiped his bloody nose with the sleeve of his shirt. Then he spit even more blood into the gravel at his feet and came at Luke one more time.

There was no need to hit the man again. Luke worried that he might kill him. So, he reached out, grabbed Carter by the coat, and slung him over his left hip. Carter landed on his back in the gravel and let out a painful groan. Luke rolled him over quickly, put his knees in Carter's back, grabbed his slender wrist, and wrenched it back.

"Ow, ow, you bastard!" Carter cried.

Luke pulled the handcuffs off his belt, slapped one side on the wrist he was holding, and grabbed Carter's other wrist, wrenching it back to the other handcuff.

"You are under arrest for a long list of offenses," Luke said as he helped Carter to his feet.

Luke placed Carter in the bed of Whitson's truck. He didn't want Carter in the cab where he might bleed on the nice new seats or do who-knows-what in there. Once he had Carter secured in the bed of the truck, which included zip ties around his ankles so he couldn't run, Luke called Sheriff Bill Miller.

"I have Ricky Carter in custody," Luke said after the sheriff answered.

"What?" Miller said, not believing what he had just heard.

"I need you to send a deputy to pick him up and get him to the jail," Luke said.

"Why can't you bring him in?" Miller asked.

"Because I am in a private vehicle and transporting him would be unsafe."

"Oh, okay. Where are you?"

Luke told him, and Miller said he would send someone right away.

"How'd you catch him clear over there?" Miller asked.

"Long story. I'll look for your deputy," Luke said and hung up. He didn't have the energy to try to explain everything to the little man with the big hat.

*

As he waited for the deputy to arrive, Luke got a small towel out of his backpack, poured cool water on it, and placed it on Carter's nose.

Carter just stared at Luke, then said, "You're still an asshole."

Luke called Captain Davis to let him know he had Carter in custody.

"That's great, Luke!" Davis said. "I'll let the Region One folks know."

"Thanks," Luke said.

"So, you'll be heading home tomorrow?"

"Yep. I'll handle whatever paperwork I need to here and should be on the road by noon."

"No need getting to the office here right away," Davis said. "Take a few days off, and we'll see you on Monday."

"Sounds good. Thanks, Cap," Luke said and clicked off.

Then he called Sara and told her all about his pursuit and capture of Ricky Carter.

"You should have shot him," she said when he got to the part about Carter rushing him.

"I would have probably missed," Luke joked. "And then I would've had to fight him anyway. I just saved a bullet."

"I would have shot him," Sara said.

Luke believed her. As a special agent with the FBI, Sara was well-trained in self-defense, and he had seen her fire her service weapon many times. She was an excellent shot. Better than he. Sara had never shot anyone in the line of duty, but Luke was confident his wife could handle herself and wouldn't hesitate to shoot someone in a life-or-death situation.

"The captain has given me the rest of the week off," Luke said. "Any ideas on what we should do?"

"That depends," Sara said. "You still have that beard?"

Luke laughed. "Yep. I'm kinda used to it now. I might just keep it."

"I think I have to work," Sara said. "But you and Jack can probably find something to do."

Luke didn't say anything.

"I really do miss you and can't wait to see you, beard or no beard," Sara finally said.

"I miss you too," Luke said. "I'll let you know when I hit the road for home."

*

It took forty-five minutes for the Stevens County deputy to arrive. Luke was pleased to see Deputy Franks behind the wheel of the SUV when it pulled up and did a U-turn to park behind Whitson's truck. He was the only deputy Luke had been involved with in the past eighteen hours he felt he could trust.

"You're the talk of the department," Franks said after climbing out of his rig. "No one thought anyone was going to find Ricky this quickly, especially you."

"Lucky guess," Luke said.

Franks looked at Carter's face. The man's nose was swollen and slightly bent to the left, and the first indications of black and blue bruising were developing under Carter's eyes.

"He came at me," Luke said.

The deputy just nodded his head like he understood. Taking

on a much bigger man was something that Ricky Carter would definitely do.

"Now that wasn't very smart, was it, Ricky," Franks said as he cut the zip ties off Carter's ankles and helped him out of the bed of the pickup.

Carter said nothing, just scowled at Luke.

Franks loaded Carter into the back of the SUV and came back to talk with Luke.

"I've read him his rights," Luke said. "He's not asked about the officer he shot, and I haven't said anything about it. I'm guessing he thinks he killed him."

"He'll ask me," Franks said. "What should I tell him?"

"Tell him he's an idiot, but a lucky one. He'll still do some pretty good time."

"I'm sure he will," Franks said.

The deputy dropped his head and kicked at the gravel for a minute.

"Listen, I want to apologize for some of our guys," Franks said. "Especially for that knucklehead Alf tipping off those guys. The sheriff didn't treat you very professionally either."

"Hey, no big deal. We got the poachers. I just hope Miller is willing to be more agreeable to working with our department in the future."

"I'm sure he will be," Franks said and started back for his rig.

"Say," Luke said. "What's the deal with him and that big cowboy hat?"

Franks stopped and thought about it for a second. "Nobody's had the guts to say what everyone is thinking."

"What's that?" Luke asked.

"All hat, no cattle," Franks said with a grin.

Luke laughed and said, "What about that six-shooter tied to his leg?"

"I haven't seen him shoot it, but rumor has it he couldn't hit a bull elephant in the butt at twenty feet. The pistol is way too big and heavy."

"Well, as long as he looks the part," Luke said.

"I guess," Franks said and turned back to his rig. "See ya back at the jail."

CHAPTER 20

E ven before Rakes was captured in Seattle, the Boise County Sheriff's Office forensics team had matched his DNA to that of the skin samples taken from under the fingernails of the woman who had been killed and dumped near the Boise River. Based on the way their necks had been broken, and with records showing Rakes in the area when the two women were killed near the Montana/Wyoming border, the Wyoming State Patrol believed he was their killer as well.

When the news filtered out of Havre about the woman who had been found dead with a broken neck when Rakes was still in high school there, authorities investigating other murders were eager to talk to him too.

As the story grew on the internet and through mass media, police in Oregon, Utah, and other Western states were soon listing

Rakes as a suspect in unsolved murders in their jurisdictions. It didn't matter that none of those women had died from a broken neck or that there was no record of Rakes ever being in those areas at the times of the deaths; he was soon at the top of everyone's list as a person of interest.

Claude Rakes was a mass murderer. There was no question about that. Mass murderer stories mean high ratings for the television networks. So, every network news did a two-minute story on Rakes when he was identified as the killer of the women in Washington and Idaho. They did a three-minute follow-up story when Rakes was captured in Seattle.

His arrest wasn't a big enough story to send one of the big-name network reporters to the Northwest like they might when a hurricane tears through Louisiana or when some nut runs down a group of bicyclists in New Hampshire. The reporter from an affiliate station in Seattle, eager for his or her big shot at being on the national news, handled that story.

When the report got out that Claude Rakes, the mass murderer who was wanted in connection with potentially a dozen or more women's deaths around the West, had escaped from a prisoner transport van in the wilds of Washington State, it blew up. Network reporters were begging their producers to let them fly to Washington State to cover the story. Satellite television trucks were fueling up for the drive to wherever the hell it was the van had crashed. Producers' assistants were looking at their phones, trying to find the nearest town to the escape, where their crews could be booked into motels.

He had only been on the lamb for nine hours, but in a very short time, Claude Rakes was about to become the biggest name on television.

"It's eerily similar to the Harrison Ford movie *The Fugitive*," one network anchor said as she wrapped up the story on the evening news just hours after Rakes had escaped. "Let's hope the authorities catch him before he kills again."

*

Luke had been home all of one day when he got a call from Captain Davis. He was enjoying a late breakfast with Sara, who took a personal day off to be with her long-absent, freshly-shaven, undercover husband, and he almost didn't take the call.

"It's Bob," Luke said as he looked at his phone buzzing on the kitchen counter.

"Ignore it," Sara said as she walked up behind Luke and rubbed his shirtless back.

"He knows I just got home, and it's a day off, so this must be something important."

"Ignore it!"

Luke gave Sara an 'I'm sorry' look and answered the phone.

"Sorry to bother you," Davis said. "But we have a situation."

Davis asked Luke if he had been following the story about the suspected killer they'd caught in Seattle who'd escaped from a DOC van that crashed up in the North Cascades.

"Nope. Haven't heard a thing about it," Luke said.

"Well, it's become a big national story," Davis said. "It seems the guy who got away may be the next Ted Bundy. Every state from here to Texas wants to talk to him about unsolved murders."

"So, what's that got to do with the Department of Fish and Wildlife?"

"The governor is now involved. He's up for a possible appointment by the president to an important post in D.C. and figures if he's in front of the cameras directing the search for the killer, it'll be good for his career."

"Did he tell you that?" Luke asked.

"No, but it's obvious. He's already on TV more than Peyton Manning, what with COVID and the massive homeless issues around the state. Anyway, he remembers you catching the Cascade Killer a few years ago and then running down those kidnappers last year. He called the director and has specifically asked that you join the search team. 'I want McCain and that yellow dog,' were his exact words."

"How would he even know about us?"

"He lived in Yakima for a while. Was an attorney here. Still keeps track of things that happen over this way."

"Ah, geez. I just got home. What happens if I respectfully decline?"

"Not an option. Tell Sara that if you go catch this guy, the governor will give you six weeks paid leave."

"Is that true?"

"I don't know. I can lobby for it. But maybe it will help with you leaving home again so quickly."

"Okay, but this is not going to go over well, no matter how much time I get off."

Davis told Luke as much as he knew about the situation and said he would email everything else he had received, including the name of the person in charge of the search for Claude Rakes and how to contact him.

When he hung up, Sara looked at Luke and asked, "When do you leave?"

"Right away. Do you know anything about this Claude Rakes guy? Supposedly killed some dancer in Spokane and was arrested in Seattle?"

"Yeah, we've been following it. No one has asked the FBI to get involved, but several investigators think he might be a suspect in who-knows-how-many unsolved murders in their states."

"Do they have any evidence?"

"The Spokane killing evidence points right at him. They have the girl's DNA from blood in his truck and can put him in the area at the time the body was dumped."

"And the others?"

"Most are questionable, although Idaho has Rakes' DNA from a murdered woman there. So that one is likely him. And maybe a couple women in Wyoming and one in Montana."

"What's his deal?"

"No one really knows. It's not a sexual thing, no rapes, and there is no rhyme or reason for who he kills. They are different ages, different hair colors, different body types. But they're all killed the same way. He breaks their necks with his bare hands and dumps them."

"Well, he's on the run in the mountains north of here, and the governor has specifically asked for Jack and me to go try to round him up. Evidently, he's a fan."

"Well, la-dee-da. I told you not to answer the call."

*

It took Luke an hour to get his gear ready. His pack was already loaded with his overnight gear, but he needed to refresh his food and water supply and make sure he had food for Jack. He threw in his backpack stove and fuel, freeze-dried meal packets for three days, along with extra clothing. It was late spring, and the weather should be fine, but in the mountains that far north, you never knew what might blow in from Canada. He also packed extra ammunition for his rifle and his pistol.

When he was satisfied he wasn't forgetting anything, he loaded it all into his state-issued four-wheel-drive Ford F-150 and went back in for Jack and to say goodbye, again, to Sara.

"Sorry about this," Luke said.

"I understand," Sara said as she gave Luke a big hug.

And she did understand. As a federal agent, she had spent many a day, and some nights, in the field when she wanted nothing more than to be home with Luke. It was the nature of the business.

"You and Jack find this guy quickly and get back here safe and sound."

"We will," Luke said and kissed her goodbye. "C'mon, boy. Let's load up."

With the big yellow Lab sitting in the passenger seat next to him, Luke backed the truck out of the driveway and headed for the highway.

*

"What do you think, boy?" Luke asked Jack. "Ready for another adventure?"

Jack looked at Luke and cocked his head like he heard the words but was trying to understand what they meant. Luke rubbed the big dog's head.

"You might as well settle in. We've got a bit of a drive ahead of us."

With that, Jack lay down in the seat, curled into a ball, and went to sleep.

CHAPTER 21

When Rakes called 911 on the officer's phone to report the accident, he told the operator they were somewhere on Highway 20 heading east, and the van was off the side of the road, not visible from the highway.

"Do you need medical assistance?" the operator asked.

"One man does," Rakes said, not mentioning there were two others dead in the van, one by his own hands.

"What is your name?" she asked, but all she heard was footsteps crunching in dirt and rocks as Rakes walked away.

He knew that reporting the accident was going to lead authorities to his trail sooner than if he had just left without calling. But something inside of him felt like the corrections officer should have help as soon as possible. He wasn't willing to sit with the man until the medics arrived, but at least the guard would have attention fairly soon.

As it was, it took the ambulance forty minutes to get there, and if an Okanogan County deputy hadn't located the wreck, the

EMTs might have never found it. When the deputy arrived at the scene, he assumed there had only been three people in the van when it crashed—the officer and the prisoner who had died and the officer who was alive in the passenger seat. So, there was no urgency in trying to locate Rakes.

It was only after one of the other deputies who had arrived on the scene called the Department of Corrections in Seattle to let them know their transport van on Highway 20 had been involved in a serious accident that anyone realized there was a prisoner missing.

"The driver was DOA," the deputy told the DOC director on the phone. "As was the prisoner. The other officer is being transported to the hospital in Winthrop."

"What about the other prisoner?"

"There's no one else here," the deputy said. "How many prisoners were supposed to be in the van?"

"Two. Can you identify the one that you have there?"

"White male, age mid-thirties, medium height and weight, long blond hair, spider tattoo on his neck."

"Ah, shit," the DOC director said and then went silent for a half minute.

"Excuse me, ma'am," the deputy finally asked. "Is there a problem?"

"Yes, there is deputy. A very big problem."

*

The Director of the Washington State Department of Corrections was acutely aware of the fact that Claude Rakes had become a person of interest in an unknown number of murders around the West. In the past twenty-four hours, she had seen the TV reports on the local and national news programs and had read a story about Rakes in *The Seattle Times* written by a reporter in Montana that was picked up by the Associated Press. The stories were giving readers the impression that Rakes could possibly be the next Gary Ridgeway. They described him as a huge man, and without coming right out and saying he looked strange, and possibly even mentally deranged, they painted a picture of a ruthless monster.

Having the man who was wanted for questioning in so many murders escape while under her watch was a disaster. She couldn't imagine how it had happened, but Rakes was evidently gone. As she looked at a map of northcentral Washington where the crash occurred, there were about a million acres of National Forest and wilderness area in which he could hide.

Could it be worse?

The director's assistant came in a few minutes later and told her about another story he had found on the internet about Rakes. Evidently, Rakes had grown up in central Montana and was quite adept at living in the wild with very few resources.

Why yes, it could be worse.

The director had a contact in the Washington State Patrol, so she called him. He immediately forwarded her call to the chief of the Patrol.

After hearing a brief recap of the situation, the chief asked, "How would you like us to help?"

"From what I understand, our van crashed in Okanogan County, but it was so close to Chelan County that deputies from both counties are either on the scene or are headed there now."

"And?"

"It would be nice to have the State Patrol there to help orchestrate this."

"Okay. We can send some officers, but we aren't equipped to be out there tracking down an escaped prisoner. I can send a helicopter to aid in the search, but boots on the ground will need to come from the sheriffs' people."

"Understood. I appreciate your help, sir."

When the State Patrol chief ended the call with the DOC director, he immediately called the governor's office.

*

Rakes had been walking steadily for hours. From the crashed van, he had crossed the highway and walked due north. Or as due north as he could. The mountainous terrain didn't allow for a straight path in any direction.

After walking for an hour or so, he stumbled onto a good hiking trail that wound along in a northerly direction. Walking on the trail was much easier than trying to cut cross-country. Rakes knew there might be a risk of running into other hikers or horseback riders, but that was a chance he was willing to take.

He crossed a small creek and considered taking a drink but remembered the time he had done so as a boy near Havre. He had gotten very sick after drinking the water straight from the stream. It was a lesson he never forgot.

Still, Rakes knew that if he was going to survive out here for any length of time, he needed to drink. A person can go two weeks or more without eating, but only days without water. He opened the first aid kit. One of the small vials in the kit was labeled "iodine." If he could find a container to boil the water and put a few drops of iodine in it, it would be safe to drink. Unfortunately, the kit held nothing that would hold water or could be used as a pan to boil it. So, he walked on, getting thirstier as he went.

Rakes heard the first helicopter before he saw it. As soon as he recognized the thumping of the blades, he ducked off the trail and into a heavy stand of fir trees. He was very aware of his orange jumpsuit and how easily it would show up in the sea of green if he didn't hide. The chopper circled the area for three minutes, then moved on. He assumed they were looking for him and wondered what else law enforcement was doing to try to run him down.

When the sound of the helicopter was so far in the distance that he could barely hear it, Rakes headed back to the trail and continued to walk at a steady pace, keeping his eyes on the brush and trees along the trail. He wasn't looking for people—he was looking for anything that might help him survive out here in the wild.

An hour later, the helicopter returned. He ducked into the trees for cover, and again, after circling for a short while, the chopper disappeared over the mountains in the distance.

As Rakes sat in the trees waiting for the helicopter to leave, he looked around. In some brush, Rakes spotted a flash of silver in the grass and leaves. When the helicopter was gone, he went over and kicked the leaves away. The silvery item was an old coffee pot that was dented and deformed. The pot had been stepped on by a horse or was somehow crushed. To most anyone who saw it, the thing looked like trash, but to Rakes it was exactly what he was hoping for.

After closer inspection, the pot looked workable. Dented, yes, but there were no holes that Rakes could see. There was some rust, inside and out, but he could clean that up.

Rakes had transformed the coat he had taken from the dead officer into a makeshift backpack. By tying the arms together and zipping the coat, he was able to sling it over one arm and his head and carry the first aid kit and the other clothing he had taken when he left the van. Rakes tossed his newfound treasure into the coat pack and got back on the trail. The next creek he came to he would build a small fire, clean the pot, boil some water, and finally, he would get a drink.

Rakes figured he'd walked for another hour or more before he came to the next creek. He looked at the sky, and based on where the sun was, he thought it was late afternoon, maybe around four o'clock.

He'd heard the helicopter again to his south but never saw it. They were definitely looking for him. Would they get a search team together on horses? If they did that, and could find his tracks, they could catch up to him within a day. Maybe they'd have a pack of hounds that tracked people come after him like they do in the movies when someone escapes from prison. He didn't know what tools the law had, but he knew they wouldn't just let him go.

Rakes had built many fires without matches over the years, mostly during his younger days. With some work, he did it again.

He used one of his boot laces tied to each end of a bowed stick and used it to spin another stick on a dry piece of wood. The friction of the stick on the wood built up enough heat that, when fed some dry leaves, it sparked a fire. Within four minutes, he had a fire going. He didn't want a big fire. Big fires create too much smoke. So, he kept it just big enough to boil water.

Before he filled the coffee pot, he used his strong hands and fingers to bend some of the dents out. He used the pot as a scoop to gather sandy grit from the creek bed. He put a scoop of water in the pot with the grit and shook it vigorously. A poor man's sandblaster.

When he got as much rust out of the pot as he could, he filled it half full of water and placed it on some rocks next to the fire. The water finally started to boil, and he let it continue boiling for what he guessed to be five minutes. Then he put three drops of iodine into the water.

As he hiked the trail, Rakes had spotted a discarded plastic water bottle. The bottle only held twelve ounces, but it would give him something with which to transport the water. While he was drinking the first pot of water out of the bottle, he had the pot next to the fire, boiling more water for later.

As Rakes sat and watched the fire, waiting for the second pot to boil, he considered his situation. He was starting to get hungry, but he knew he could deal with that. He could keep looking for and scrounging items to use to trap small animals and birds to eat at some point. The more pressing matter in his mind was who was coming after him, and how close they might be. The farther he could get from the van, as quickly as he could, the better his chances of making it to Canada.

When the second pot of treated water cooled, Rakes poured it into his bottle, drank the remainder of the water in the pot, and threw the pot and full bottle of water in his pack. Refreshed by the short rest and hydration, he got back on the trail, put his head down, and walked.

CHAPTER 22

It had taken Luke almost four hours to get to the crash site on Highway 20. It was a circuitous route from Yakima, over Blewitt Pass to Wenatchee, up the west side of the Columbia River to Brewster, then up through Twisp and Winthrop. It was a beautiful drive, but Luke wasn't paying much attention to the scenery.

Just outside of Wenatchee, Luke stopped for fuel and to let Jack out to do his business. As he waited for the gas pump to click off, he pulled up the email from Captain Davis about what to expect when he got to where he was headed.

> *Luke,*
>
> *Claude Rakes has been on the run since 11:15 yesterday morning. He was in an orange DOC jumpsuit when he disappeared, but may have taken some clothing from the deceased in the van. He has taken a first aid kit from the van, meaning he may be injured. Reports from Montana say that Rakes is a skilled survivalist in the*

wild. He is not armed, but he kills with his bare hands, so treat him as extremely dangerous. No one seems to have any idea which direction he went. State Patrol has been flying over the region but they have spotted nothing.

Officer in charge of the search for Rakes is Okanogan County Sheriff Mel Chambers. Seems competent. Knows the Gov. has requested you and is expecting you. Keep in touch the best you can.

Good luck. BD.

When Luke arrived at the scene of the accident it was still a beehive of activity. There were state patrol officers directing traffic, and sheriffs' rigs from both Okanogan and Chelan Counties parked here and there.

Luke found a hole to park in, told Jack to stay, got out, and headed to where a group of officers and other folks were looking over the edge of the road. Sitting on the shoulder was a big tow truck pulling the crunched DOC van up the hill.

"You McCain?" a voice in the crowd of people asked.

Luke looked around and saw yet another sheriff in a cowboy hat. But this guy wore it right, and it seemed to fit.

"Yes, sir. Sheriff Chambers?"

"That's what my paycheck says each week. Call me Mel," the sheriff said with a friendly smile and shook Luke's hand. "Glad to have you here. I guess the governor is a good friend of yours, huh?"

"Never met the man," Luke said. "Only know him from TV."

"Well, I'll be damned if I didn't get a call from the man himself, asking me to make you part of our search team here."

"I feel honored, I guess."

"You should. He was quite enamored with your past work."

"You know what my wife said when I told her the governor had asked me to go help find this Rakes fella?"

"No."

"She said, 'Well, la-dee-da.'"

Chambers laughed. "Didn't impress her much, huh?"

"Nope. But here I am. So how can I help?"

"Let's go over here and chat for a minute," Chambers said.

The sheriff stood six feet tall, was a fit one hundred and eighty-five pounds, and had an easy gate to his walk. Black sideburns with just a touch of gray grew down past his ears. Dark eyebrows rode just below a wrinkle on his forehead and above dark brown eyes set evenly on each side of a thin nose. The hat covered Chambers' head, so Luke had no idea if he had a full head of hair or not. Luke thought the man would have fit in perfectly on the set of *Yellowstone*, standing next to Kevin Costner.

He followed the sheriff to his SUV, and the two men leaned up against the rig.

"Here's where we are," Chambers said and proceeded to tell Luke what had happened since his deputy first arrived at the scene twenty-six hours earlier.

He told Luke that there had been two corrections officers hauling two prisoners from Seattle to Spokane. The officer who had survived the crash was in serious condition at a hospital in Wenatchee after first being treated in Winthrop. He was still sedated, and no one had had a chance to talk to him yet. Chambers said one prisoner had died at the scene, but there were strange circumstances to his death. He was out of his handcuffs and leg manacles when the deputy arrived, and he didn't seem to have any serious injuries other than a possible broken neck.

"You think Rakes could have killed him?" Luke asked.

"We think it's a good probability," Chambers said. "But why kill a fellow prisoner and not the officer?"

Luke thought about it but didn't have an answer.

"And we believe it was Rakes who phoned 911 to report the accident," Chambers said. "Now how weird is that?"

"Doesn't make much sense, does it?" Luke said. "Who knows how long the van might have been here before someone found it, if it wasn't called in. He could've had a two-day head start going wherever it is he's going."

"That's the other thing," Chambers said. "We have no idea which way he went. Unfortunately, by the time we tried to find his footprints, there had been at least eight people down around the van, up and down the hill. The area was covered in nothing but boot prints."

"State patrol hasn't seen anything from the air?" Luke asked, but he already knew the answer to the question.

"Nope. The forest is pretty thick in some of this country. He could be all kinds of places where he wouldn't be seen from the sky."

"So, what's your plan, sheriff?"

"We already have a deputy and a guy with his dogs looking to the south. The man swore his hounds cut scent headed that way, so they've been searching that direction for the past eight hours. I get a report from the deputy every hour. The dog guy still thinks they're on the right scent, but I have my doubts. We've worked with him before. His dogs are pretty good at finding a problem cougar or bear now and again, but this is their first manhunt."

"Maybe Jack and I should look to the north. Any thoughts that Rakes might try to get to Canada?"

"Who knows. Not that it would do him any good. Canada doesn't want a mass murderer running around up there any more than we do down here."

"Well, I need to do something. Governor's orders and all. We'll go that way and check around a bit. If we find something, I'll radio you."

"That'd be great. You need another person to go with you? I can supply a deputy who can run up and down these mountains all day. He's a freak of nature."

"Let's wait on that," Luke said. "Let me see what my dog and I can find. I'll radio in every hour?"

"Make it on the half hour," Chambers said. "I've got the deputy with the hound guy checking in on the hour."

"10-4," Luke said and headed to his truck to get Jack and his gear.

"I'll let the governor know you're on the clock," Chambers said with a laugh.

The first thing Luke did when he pulled his pack out of the truck was to dig his GPS unit out and turn it on. As soon as it had connected to the satellites, Luke marked a waypoint for where his truck was parked. He knew his way around in the mountains better than most people, but if the weather changed and fog and rain or—heaven forbid—snow blew in, he wanted to be able to get back to his rig.

Luke let Jack out and told him to sit and stay while he put his backpack on. He was just getting buckled into the pack when he looked up and saw a huge CBS television truck pulling off the highway. The rig was as big as a Greyhound bus and had at least three satellite dishes sitting face down on top.

"Oh boy," Luke said to no one in particular. "Here we go."

Luke grabbed his rifle and patted his leg to bring Jack at heel. They worked their way around a couple sheriff's rigs, checked both ways for traffic, crossed the highway, and headed up the hill.

Sheriff Chambers watched Luke and Jack disappear into some trees and then headed to the TV truck. Where was the governor when he needed him?

*

Mostly out of blind luck, Luke found Rakes' tracks fairly quickly. Or he assumed they were Rakes' tracks. The footprint in some soft soil was big, made from a heavy person, most assuredly a man. In the notes Davis had sent him was a description of Rakes, including his last known height and weight based on his Montana driver's license.

According to the license, Rakes was six foot seven inches tall and weighed three hundred and fifteen pounds. Someone that size, Luke figured, would have a shoe size of thirteen or fourteen, or even bigger. Luke's own shoe size was twelve and a half, and the print he was looking at was a good two inches longer than his.

Luke brought Jack over to smell the area where the print was, but he seemed uninterested. It had been almost twenty-seven hours since Rakes had gone through here, if it was Rakes, and Luke assumed the scent was totally gone. It would be quicker to have Jack tracking with his nose, but it was going to be up to Luke to stay on the footprints with his eyes, at least until they closed the distance enough to get some fresh scent for Jack to follow.

Luke slowly worked on the puzzle. He would find a track every twenty or thirty yards, but then he wouldn't find another for a hundred yards or more. The tracks were working around a hillside and were headed in a northerly direction. He lost the tracks twice, but by crisscrossing back and forth, he picked them up again. The second time he lost then relocated the tracks, they headed downhill to the east. When Luke looked that way, he saw the reason for the direction change. Down below, he could see a well-used trail.

"C'mon, boy," Luke said to Jack and turned and headed to the trail.

He didn't pick up Rakes' tracks right away, but once he saw that the man was heading up the trail, it was much easier to follow, and Luke and Jack moved along quickly. As he hiked, Luke thought about what they were getting into. If Rakes was in decent shape, he could maybe hike two miles an hour. Two miles an hour multiplied by the nearly thirty-hour head start, that was sixty miles. Luke backed out some time for rests and water breaks, but that still put Rakes fifty miles ahead of him. That would also put him close to, if not inside, Canada.

But a big guy like that, a truck driver, sitting all day, Rakes couldn't be in that good of shape. Plus, most of the walking so far had been at least gradually uphill, sometimes up steep grades. Luke did some more calculations and figured that at best Rakes was only twenty miles ahead of them. If he had stopped to sleep during the night, that would put him even closer.

Luke liked those calculations better, and it spurred him on. He had to be in better shape than Rakes. If he could push it to three or even four miles an hour, he would catch up to the fugitive sometime tomorrow. That is if everything went smoothly.

*

At 4:35, Luke's radio crackled.

"Chambers to McCain."

Luke checked his watch. He had forgotten to radio in on the half hour as the sheriff had asked.

"Go ahead," Luke said.

"How's it going?"

"Yeah, sorry about missing the call in. I lost track of time. I've found some prints that could be Rakes. We're following them now."

"Roger that," Chambers said. "Our hound guy has finally decided his dogs are on a lone wolf, of all things. You want me to have him come your way when he gets back here?"

"Negative," Luke said. He had dealt with another hound guy once before, and it hadn't been a great experience. "His dogs will need a rest. I think Jack and I are okay."

"Give me your coordinates so I can put your location on the map," Chambers said.

"Hold on," Luke said as he pulled his GPS out. Then he read off the longitude and latitude.

After a minute, Chambers came back. "If it is Rakes, he is definitely headed toward Canada. I'll get these coordinates to the State Patrol. They can get their chopper up that way and concentrate the search to your north."

"Roger that," Luke said.

He wanted to say that it was most likely a waste of time. They might spot Rakes, but Luke seriously doubted it.

"What's your plan?" Chambers asked.

"I'm going to stay on these prints and hope I find something that tells me I'm on the right track."

"10-4. I'll let your buddy, the governor, know you are in hot pursuit."

"You might hold off on that for a bit longer. If he makes some statement to the television reporters and I'm wrong, he'll have egg all over that pretty face of his."

"10-4. Check in in an hour."

"Roger that."

CHAPTER 23

Rakes hadn't walked this much since he was a kid, and it was starting to wear on him. He had slowed his pace, and he was stopping more often to rest. He replenished his water twice more before it got dark. He didn't want to build a fire during the night hours in case someone was watching from a plane. They might even have satellite capabilities to look down from space and find him.

He had read an article describing the extremely powerful cameras that were loaded on the government satellites circling overhead. The magazine story said the cameras could read the serial numbers on a dollar bill lying on a sidewalk, and they could be trained on anything or anyone at any time. If that was the case—and Rakes had no reason to believe otherwise—they could certainly see him walking on a trail in the middle of nowhere. That is, if they knew where to look. With those thoughts running through his mind, any time the trail would pass through a meadow or left the canopy of trees, he would move off the trail and stay in the trees.

Rakes had found another discarded plastic water bottle and now carried two bottles filled with boiled water. Those kept him hydrated but did nothing to stave off a growing hunger. As hungry as he was, Rakes was even more tired. Just before dark, he left the trail and followed a small stream downhill. He was looking for a big log that was lying on semi-flat terrain and found just what he was looking for after walking only seventy-five yards or so.

In his youth, on the prairies of central Montana, Rakes had built many shelters. Some he dug out of the dirt or in the cutbank of a dried creek bed. Others he built from the downed cottonwood trees that grew along the streams in the area. The log he found off the trail was a fir tree, but it would work as well as a cottonwood, maybe even better. He broke branches off the downed tree and used the end of the bigger dead branch to dig out a man-sized depression right up against the log. Rakes used his overpowering strength to break green bows off some smaller fir trees and placed them in the depression. Then he rounded up some shorter logs and leaned them over the fir bow bed at a forty-five-degree angle up against the bigger log.

When he was done, he had a decent bed to lie on and a roof over his head, such as it was. It wasn't a log cabin or any place Rakes would want to spend more than a night in, but it would keep the bugs off him. More importantly, the makeshift shelter would keep him hidden from anyone trying to find him, including those pesky satellites orbiting above.

After drinking one of his bottles of water, Rakes lay down on the bows and pulled the extra coats out of his pack, using them as blankets over his upper body. As he lay there, he listened to the sounds of the wilderness. Crickets chirped, tree frogs croaked, and the little stream babbled away. Rakes was just drifting off to sleep when he heard the eerie howl of a creature in the distance.

He wasn't superstitious, but Rakes wondered if the howl might be from a sasquatch. Then he remembered there were wolves in this part of Washington. When two or three more howls rolled down the canyon, one over the top of another, he decided that, yes, those were wolves, probably in a pack. Maybe they had just killed a deer and were celebrating.

Until then, Rakes hadn't worried about the creatures that lived in the area he was now traveling through. He had never been afraid of anything with four legs. A couple of times, neighbor dogs had tried to bite him, and he'd dealt with them the same way he had the women he'd killed. With his big hands and powerful arms, he had grabbed the dogs by the throat and snapped their necks.

A pack of wolves would create a different challenge. He believed he could handle one, but not a bunch of them. He would have to be wary and watch for wolves.

The thought of the wolves eating on a dead deer interested Rakes. Was there a chance of coming onto one of their kills? If so, he could steal some meat to cook and eat. That would be much easier than setting a snare for a rabbit or squirrel. Snares worked fine. Rakes had used them frequently back home when he was younger. But they took time and patience. He had the patience, but he didn't have the time. It might take a day or more to wait for something to get caught in a trap.

Rakes also had nothing with which to build a snare. He was constantly looking for items he might scrounge that he could use for his survival as he hiked the path, but besides the dented coffee pot and the two plastic water bottles, the pickings had been very slim. All he needed was some discarded wire or maybe some string or cord, and he could create his snare. He would keep looking.

Those thoughts were turning in his head when Rakes fell asleep.

*

Birds chirping and chipmunks scurrying about had replaced the sounds of the night. Rakes still felt sleep-deprived, and the natural sounds of the woods were soothing to him. He fought to stay asleep and dozed restlessly. But not for long. His subconscious started screaming at him to wake up when another sound echoed through the trees.

Rakes didn't sit up or move a muscle, but he opened his eyes. He could see daylight through the cracks in the logs of his lean-to. He listened intently. What had he just heard? Was it a person?

"Hahahaha!"

There it was again. It sounded like a woman laughing. Or was it a bird chattering? Then there was talking. Definitely a woman's voice. Followed by a man talking.

Rakes stayed as still as death. The voices were getting closer. Were they members of a search party looking for him? Or were they hikers walking the trail he had been on just hours before?

"How long until we are back at the trailhead, Travis?" the woman's voice asked.

"We should be back by mid-afternoon," the man's voice answered.

Rakes could hear footsteps as the hikers clumped along the trail. He risked catching a look at them as they walked by. The woman was leading the way. He could only see the upper half of her body. She was wearing a green coat and a white visor and carried a tall pack on her back. The man followed closely behind. He wore a brown jacket and a look-alike white visor. He, too, carried a tall pack that appeared to be loaded with gear.

The instant Rakes saw the packs, he thought about everything that might be inside of them. There had to be food and matches and water. He could run them down and see if they would be willing to give him some supplies. But then they would know where he was, and they could let the authorities know if they ran into anyone. Best to just let them go.

As quickly as the couple had come into view, they were gone. Rakes could hear their footsteps fading away, and he heard the woman say something he couldn't understand a few minutes later. Then he heard nothing but the birds chirping and the creek burbling.

When he was sure the hikers were not coming back his way, Rakes got up. He relieved himself and drank some water out of the second bottle. He was almost out of water, so he decided to build a fire right there and boil some more.

It took five minutes to get the fire started with his string bow. He kept the bow stick in his pack but had to take one shoelace out of his boot each time he used the bow. Rakes had seen kids wearing sneakers without shoelaces all over the place in Great Falls. They seemed to have no trouble walking, so he tried to do the same with one boot. The boot kept slipping off his foot, and in a matter of fifty steps down the trail, he was already feeling a hot spot developing on his heel where the lace-less boot was rubbing. In all, with constructing the bow, getting the fire started, and boiling enough water to fill both of his bottles, he was there an extra half hour.

Rakes had no idea if the authorities were following him, but he saw the helicopters flying around, so he believed they were. Whenever he stopped to rest, he would listen for the bawling of hounds on his tracks, but he never heard dogs or anything else that might mean they were getting close.

Still, he knew he needed to keep moving. The deeper he got into the wilderness, the better his chances of getting away.

*

The cougar was lying in the shade just below a rock outcrop above the trail when he saw something walking along. It had been five days since he had eaten, and this creature walking below him seemed slow and meaty. It might just make for a feast.

The mountain lion had never seen a human before, nor had he smelled one. As the figure moved up the trail, the cougar slipped out from under the rocks and moved silently down the hill. The cat was definitely curious. He dropped to his stomach and watched from behind as the thing walked up the trail.

Staying low, the cougar crept along behind the thing as it walked. If he was going to try to attack, he would need to get closer. The tip of the cat's tail flicked back and forth when he paused to watch the creature plod on ahead of him.

*

The trail turned up the hill, and Rakes slowed his pace. His legs were already aching from the miles he had put in since leaving the van the day before, and the hills were taking their toll. Halfway up, he stopped to catch his breath. When he stopped, he thought he heard something. No, he hadn't heard something—he *felt* something. Rakes looked around and saw nothing. He searched harder, looking for a deer or maybe one of the wolves he had heard in the night. Still nothing.

Rakes took a drink from one of his bottles, wiped his forehead with the sleeve of his jacket, and started up the hill again, with his senses on full alert.

As he walked, he wondered if someone was watching him. Could someone have him in the sights of a high-powered scope on a hunting rifle? Or maybe someone was watching him through a spotting scope—possibly the police?

Rakes again thought about the satellites. Could he really feel them watching?

With those thoughts going through his mind, he quickly moved from the trail to get into the trees. The second he moved, he heard something rushing him from behind. He started to turn and was hit by something moving with amazing force.

*

The cougar stayed low in the grass just off the trail. He had moved to within ten yards of the two-legged creature. When the thing stopped and turned to look in his direction, the cougar melted even lower into the grass. His golden coat made him virtually invisible.

Then the creature made a sudden move, as if it were running away. That was all the cougar needed. In two quick pounces on his powerful legs, he was on his prey.

The cat had learned how to take down deer and elk calves from his mother. She had taught him to attack from the back and bite the animal in the neck. But this creature was built differently.

The first thing that came available to bite was about the size of a deer's neck, but there was no head attached. He bit hard and dug his claws into the creature's back.

*

Rakes yelled when the cougar hit him, as much from the startling quickness with which the cat had attacked as from the pain in his left forearm where the cougar had clamped his strong jaws. He stumbled a few steps, but once the shock of the initial hit subsided, Rakes quickly went on the offense. With his free hand, he reached around and grabbed the cat by the scruff of the neck. Rakes wanted to break the animal's neck like he had done with the neighbor dogs, but the cougar was not letting go of his forearm.

Using his considerable weight advantage, Rakes turned, with the cougar on his back, and fell to the ground. Just before he hit, he pulled the cat under his body. Three hundred pounds landing on the cougar definitely had an effect. Rakes could feel the animal deflate, but it continued to bite into his arm. The claws in Rakes' back, which had had to cut through a backpack and a coat, were doing little damage. The cat let go with his paws when Rakes landed on him.

With the cougar basically unable to move under his weight, Rakes moved his right hand to the front of the cat's neck, and with incredible strength boosted by a surge of adrenaline, he closed his fingers around the cougar's throat. Rakes squeezed, imagining where the animal's windpipe would be, and didn't let go.

The cougar, now realizing he was in trouble, started struggling. He released his hold on Rakes' arm and clawed at whatever he could reach to try to make the man let go. It was useless.

Rakes' fingers were burning, and his hand was cramping. Would this cat never die? Finally, he felt the cougar's body go limp. Even then, he didn't let go of the animal's throat. He kept squeezing for another minute, then two. Just to make sure the animal was dead.

He rolled off the cougar, prepared to fight it off more if necessary. But when he looked at the cat's face, he saw something he had seen many times before. Rakes had seen it in the kittens he'd killed in the barn. He had seen it in the neighbor dogs he had killed. And he had seen it in the faces of five women—and that idiot Jenkins. Blank, dead eyes staring into nothingness told him the cougar was no longer among the living.

CHAPTER 24

A short time after his conversation on the radio with Sheriff Chambers, Luke found where a small fire had been built near the trail by a creek. He also spotted several big shoe prints in the dirt. Luke put two and two together and figured Rakes was boiling water. The fugitive obviously had left the van with no supplies other than the first aid kit, so he had nothing to drink. Rakes was savvy enough to know that drinking untreated creek water would most likely infect him with giardia, so he was boiling his water.

Luke wondered what he was using as a pot. He must have stumbled onto an old campsite and rummaged something up. There may have been matches in the first aid kit, but if not, Rakes was building fire with just his two hands. Not many people in today's techno world had any idea how to do that. Luke was impressed. And he was concerned. It seemed that Rakes had the knowledge and ability to stay out here for an extended period of time if he had to.

All Luke could do was keep after the man and see what developed.

*

The State Patrol helicopter flew overhead about forty minutes after Luke spoke with Chambers. They were flying low, and when Luke saw the pilot, he gave a wave. The pilot waved back and kept moving up the canyon.

For the last two miles, the trail had stayed in the bottom of a big, wide canyon. Fir trees filled the bottom of the canyon, and where Luke could see up one side or the other, large aspen patches were interspersed among rocky bluffs. Even though he hadn't seen any, Luke thought it looked like great mule deer country. Maybe he and his buddy Cale would come up this way in the fall to hunt.

On the half hour, Luke checked in with Chambers, but the radio conversation was short. Nothing much to report. Luke didn't mention the fire. He still wanted to be sure he was on Rakes' tracks.

Fifteen minutes after the last radio call, Luke spotted someone on the trail ahead. He looked closely and saw two hikers walking toward him—a man in his mid-twenties walking ahead of a woman of about the same age. They were wearing hiking boots over socks up to mid-shin, tan shorts with pockets everywhere, and pastel-colored t-shirts. The man's shirt was blue and the woman's was peach. They had jackets tied around their waists and were both wearing white tennis visors on their heads. Each seemed to be struggling under bulging backpacks that rose a foot over their heads.

When the man in the lead finally spotted Luke, with Jack standing by his side, he was startled but said, "Oh! Hello."

"Great day for a hike, huh?" Luke said.

The woman stood behind the man like he might need to save her from unwanted advances from this stranger on the trail.

Luke noticed her apprehension, pointed at the imprinted badge on his shirt, and said, "I'm state police."

She looked at the badge and then at Luke's pistol in the holster

169

in his belt and the rifle slung over his shoulder. She still wasn't at ease. But the man was.

"What's going on up here that needs policing?" he asked.

"Looking for someone," Luke said vaguely. "Have you seen anyone else on this trail since you've been on it?"

"That's what the helicopter is all about, isn't it?" the man replied without answering Luke's question. He turned to the woman and said, "I told you they were looking for someone."

Luke asked again about seeing anyone else.

"No, sir. Not a soul," the man said. "Although we did see where someone had built a little fire next to a creek by the trail about three miles up that way. It looked fresh."

Luke wondered how a fire could look fresh, but he didn't ask. He would see it for himself soon.

"It kind of pissed us off," the man continued. "Fires are illegal outside of established campgrounds in the National Forest, right? Why would someone do that?"

"I don't know," Luke said. "But I'll look into it."

The woman looked at Jack, sitting by Luke's side. "Does your dog bite?"

"Not unless he is protecting me from something or someone."

Both the hikers looked back at Jack, the big, happy dog with his tongue hanging out. Luke could see they were not impressed.

"Is the person you are looking for dangerous?" the woman asked.

Luke wondered why someone who seemed scared of her own shadow would come out into the wilderness in the first place. He couldn't lie to the lady because he didn't want them to stumble into Rakes without some advance notice that he could be dangerous. Luke didn't tell them he was wanted for multiple murders and that the victims were all females. That might send the woman screaming down the trail.

"Yes, he is. He escaped from a jail transportation van. If you see a big man by himself, dressed in orange, stay clear of him."

"Bigger than you?" the man asked.

"Yes, bigger than me."

"Wow," the woman muttered. "Let's get outta here, Travis."

Luke wished the hikers happy trails and watched as they labored down the hill, under who-knows-how-many pounds of camping gear on their backs.

"Let's go, Jack. We'll see if we can find that fresh fire pit."

*

The dead-out fire was exactly where the hikers said it would be. Luke felt the ashes. They were cold. Probably made the day before.

As he and Jack moved up the trail, Luke kept an eye out for the large boot prints that he assumed belonged to Rakes. The hikers' tracks had covered most of the prints, but Luke found some partial boot prints, so he knew Rakes was still on the trail.

A few times, Luke noticed the tracks just disappeared, but then they would reappear down the trail. He thought about that and looked around. Whenever the tracks left the trail, it was where there were no trees overhead. That was another reason he thought he was on Rakes' tracks. The boot prints were large, made by a big man. The person he and Jack were following was building illegal fires, most likely to boil water because he had no supplies. And now the man seemed to be avoiding open spaces, moving to the trees where he couldn't be seen from the air. Luke didn't think about the possibility of satellite observation.

They walked by the lean-to shelter Rakes had built the night before. It was well-camouflaged and far enough off the trail that they didn't see it. But they did find the dead cougar.

They were moving along on the trail when Jack stopped and his hackles went up. A low growl rumbled from his throat. Luke had seen Jack do this many times before, so he took his rifle off his shoulder and stayed ready.

"What is it, boy?" Luke whispered to Jack.

The yellow dog just stared into the trees, ears forward, emitting the low growl. Luke could see Jack's nostrils moving left and right as he picked up whatever scent it was that was causing him concern.

Finally, after two minutes of standing there, Luke started walking in the direction Jack was looking. He urged Jack to come along, but he just stood there, almost like he was on point.

Luke kept the rifle ready. Jack had alerted him to bears in the brush before, and Luke thought that might be what he smelled now. He looked for a black or brown body in the brush but saw nothing. Then he looked up into the trees because black bears will climb a tree when threatened. Nothing there either.

Jack slowly moved up next to Luke and then went past him. He stopped just short of some long grass and stood and growled louder. Luke walked up and saw a long tail sticking out of the grass twenty feet away. A closer look revealed a cougar attached to the tail, lying in the grass and unmoving. Luke moved in and poked the prone cougar with his rifle barrel. Still, it didn't move. The cat's eyes were open, and it was obviously dead.

"That's weird," Luke said more to himself than Jack. The dog still wasn't sure he should be this close to the cougar.

Over the years, Luke had dealt with many cougars. Some he had tranquilized and transported away from houses and farms. Others that had taken to killing goats or other livestock, he had had to shoot. And he had checked cougars that had been killed by hunters over the years. In that time, he had seen big mature cougars and younger cats that weren't nearly as large. Luke picked up the dead cat and figured it weighed sixty or seventy pounds. A look at its teeth, along with its weight, told Luke this was a young male.

The cougar was of the age that it would be traveling, looking for a new home area. During that time, they still hunt to eat, but it can be difficult for them to find deer, their preferred prey. This is the age when cougars sometimes will move into areas inhabited by people, looking for an easy meal. Dogs, cats, goats, and sheep all become targets. Once in a blue moon, a cougar will even take on a human.

Luke remembered reading a story a few years earlier about a man in Colorado who had been jumped by a young cougar while he was out jogging. The man fought the cougar, trying to stab it and beat it with a rock. He finally killed it by holding the cat down and stepping on its neck, eventually suffocating it. The photo of the man looked like he had been in a fight with, well, a cougar. He had deep lacerations on his face where the cat had scratched him during the battle.

Is that what had happened here? He examined the cougar's body. There were no bullet holes or any other marks that would indicate a fight with another animal. The thing looked like it had just tipped over and died.

Luke went back to the trail and tried to find any prints or scuff marks that might show what had happened. He found the big man's tracks and backtracked those until he found cougar tracks just off the trail. Luke walked back up the trail, found where the grass was torn up and matted down just off the trail. He found blood on the grass.

All he could figure was that cougar had attacked the man with the big feet, probably Rakes, and the man had killed the cougar. There was no blood anywhere on the cougar's body, so it seemed logical that the cat had bitten and scratched the man, and that is where the blood had come from.

Luke thought about that for a minute. Could he kill a cougar with his bare hands? He guessed if it was life and death, he could. The jogger in Colorado had done it. Still, it would take some strength, and some luck. But if what Luke had read was true, that Rakes was breaking his victims' necks with his bare hands, he would be formidable in a hand-to-hand battle. Luke hoped he wouldn't find out just how tough that would be, if, no, when he caught up with the fugitive.

They left the cougar where it lay and started up the trail again. On the half hour, Luke radioed Sheriff Chambers.

"How's it going, Luke?"

"I'm pretty sure I'm on Rakes' trail. He's building little fires near creeks to boil water, so he has something to drink. Anyone else without water would be walking back to the highway, rather than away from it."

"I agree," the sheriff said. "Listen, things are getting kind of crazy here. Three more television trucks have arrived, and they are all looking for a story. One of the networks is even talking about chartering a helicopter to start looking for Rakes themselves."

"They can have at it," Luke said. "It won't bother what I'm doing. The person we're tracking leaves the trail anytime there isn't enough canopy to keep him hidden. They'll never see him. It would be a waste."

"Yeah, but it would get them out of my hair."

There was dead air for a half minute, then Chambers said, "And even better news is the governor is coming at some point. He received word about all the network trucks here and, well, you know. It's good for his image."

"Again, won't bother me," Luke said. "As long as he stays there with you."

"That's just the thing. He has asked me to form a posse. He wants riders on horseback. Just like the old west. He's serious about catching Rakes."

In his seventeen years with the Department of Fish and Wildlife, Luke had never known a sheriff's department to form a posse. Evidently, now he was going to have to deal with a second one, just days after the first.

"He's the boss," Luke said. "But can you hold him off for a day? I really feel like we're gaining ground on this guy. I believe he is out of shape, carrying a lot of weight. I don't think he has anything to eat. He must be hungry and getting tired. If we are on Rakes' trail, and I think we are, we are going to catch up to him tomorrow."

"I'll see what I can do, but I have to have the riders here when the governor arrives. Those are my orders."

"Roger," Luke said. "Hey, can you give my captain a call and update him on what's happening and ask him to call my wife? She'll want to know that the dog is doing okay."

The sheriff laughed. "Will do. If I hear anything differently about the posse, I'll let you know."

"10-4. McCain out."

CHAPTER 25

Rakes had taken the cougar's carcass and tossed it fifty yards off the trail. He seriously thought about packing it with him. He knew people ate cougars and he was hungry. The thought of eating the cat didn't bother him one bit. His only problem was he had no knife, so skinning the animal to get to the meat would be difficult.

If he thought he might run across something sharp enough to butcher the cougar within the next mile or two, he would have thrown the dead cat over his shoulder. But packing an additional sixty pounds up and down hills for an extended period was going to be too much. He was getting more tired by the mile.

Rakes drank when he was thirsty and rested often. He built another water-boiling fire at the next creek the trail crossed. All of this was slowing him significantly. Plus, the shadows were getting long, meaning it was late in the day. It would be getting dark in an hour. He should look for another good spot to build his shelter for the night.

His arm ached from the mountain lion bite, and he had some deep scratches on his right leg where the cat had clawed him as he was strangling it. Luckily, he had the first aid kit. After washing the wounds with water from his bottles, Rakes applied some antibacterial ointment to the bite and the scratches. He wrapped his arm, because those wounds were the deepest, and put two bigger adhesive bandages on the lacerations on his leg.

Rakes knew that house cats were notorious for carrying all kinds of bacteria in their mouths and on their claws, which could cause serious infections. He wasn't sure if cougars did as well, but he would watch the wounds closely and keep them clean and doctored up for as long as his supplies lasted.

As he walked up the trail, he started humming the tune to "Cat Scratch Fever," the Ted Nugent song from the late 1970s. It was Rakes' subconscious telling him he would need to pay attention to his body temperature as well.

*

It took Rakes a half hour to find a usable spot to build a lean-to against a downed log and another forty-five minutes to gather all the materials he needed for it to be semi-comfortable and hidden from the trail.

When he finally finished the shelter, it was completely dark. The effort to collect the logs and branches and to put the shelter together zonked him. He knew he should build a fire to boil water, but he was just too tired. He needed to rest.

When Rakes lay down, his arm started aching even more, and his stomach started rumbling. He had seen some pain reliever tablets in the first aid kit when he was searching for bandages and ointment, so he dug the pain pill vial out of the kit and swallowed three with a gulp of water. He had nothing for the hunger pangs.

It took twenty minutes for the pain pills to start taking effect, and even though his arm still throbbed, it was not as bad, and Rakes finally fell asleep. Unfortunately, it wasn't a restful sleep.

He had been asleep only a short time when the howling of

another—or maybe it was the same—pack of wolves awakened him. The canines were close. Rakes wondered if they'd smelled him. And if they had, would they come for him?

His stomach rumbled, and that made him think again about finding a wolf kill where he could scrounge even a few bites of meat, like a magpie or crow might. Anything would be better than nothing.

Finally, the howling stopped, and Rakes nodded off again. Entering REM sleep brought on a dream. It was in living color, only the star of the dream was not living. It was that idiot James Earl Jenkins. In the dream, he came back to life, leaped up off the floor of the wrecked van, and grabbed Rakes by the throat. Jenkins was squeezing Rakes' windpipe just as Rakes had done to kill the cougar.

"You are going to die tomorrow, shovel," Jenkins said. "Then I will see you in hell!"

Rakes startled awake. He felt his forehead. He was sweating, but he didn't have a fever. Or at least he didn't think he did. The dream was definitely a fever dream though. It was so vivid. He thought he could even smell the stench of Jenkins' rotten breath.

There were no more dreams, but Rakes woke up every hour or so. His arm hurt. His legs hurt, both from the scratches and the hiking. His stomach gurgled. And every time he woke up, he thought about the message Jenkins had delivered.

Just like when the foul woman he'd killed in Havre came to him in the dream at the motel, the Jenkins dream was a message from his subconscious. The law had to be after him. And they must be getting close. He was going to need to be extra careful.

*

Luke had also set up camp just before nightfall. He had considered staying on the trail, trying to get closer to Rakes, but decided that expending energy in the dark would be unproductive. Plus, he was tired. He figured he and Jack had covered close to ten miles by pushing hard. They weren't running up the trail, but they were moving much faster than a normal hiking speed.

After putting up his one-man tent near the creek, Luke pulled out his Jet Boil stove, filled the small cooking pot with water, and had it boiling in a minute. He let the water boil for three minutes, then poured the hot water into a packet of freeze-dried macaroni and cheese.

As he waited for his dinner to cool, Luke pulled out a small bag of kibble for Jack and fed him in a collapsible bowl. Jack ate like he hadn't had food in a month and was done before Luke's pot of mac and cheese was cool enough to eat.

"Slow down, buddy," Luke said to Jack as he gobbled up the food. "No one is going to take it from you."

His words fell on deaf ears. As soon as Jack finished licking the last crumbs from the dish, he looked up to Luke for more.

Luke gave the yellow dog one of the doggy energy bars he had packed and said, "Here's a little dessert."

Luke carried a water purifying bottle that sucked stream water through a filter system, and he used it often to keep his bottle full. But to save a little time, he boiled another pot of water to replenish his bottle before going to bed.

His tent had a rainfly, but Luke could see about a zillion stars in the sky, so he figured he wouldn't need it tonight. That was a decision that had bit him in the past, but he decided to take the chance. He rolled his compressed foam pad out on the floor of the tent and then put his sleeping bag on top of it.

"Okay, boy," Luke said to Jack. "Time for bed."

Jack followed Luke into the tent and immediately plopped down on the sleeping bag.

"Oh no you don't. That's for me. Now scooch."

The big dog obliged, cozying up next to Luke when he was settled in the sleeping bag. That didn't bother Luke at all. He liked feeling Jack next to him. He knew the dog would alert him to anything or anyone who might come along in the night.

As he lay there thinking about the day, he started to question whether they were really on Rakes' tracks. Who else could kill a cougar with their bare hands? And why was the man leaving the trail to stay under cover? It was the boiling water deal that again convinced Luke they were on the tracks of the fugitive.

He thought about his last radio conversation with Chambers. Sending deputies on horses did not seem like a good idea. Would he like to have another person or two with him when he did catch up to Rakes? Yes, certainly. But if not, he was confident he could handle the situation.

Luke was just about to sleep when he heard a pack of wolves start howling in the distance. Jack raised his head and listened.

"It's okay, boy," Luke said. "They aren't close enough to bother us."

He had heard wolves before, but their long, lonesome howls always gave Luke the chills. He wondered if Claude Rakes was also listening to the wolves, wherever he was.

*

Luke slept well and was awakened by robins chirping in the gray light before sunrise. The birds always seemed happy to see the first signs of a new day's arrival, and they let the world know about it.

He opened his eyes to see Jack staring at him. "Okay, I get it. Time to get going."

Luke unzipped the door to the small tent and let Jack out. The dog hurried off into the trees.

"Stay close," Luke said, knowing full well his idea of close and Jack's were two different things. But he could always count on the dog coming back as soon as he heard Luke whistle for him.

He set up the backpacking stove again and boiled some more water. He had no idea what the day was going to bring, but if he was right, and they were going to catch up with Rakes, Luke wanted to be fueled up.

While the water was boiling, Luke stuffed his sleeping bag into its sack, rolled up the pad, and dismantled the tent. It all went neatly back into his backpack.

Luke dumped the hot water into a pouch of dried scrambled eggs and sausage and stirred it around. Jack must have smelled the food because he came running back just as Luke was digging in. When he was done eating, he gave Jack some more kibble and another doggy energy bar.

He looked around their little campsite for anything that he might have missed, pulled the pack over his shoulders, grabbed his rifle, and headed for the trail.

"C'mon, Jack. Let's go see if we can find this Rakes fella."

*

The robins had awakened Rakes as well. But he wasn't quite as optimistic as Luke had been about the day ahead. He had slept only briefly here and there throughout the night. His nightmare featuring Jenkins kept popping into his head, and his arm and legs were throbbing. He was tired. Physically and, to his surprise, emotionally.

After he climbed out of his shelter, Rakes went to work getting a fire started. As he held down the spinning stick that went into the board where the embers were created, his left arm gave way. Rakes winced with pain. Something was wrong. He moved his left wrist, and as he did, the pain intensified. The cougar bite was deep, and the only thing he could think was that it had clipped or bruised a tendon. It didn't make the arm useless, but if he had to fight off another mountain lion, well, he didn't want to think about that.

After a bit of a struggle, he got the fire going and put the pot of water on to boil. As the water was heating, Rakes tended to his injuries. He applied more ointment to the puncture wounds and rewrapped his arm. He washed the lacerations on his leg and put new bandages on them.

Rakes was really hungry. Normally, he could have gone a day or two without eating. But out here, burning calories by the thousands, he needed something to fuel the fire. He looked around for some berries or anything to eat. It was too early in the year for berries, he knew, but still he looked.

Finally, he spotted some wild sunflowers. Rakes remembered someone eating the leaves and flowers of that plant on one of those survival television shows, so he went over and picked a leaf. He wiped it off and stuck it in his mouth and chewed. The flavor wasn't great, but it wasn't terrible either. He plucked some of the yellow petals from the flower and ate them.

The gal on the TV show had said it was alright to eat some but not a lot of the sunflowers, as it could send your guts into major malfunction. So, he ate just a little, and it seemed to tame his hunger. If he got through the morning without puking or diarrhea, he would eat some more later.

Rakes kicked some dirt on his fire, grabbed his stuff, and started walking again.

*

Luke radioed in to Chambers and listened as the sheriff brought him up to speed on all the happenings at the scene of the van crash, which had now turned into communication central. He told Luke that the governor would be arriving sometime via helicopter. The posse had been formed and included three men and two women. Two were deputies of his from Okanogan County, and two were Chelan County deputies. The fifth person was a wrangler from Twisp who was providing three of the horses. The two women deputies had their own horses.

"The wrangler knows this country and has ridden around in it most of his life," Chambers said.

"Ah, man. Any chance to keep them there for a while?" Luke asked.

"I'm holding them, but this was the governor's idea. Who knows what will happen when he gets here."

"I really think I'm getting close to Rakes. Any chance I can talk to the governor when he gets there?"

"I'll see what I can do," Chambers said. "He told me he thinks you are doing a helluva job, but he wants to send in reinforcements."

"Great. Nice to have him on my side."

"By the way, I heard back from your captain," Chambers said. "He said your wife was glad to hear that yellow dog of yours is doing well."

"Well, that's comforting," Luke said. "Holler at me if the governor wants to chat. Otherwise, we're going to go find our man."

"Good luck," Chambers said and signed off.

CHAPTER 26

The television trucks were parked nose to tail along the shoulder of Highway 20 where the transportation van had been forced off the road and into the trees. ABC, NBC, CBS, and CNN were all there filing reports for their early morning shows and evening news broadcasts. Washington State Patrol officers had been stationed at each end of the area and were directing the looky-loos and other traffic around the trucks.

In the twenty-four hours since Claude Rakes had mysteriously escaped from the van, America had become enthralled with the disappearance of this mass murderer and the effort to try to round him up. On the day Rakes disappeared, one of the networks had started running a small digital clock that stayed in the upper-left corner of the screen throughout their broadcasts, clicking over each second. It sat next to the words "Hunt for a Mass Murderer."

A pretty, dark-haired reporter approached Chambers and asked if he would be willing to be interviewed on camera for her six o'clock news report. The woman, who might have been thirty, was rail thin, because the TV cameras add ten pounds, and had perfectly arranged teeth covered in dazzlingly white veneers. The teeth seemed even whiter, if that was at all possible, because they were surrounded by bright red lipsticked lips.

"We're in hour nineteen of the hunt for Claude Rakes," the woman reporter started off, looking into the television camera. "Rakes is now wanted for questioning in the murders of women in eleven western states. I have with me Okee-noggin Sheriff Melvin Chamberlain who is in charge of the search for the fugitive. How is the search going, Sheriff?"

She stuck her microphone in Chambers' face.

"We have a search team with hounds scouring the forest to the south, and one of the state's best trackers and his dog are working to the north," Chambers said with his most serious face.

"This is big country, sheriff. You think one man is enough to try to find such a despicable murderer?" the woman asked with a dazzling smile and a bit of an attitude.

"We are forming a team of deputies on horseback that will join the search in the morning and—"

"You mean like a posse?" the reporter interrupted.

"Well, yes, it could be called that. They can cover more ground on horseback. And we have had the State Patrol helicopter searching a twenty-square-mile radius for several hours today."

The woman pulled the microphone away from Chambers, turned to the camera, and said, "It sounds like Claude Rakes may be out here for days or even weeks. Let's hope there are no unsuspecting campers nearby, as they could end up as the next victim of a known mass murderer, loose in the wilds of Washington State. From the scene of the escape, I'm Tiffany Brooks reporting."

Chambers listened to the woman's wrap-up of the story and wanted to reach out and slap her.

"Thank you, Mr. Chamberlain," Brooks said with her fake smile. She turned to her cameraman and asked, "How was that?"

"I think you got his name wrong," the cameraman said.

"Oh well. No one will notice," Brooks said. "Let's go get some footage of where the van hit the tree."

One of the other networks dubbed their coverage of the search for Rakes as "Mass Murderer Manhunt." That one seemed to really resonate with the viewers across America. Other media members liked it too. The next day, several newspapers in the larger cities around the country were using Mass Murderer Manhunt as their headline for the stories on the search for Rakes. Others just used the word Manhunt. Or Manhunt in the West.

Three more TV reporters at the scene interviewed Chambers and asked pretty much the same questions. He gave the same answers. In none of the interviews did he mention that the search team with the hounds had struck out, and the dogs were now lounging in their crates, their handlers waiting for orders to try someplace else. Nor did he say that the WSP helicopters were basically useless and a waste of taxpayer dollars. He wanted to tell them all that Luke was likely on Rakes' tracks and could have him under arrest as early as tomorrow, but he didn't do that either.

*

The governor arrived the next morning with much fanfare. Someone had tipped off the television crews that he would be arriving at nine o'clock via helicopter and would be landing near the highway just down from where the TV trucks were parked.

The State Patrol had blocked the highway, much to the chagrin of several truckers who were on deadline to get goods delivered to the west side of the state. They could wait. This was for the good of all the people of the state, or so they said.

The governor, dressed in blue jeans and a white button-down collar shirt under a blue denim jacket with fuzzy fake wool around the collar, ducked down out of the chopper and marched right over to a spot where the TV cameras had been told to stage. Two women and a man dressed similarly followed the governor dutifully out of the helicopter. As they walked, the chopper lifted off and turned sharply away, blowing dust and leaves all over the governor, his minions, and the TV crews.

Once the chopper was out of earshot and the debris had settled, the governor said, "I'll be making a statement and then I will happily take questions."

One smartass camera guy said, "So you're making a statement about making a statement."

Everyone laughed, except the governor. This was far too serious a situation for humor.

"The police agencies in Washington and I are taking the escape and the need to capture Claude Rakes seriously. I personally requested Washington State's best tracker, a special officer from our Department of Fish and Wildlife agency, to attempt to find the fugitive. The officer has been tracking Rakes in the wilderness for nearly twenty hours, and the word I have received is he is closing in on the killer."

There was a murmur in the crowd of reporters.

"To assist the state officer, I have requested a posse of deputies on horseback to be formed. This group of skilled and brave officers will join the hunt as soon as I give the word. We believe we will have this murderer in custody within hours."

At the end of his short speech, all the reporters started barking questions at the governor, most of which he had already answered in his statement.

When there were no more questions, the governor turned to Chambers and said, "Sheriff Chambers, let's get our posse going."

Chambers, who had talked to the governor by phone earlier, had it all set up. He had told the wrangler and the deputies to be ready to ride as soon as the governor was done talking to the reporters. The TV cameras swung around to Chambers, who looked every bit the part in his cowboy hat. He raised his hand with a finger pointed in the air and spun it around. The five riders spurred their steeds, and the horses galloped across the road, up a slight embankment, and off into the trees.

"Shit!" one of the camera operators said. "I missed that. Can we do it again?"

As soon as the posse was off and running, the governor's helicopter swooped back in and landed. The governor's staff members ran for the chopper, but before he joined them, he walked over to Chambers.

"Thanks, sheriff," the governor said, shaking Chambers' hand. "Let me know as soon as we have this guy in custody."

"I will, sir," Chambers said. "Fly safe."

The helicopter was still in sight, thumping off over the mountain when Chambers radioed for Luke.

"Yeah, go ahead," Luke said.

"Good news and bad news," Chambers said.

"Okay."

"The governor and I both called you Washington State's best tracker on national television."

"So, what's the good news?"

"The governor just turned the posse loose. Five riders coming your way."

"Super," Luke said. "Do they know where they are going?"

"I gave them your coordinates from last night. I figured that would get them close enough."

Luke calculated how long it would take the riders to get to him. "That doesn't give me much time."

"Sorry about all this, Luke. The posse is on channel two on the radio if you want to communicate with them."

"Okay, thanks. I'll check in later."

"Good luck."

*

Sara McCain had watched the evening news the night before and the morning shows on the network television stations. The reports about the search for Claude Rakes didn't give her anything she didn't already know from talking to Captain Davis who was checking in with her whenever he heard from the sheriff up north.

She was amazed at how much time the networks were giving to this story. They all had delved into Claude Rakes' life. Some repeated the stories that had played before Rakes had escaped, and many updated their stories. They talked to people in Havre who went to school with Rakes and supposedly knew him well. They talked to his former teachers. And they talked to his boss at the trucking company in Great Falls.

They also talked to the Wyoming State Patrol officer who had found the bodies of the two women who had had their necks broken and their mouths formed into eerie smiles. They talked to the Boise County sheriff who had investigated the murder of the woman found with a broken neck in Idaho, and they talked to the Spokane County deputies who'd identified Rakes as the suspect in the murder of the girl there.

They tried to talk to the kid who had watched Rakes dump the body off the bluff, but even though he was beyond eager to tell his story and be on TV, his parents were concerned that Rakes may not be captured and their son would be in danger.

The network reporters also talked to investigators in Oregon, Utah, New Mexico, and Colorado who were wanting to talk to Rakes about several unsolved murders of women in their states. Viewers were eating it up.

So far, the stories hadn't mentioned Luke by name. Sara was good with that and knew Luke would be as well. She worried about Luke, but she also knew he was good at his job. He had tracked down murderers and kidnappers before, and she was confident he would do it again. Having Jack with him also made her feel better. Their dog was an extra set of eyes and ears for Luke, and he also had a great nose. They were a good team, and Sara was convinced they would have Rakes in custody within the next twenty-four hours.

CHAPTER 27

Adam Wisner had also been watching the news about the search for Claude Rakes from his apartment in Rathdrum, Idaho. He switched from ABC to NBC to CBS and to the cable news stations to get every bit of information he could. Unfortunately, the reporters were telling him nothing new. They all said the same thing and interviewed the same people.

He wanted more. He needed more. So, Wisner called in sick at the welding shop where he worked, threw some food and drinks into a cooler, grabbed the .270 rifle he had inherited from his grandfather, and loaded that stuff, along with some ammunition, into his Ford pickup and headed for the interstate.

Wisner had driven through northern Washington several times and knew pretty much where the van carrying Rakes had crashed. Plus, he figured with all the TV trucks and police vehicles around, he would know exactly where it was when he saw it. He estimated the drive would take him about three hours.

He lit a cigarette, rolled down the windows, tuned his radio to the country music station, and headed west.

*

Rakes walked for three hours. The trail had climbed continuously up the side of a mountain before it turned and went around it. On the other side, he found he was now going to be walking downhill, which lifted his spirits somewhat. Before he left the other side of the mountain, Rakes stopped for a rest. He drank some water and watched his backtrack. He couldn't see very far because of the trees, but from what he could see, there was nothing moving. He couldn't see anyone on the trail below, but he knew someone was out there.

The flowers and leaves Rakes had eaten staved off the hunger for a while, but soon his stomach started rumbling, and his guts were churning. He drank some more water, emptying his first bottle and half the second.

His leg hurt some, but his arm was really pounding. When Rakes looked at his left hand, he noticed that it was a reddish color. Different than his pale right hand.

And, instead of feeling hot from all the walking uphill, he felt chilled. He knew that was not good.

Rakes kept pushing. The downhill walking was easier, but he was getting winded more often. He stopped to rest every ten minutes. He was sweating more too from the hiking and from what he perceived was a fever that was trying to push something bad out of his body.

It took an hour of hiking before the trail down the mountain crossed another creek. It was a welcome relief. Rakes immediately kneeled and splashed icy water on his face and used the dented pot to pour water over his head.

He hadn't urinated all morning and was becoming dehydrated. He had to have water to drink, and he almost took a chance and drank the cold, clear water directly from the stream. But he talked himself out of it and went about starting another fire.

Rakes' left arm was starting to swell, and as stiff and sore as it was, it was almost useless. But he had to have fire to boil the water. He forced himself to make the arm work, almost screaming at the pain of holding the fire stick while the bow and shoestring spun it back and forth. When the little pile of leaves and needles finally started smoldering, Rakes was exhausted. Once the flames were licking at the small branches he added to the fire, he lay back on the ground. How many more times was he going to be able to do this?

As he waited for the pot of water to boil, he started thinking about his situation. He needed food and he needed rest. One was going to be much easier to attain than the other.

When the water cooled, Rakes drank the whole pot. Then he filled it a second time and put it on to boil. As he lay there waiting for the second pot, Rakes closed his eyes. In seconds he was asleep. It felt so good.

The pot was at a rolling boil when he woke up. How long had he been asleep? He wanted the water to boil at least three minutes to kill the bacteria effectively, but he had no idea how long it had been boiling. So, he let it boil for another few minutes.

Once he had filled his bottles, Rakes snuffed out the fire. But instead of hitting the trail, he wandered down the creek fifty yards to where a giant tree had fallen. It was the perfect spot for a shelter. He knew he should keep moving, but he was just too tired.

Reinvigorated by the idea of sleeping, he gathered up the logs he needed to create his lean-to. The grass under the log was long enough to offer some relief from the hard ground, so Rakes didn't gather any bows on which to lie.

The cougar bite on his arm was hurting less, but now his left hand was aching. It had swollen more and was turning a reddish-purple. His cold sweats were coming more regularly.

Rakes climbed into the shelter and lay down. Despite the pain in his hand, he fell asleep quickly. His last thought before falling asleep was to wonder just how close the law might be.

*

Luke had pushed hard up the trail for most of the morning. He kept an eye on the tracks in the trail and knew he was still following the big footprints of the man he assumed was Rakes. He had radioed one of the deputies in the posse and was told they had hit a snag. One of the wranglers' horses had come up lame, and he, along with the deputy riding the horse, were taking the injured horse back to the highway. That left three riders, the two female deputies on their own horses and one male deputy on the other wrangler's horse.

"We're not as familiar with this country as Tuffy is," a deputy named Jessica Hart said. Tuffy was the wrangler, Luke surmised. "So, we're kind of feeling our way."

Luke gave her encouragement but also told her that he was doing fine on his own. "Don't push it," Luke said. "No need to get another horse—or worse, a rider—hurt."

They agreed to stay in touch, and Luke signed off after telling them to be careful.

It wasn't long after the radio call that Jack went on alert as they hiked along the trail. He stopped, ears forward, and looked into the trees. Luke could hear him sniffing the air. But the dog's hackles weren't up. That meant it probably wasn't an animal like a bear or a cougar.

Luke looked ahead and saw they were coming up on another creek crossing. He urged Jack on, and the two of them slowly walked that way.

He had gotten used to seeing evidence of the small fires that Rakes had been making, presumably to boil water, so it didn't surprise Luke to find another. But Jack was definitely smelling something new or different here.

"What is it, boy?" Luke asked as he pulled his rifle off his shoulder.

Jack was looking down the creek, so Luke looked that way too. At first, he didn't see anything. Then, he spotted something that didn't look quite right. Someone had leaned a dozen smaller logs up against a big downfall. It was some kind of shelter.

With his rifle ready, Luke slowly walked toward the shelter. He stepped lightly, feeling the ground with his feet before he put his full weight down. He didn't want to break a branch and alert whoever might be in there to their presence. He had whispered to Jack to heel, and the dog stayed close at Luke's side.

He hadn't taken the time to feel the fire, but Luke had to assume since the shelter was close to the fire that it had been constructed by Rakes. It was mid-day, and there was no reason to believe Rakes was still in the shelter, but he might be. He couldn't take any chances.

As he got closer to the shelter, Luke stopped and listened. If someone were sleeping in there, he might hear breathing or light snoring. He heard nothing. But Jack started his low, rumbling growl. Luke didn't risk saying anything to the dog, so he reached down and touched his head. Jack stopped growling.

When he was five feet from the shelter, Luke stopped again and pointed his rifle at the lean-to of logs. Again, he waited and listened. Nothing.

"State police. Come on out of there," he said with authority.

Luke waited for a minute, but there was no response. There were three possibilities here. One, no one was home. Two, the person inside was a seriously sound sleeper. Or three, he was dead.

There was only one way to find out. Luke stepped closer and maneuvered the barrel of his rifle around, sticking it between two of the logs. Then he pushed them apart.

CHAPTER 28

WHOMP! He had no idea what had just hit his windshield. It certainly snapped Adam Winsor out of his driving trance. He looked in the rearview mirror and saw about a thousand feathers swirling around as a feral pigeon flopped on the centerline.

Winsor carried the youthful build of a teenager even though he was twenty-one. He was slender, and stood five-foot-eleven. He had blond hair and a narrow face, which was home to some scraggly blond whiskers. He was trying to look his age, but the light hair on his lip and chin was sparse and difficult to see unless you were right up close to him.

His blue eyes were the color of robin's eggs, which would have made the girls swoon, but unfortunately, his eyes didn't look in the same direction. Winsor was afflicted with Strabismus, a condition in the eye muscles that kept the eyes from looking at the same spot at the same time. Famous actors like Topher Grace and Steve Buscemi among others had the condition, but that never was much help to Winsor when it came to having confidence in the way he looked.

Even with his wonky eyes, Winsor had become a crack shot. As a young boy, he had hunted tweety birds with a BB gun, then squirrels and rabbits with a .22 rifle. Finally, he had become skilled with the .270 caliber Winchester Model 70 he had inherited from his grandfather. Many a deer, both legally taken during hunting season and some during other times of the year, had died from a well-placed shot from granddaddy's rifle in Winsor's hands.

Even though they had told him and his classmates in grade school that smoking would kill you, Winsor was a pack-a-day guy. Marlboros were his brand. And as he drove, he smoked one after another.

He checked the clock on his dashboard. He should be arriving at the site of the prisoner van crash in an hour.

Mel Chambers tried to call Luke on the radio two different times. Either the radio was turned off, or he was down in a hole or some other place where the radios wouldn't reach. Whatever the reason, Luke wasn't answering.

The sheriff wasn't really worried about Luke. More than anything, he was just desperate for some news, any news, that he could pass on to the governor. It had only been five hours since he had flown off in the helicopter, but the governor was expecting some kind of resolution to this situation, and his people were calling every half hour for updates.

That was on top of the persistent pestering by the news people, which now included three different news correspondents who were feeding stories to the Associated Press, Reuters, and United Press. They wanted updates now, but Chambers had very little to tell them. Finally, he sent one of his deputies around to each of the trucks to tell them the sheriff would speak to the media at noon to bring everyone up to speed on the search for Rakes.

He had heard from the posse and knew that it was down to

three deputies after one of the horses got hurt. There was some concern on the part of the deputy leading the group that they might not be on the right track.

Chambers told them to keep looking, but if it got too late, or they were worried about anything else, to turn around and come back.

"We don't need anyone getting hurt out there," Chambers told the deputy.

"10-4," the deputy said. "We're going to stay after it."

She was aware that she was likely being judged because she was a woman. Not by the sheriff—she knew he had one hundred percent confidence in her—but by others. It was inevitable. She had seen it since her first day in the department.

"Roger that," Chambers said. "Stay in touch and let me know immediately if you catch up to Officer McCain."

*

At noon, Chambers stood in front of a half dozen TV cameras, with microphones stuck in his face. He still did not have much to tell the reporters, but he did tell them a little more about Luke and what he was doing.

"Our tracker is convinced he is on Rakes' heels right now," Chambers said. "He is of the opinion that he will have the fugitive in custody before sundown if everything goes okay."

Then the sheriff added one of those cover-your-butt statements.

"But everyone needs to realize this is the wilderness, with dangerous animals and problems around every corner, so we need to be patient. A hundred things could go wrong out there."

"What kind of dangerous animals?" Tiffany Brooks asked, an even darker shade of red lipstick surrounding her perfectly white teeth.

"Well, there are at least three packs of wolves in this area that we know of," Chambers said. "There are cougars throughout the Cascades from Oregon to Canada, and there has been more than one report of grizzly bears in the higher elevations near here."

"Wolves don't attack people, do they?" one of the other reporters asked.

"Not normally," Chambers said. "But they will if they get hungry enough or are put in a situation they feel they can't get out of."

"We've heard your tracker is Luke McCain, the wildlife officer who caught that serial killer down around Yakima a few years ago," another reporter said. "Is that true?"

No sense denying it. One of the governor's people had probably dropped the name.

"Yes, it is Officer McCain, along with his yellow Lab, who are tracking Rakes at this moment. Our posse is still headed to assist Officer McCain as he closes in on the fugitive."

"Why don't you just fly a helicopter up there?" Brooks asked. "That seems like it would be quicker."

"That country up there is wilderness, Miss Brooks," Chambers said, talking to her like a teacher might talk to a third grader. "There's not a flat spot within twenty miles, and trees cover almost every inch of it."

He wanted to say, "Stop asking stupid questions," but he thought she got the message.

Brooks frowned. She didn't like her good idea being shot down so quickly.

There were a few more questions regarding the posse and how long it might take to get Rakes back down here when he was caught. Chambers answered them truthfully and succinctly. Then he sent them back to their TV trucks with a "That's all. We'll let you know the second we get word from our deputies that we have captured the fugitive."

Chambers was extra careful to not call Rakes a killer or murderer in his remarks to the media. The man was still innocent until proven guilty in the eyes of the law. The TV reporters on the other hand weren't so generous.

The running clock up in the corner of the cable news network clicked over to 29 hours, 12 minutes, 33 seconds.

CHAPTER 29

Luke tensed as he started to move the logs apart on the shelter. He believed Rakes was unarmed, but he needed to be ready for anything. The logs parted and there was . . . nothing. He relaxed a little and stepped back.

He was disappointed to find the shelter empty, but he wasn't surprised. Rakes was too good to be caught in the middle of the day sleeping. But it would have been nice to get him back in custody.

Luke searched the area and found a few blood drops in the grass around the shelter and some discarded medical tape and two bandages stained with blood. That told him that Rakes had more than just scratches from the battle with the mountain lion. The wounds had to be hindering the man's progress.

He walked back to the fire and felt the ashes. They were cold, which is what Luke expected. He pulled his filtered water bottle out of his pack, drank the remaining water, and replenished his supply in the creek.

He had to be gaining on Rakes. But by how much? He wasn't sure, but one thing he did know was that he wasn't gaining on him by sitting around. He called Jack, and they were off again, following the big boot tracks on the trail.

*

Rakes slept into the afternoon. When he awoke, he didn't know how long he had been asleep. When he climbed into the shelter, the sun was almost overhead. Now it was pushing hard to the west.

He took a quick inventory of his injuries. His lower right leg was sore but seemed better. His left arm was stiff and still very sore. His left hand caused his biggest concern. It was swollen more than before, and it no longer hurt because it was numb. His fingers were so fat from the swelling he could hardly move them. Rakes knew his little tube of antiseptic gel wasn't going to fix whatever was going on with his hand. He needed medical attention.

As he lay there thinking, he realized he was at a crossroads. Or maybe it was the end of the road. If he had a pistol, he might just put it to his temple and pull the trigger. His little camouflaged shelter would be his tomb, where the authorities would never find him.

Rakes smiled thinking about it. He would just disappear in the mountains, and no one would have any clue what happened to him. He would be like D.B. Cooper or the convicts who escaped from Alcatraz. It would be just another mystery about a wanted man who vanishes. Years from now, people would secretly be rooting for him, hoping he was living a happy life in Canada or Mexico or someplace exotic.

Unfortunately, that was all just a pipe dream. Rakes had no gun with which to commit suicide, and the facts were that if he were to die in these mountains, it was most likely going to be a slow, painful, miserable death. Gunshot to the head or not, if he stayed in his shelter, he was going to die.

His leg felt better, so he forced himself to get up. When he stood, he almost fell right back down. He was dizzy. And as soon as his arm moved to his side, his left forearm and hand exploded with pain. When he looked at his hand, he fully expected to see blood shooting out of his fingers.

It was the last conscious thought Rakes had before he passed out.

*

Luke's radio crackled.

"Officer McCain, this is Deputy Hart."

"Go ahead, Hart," Luke said into the radio.

"We believe we're now on your trail. We're following boot prints with some dog tracks scattered around."

"That's gotta be us," Luke said. "Have you hit any dead fires near a creek crossing?"

"10-4. Just passed one."

"Okay, well, keep on coming. I won't wait for you. On horses you should catch us within a couple hours."

"We need to give our horses a break here in a bit, so not sure it will be that soon. If we don't catch up to you before dark, we're going to set up camp."

"Good idea. I'll do the same."

Luke put his radio on his belt and pushed on. He and Jack were working up the side of a mountain, and as he looked up the hill, he could see the trail going around the side and disappearing into the trees.

It was getting late in the afternoon, but they were still making good time. They took a quick rest when they reached the point where the trail started to drop down the hill. Luke didn't know for sure, but he believed he was gaining on Rakes.

The sun was just starting to slip behind the highest ridge when Luke found another fire next to a creek. He kicked at the ashes and saw a few bright orange sparks. Now he knew they were getting close.

Luke whistled for Jack and started up the trail. But Jack was nowhere to be seen. Luke stopped and looked and listened. As he stood there and waited, he looked down at the trail. It had been months since the last rain, and the trail was extremely dry. That is why he had been able to follow Rakes' tracks so easily. The spot in the trail where he was now standing was not just dry, it was dusty. But there was something missing.

He had become so used to seeing the big boot prints in the trail, he hadn't been looking that hard. But as Luke looked more closely, there were no prints. He walked a few yards ahead. No prints. Then he walked back to the fire. There were prints there.

Rakes had detoured off the trail.

Luke looked around for Jack. He spotted the yellow dog down a slight hill, standing dead still, looking at another lean-to shelter. Rakes hadn't been in the last one, but based on the tracks, the fugitive was likely in this one, and Jack could smell him.

*

Again, Rakes had no idea how long he had been asleep. In fact, he didn't remember going to sleep and really didn't know where he was. He was burning up with fever, and his undershirt was soaked in sweat. He started to reach over to touch his shirt, but his arm would barely move. His hand was like the end of a club, huge and red.

He tried to remember what had happened, and as he was forcing his brain to come up with some answers, he heard an animal growling. Instantly, Rakes remembered where he was and what had happened. He remembered being in the shelter and contemplating suicide. He couldn't believe it. The wolves had found him and now he was going to be killed by them. He was okay with dying, but not like this. Rakes wasn't going to let them take him without a fight.

His left arm was useless, but his right arm and legs were usable to some extent. Maybe there was only one wolf. He could take on one. If there were more than one, well, he would just have to do his best.

He heard the low rumbling growl again.

If only he had a knife, or even a big sharp stick. But Rakes had nothing. Only his bare hands. More accurately, only one bare hand.

He decided his best defense was to stay in the little shelter. Let the wolves try to get in to him. They would, he knew, eventually get through the logs, but maybe they'd get tired doing so. Rakes just lay there and didn't move.

∗

Luke took his rifle off his shoulder and moved slowly down the hill to the shelter. Like before, he watched his steps so as not to step on a pine cone or a dead stick. As he got close to Jack, he could hear the dog growling. Luke silently moved up to Jack as he stood ten feet from the lean-to. He touched Jack's head, and the dog stopped growling.

"Mr. Rakes, I'm a state police officer. I've come to take you in."

There was no movement from the shelter. But Jack's ears were forward. A low growl came from his throat again. Luke knew the man was in there.

"I know you are in there, and I know you are hurt. We can make this easy or we can make it hard. What do you want to do?"

∗

When Rakes heard the man's voice, he was almost relieved. The wolves were not there to eat him. His dream of making it to Canada and making a new life for himself was over. He knew from the minute he had killed the woman in Havre, this day would eventually come.

His hand hurt so badly that he wanted to cut it off. He was tired. He was thirsty. And he was hungry. He figured that even with all that, he probably had one good fight left in him. But the lawman was assuredly armed. And there must be a dog out there.

Finally, Rakes said in a slow drawl, "I'm coming out. Please don't shoot."

∗

Luke heard Rakes speak and got his Taser ready. He didn't want to shoot the fugitive, but he needed to be ready if the man attacked him or Jack.

"I won't shoot. Come on out."

Three of the logs pushed to the side, and Rakes attempted to stand up, but he fell back. Luke looked at the man's left arm and hand and saw that something was seriously wrong with them.

"Here," Luke said, stepping toward the shelter where Rakes was struggling to stand. "Let me help you. Just know I have a Taser in my hand that will put about fifty thousand volts through you."

"Don't shoot," Rakes said again. "I won't fight-cha."

Luke stepped closer and grabbed Rakes by the right arm and helped him to his feet. He was impressed with the size of the man. Even in Rakes' weakened state, he wouldn't want to have to tussle with the guy.

"That's quite a wound you have there. Did that dead cougar I found back there do this?"

"Yessir, it did," Rakes said slowly. "It prob-lee wished it hadn't tangled with me when it was all over with."

"I guess not," Luke said. "I'm no doctor, but I'd say you have a pretty bad infection going on in that hand."

"Hurts like hell, and I've got the fever," Rakes said. "Something in the cat's teeth is my guess."

Luke helped Rakes slowly walk back up the hill to where his fire had been earlier. He kept the Taser at the ready just in case.

"My name is Luke McCain. I'm a game warden. That yellow dog is Jack. He's the one that found you."

"I heard him growlin' and thought the wolves were going to finish me off."

"If the wolves didn't get you, this infection might have. We'll get you to medical attention as soon as we can."

"I'm tired of running, Officer McCain. And I'm really tired of walking. I'm not sure I can make it much farther."

"There are some deputies coming our way with horses. We'll be able to get you back down the trail on one of them."

Luke sat Rakes down next to the small fire ring and leaned him against a stump.

"Let me get a fire started," Luke said and handed Rakes his water bottle. "Here drink this."

"Thanks," Rakes said. "I've had nothin' to eat except a few leaves since I left Seattle, however many days ago that was. Seems like a week."

Luke dug into his pack, pulled out an energy bar, and handed it to the big man.

"We'll cook up some freeze-dried meals when the fire gets going."

"Thank you," Rakes said as he ripped the paper off the energy bar.

By the tone in his voice, Luke knew he meant it.

CHAPTER 30

When Adam Winsor arrived at the scene of the van crash, he was surprised by the number of TV trucks and cops parked all around. A state patrolman was directing traffic and waved him through. He slowly moved along the highway behind a string of cars and semi-trucks and trailer rigs.

As they inched along past all the parked rigs, Winsor looked around. There were lots of trees in the area, almost too many. He would need to park someplace and get out to do some scouting. He also needed to find out what was happening. The last he had heard on a report from a radio station out of Omak was that the governor had some super-tracker out after Rakes and that the local authorities hoped to have the man in custody this afternoon. Even if they did catch Rakes this afternoon, Winsor figured they wouldn't have the man back here to the highway before sometime tomorrow.

He drove past all the TV trucks and found a Forest Service road about a mile up the highway and turned onto it. He found a place to park and walked back to where everything seemed to be happening. If he stayed on the periphery, he should be able to hear what was going on and get an idea when he would need to be wherever it was he was going to be.

*

Sheriff Chambers hadn't heard from Luke in hours. But he had talked to Deputy Hart, who had talked to Luke, so he knew that Luke was still out there searching.

"We're watering the horses now," Hart said over the radio. "Then after a bit of a rest, we'll keep moving toward McCain. We're on his tracks and should catch up to him within the next couple hours."

"Sounds good," Chambers said. "Keep your eyes open and holler when you catch up to McCain."

"Will do," Hart said and signed off.

After a half hour, the riders saddled up and moved up the trail. They had only been riding fifteen minutes when Hart's radio sounded off.

"Deputy Hart? Luke McCain here."

"Go ahead."

"I have Rakes in custody. He's in tough shape. We're going to need to get him out of here on horseback. Hopefully, one of your posse members will be willing to give up their ride and be able to walk out."

"I think we can make that happen," Hart said as she looked at the other deputies who both nodded in agreement.

"I have no idea how far away you are, but when you head up a pretty good grade and then around a hill, you'll only be a mile or so away once you start descending the other side."

"Roger that," Hart said. "I'll radio when we are heading down the hill."

"It'll be close to dark when you get here. Are you geared up to spend the night?"

"Affirmative. Unless you want to try to walk back out tonight."

"Let's play that by ear. Talk to you soon."

"10-4," Hart said.

*

After talking to Luke, Hart radioed Chambers and gave him the good news about Rakes being in custody. She told him she didn't know if they would try to ride him out of the mountains tonight or in the morning.

"Let me know as soon as you decide. The governor is going to want to be here when you are going to get here."

"Of course, he is," Hart said. "We still have a ways to go before we meet up with McCain. Sounds like Rakes has been injured somehow and will need to ride out."

"Should I send another rider with a second horse?"

"No, we can handle it. Reece said he'll give up his horse and walk."

"10-4. Thank him for that."

"Will do, and we'll let you know when we are back on the trail toward the highway and give you an ETA."

"Excellent. Thanks, Hart. Good job."

"We didn't do anything, sir, but thank you. It's McCain who found the guy."

"Understood. But he can't get Rakes back here without you. See you soon," Chambers said and signed off.

As soon as he was off his radio, Chambers called the governor's office. The man himself wasn't available, but one of his executive assistants was, and Chambers filled her in on what was going on in the mountains.

"So, he's in custody right now?" the woman asked in confirmation.

"That's correct, we'll let you know when the posse will have Rakes back to the highway as soon as we know."

"The governor has an important meeting from ten to noon tomorrow. Try not to bring him out then," the assistant said.

Chambers wanted to scream but instead calmly said, "Ma'am, we will get the fugitive out when we get him out. If the governor wants to be here, he'll have to figure it out." Then he hung up on her.

Next, he had a deputy go around to all the TV trucks and let them know he had some news on the search for Rakes and would speak to everyone in ten minutes.

*

Winsor positioned himself in a group of trees on the opposite side and uphill from the TV trucks. He watched through his binoculars as a pretty, dark-haired reporter flitted about, talking on the phone. Man, what he would like to do with her. Other than that, it was quiet.

After sitting and observing for a little more than an hour, Winsor watched as a deputy came along and knocked on each TV truck door and talked to someone inside for a minute or two. Then things started to happen. Cameramen and women gathered up gear and hauled it down to where an Okanogan Sheriff's SUV was sitting. Reporters, including the tall dark-haired gal, now all in makeup, hustled down to the SUV. Something was happening.

Winsor hurried off the hill and got in with the crews heading down to the sheriff's rig. He stood in the background behind the TV cameras where no one paid any attention to him.

When everyone was ready, with their microphones extended into Chambers' face, the sheriff began to speak.

"Claude Rakes was captured at four fifty-seven this afternoon. He is in custody of state police Officer Lucas McCain, who had been tracking him for the past thirty-one hours. Three deputies on horseback are en route now to assist Officer McCain in bringing Rakes out of the mountains. We are not sure exactly when the officers with Rakes will arrive here, but as soon as we know, we will let you know."

"Sheriff Chamberlain, Sheriff Chamberlain," Tiffany Brooks shouted. "Any guess on when they will arrive here?"

Chambers said through tight lips, "I just said we are not sure and will let you know when we know."

"Do you know how Officer McCain caught him?" another reporter asked.

"We have received no details on the capture. We just know he is now in custody."

The reporters asked a few more questions, but after Chambers told them several more times that he had no other details, they relented and went off to do their stand-up reports, where they talk directly into the TV camera and repeat what Chambers just said.

As soon as the word hit the national networks, they all built promos to start airing immediately, pimping their coverage of the capture of mass murderer Claude Rakes. The station with the running clock stopped it and start flashing the word CAPTURED in bold red letters over the clock.

Other stations ran a constant scroll along the bottom of the screen with the words MANHUNT IN WASHINGTON OVER? AUTHORITIES REPORT MASS MURDERER CLAUDE RAKES IN CUSTODY. Viewers paying particular attention to Tiffany Brooks' report would see a young, skinny, blond guy lurking in the background.

Like the rest of America, Winsor now knew that the infamous mass murderer, currently wanted in thirteen states for questioning about unsolved murders, was finally back in the custody of Washington State police officers.

Winsor slowly worked his way back up to his perch in the trees and watched and waited. He needed to do some more scouting, but he would be ready when the tracker Luke McCain and Claude Rakes made it out to the highway.

*

When Hart and the other two deputies rounded the mountain and hit the flat before heading down the hill, she radioed Luke.

"We're about to head down the hill," Hart said after Luke answered. "We should be there shortly."

"Sounds good," Luke said. "We'll figure out what we want to do when you get here."

"10-4," Hart said and signed off.

CHAPTER 31

"I've never had freeze-dried food before," Rakes said slowly after he finished off a pouch of spaghetti. "It's pretty good."

Rakes had trouble holding the packet and the plastic fork Luke gave him, but he was hungry enough that he managed. Normally, Luke would have always had someone of Rakes' reputation in handcuffs, but after assessing the situation, Luke couldn't bring himself to put the cuffs on Rakes' left wrist. Not that a handcuff would have fit anyway.

Luke had taken a towel from his pack, soaked it in the ice-cold creek, and wrapped it around Rakes' hand. That seemed to help a little with the swelling. And according to Rakes, it helped some with the pain.

"Yeah, freeze-dried food tastes like French cuisine when you're hungry," Luke said. "You want another?"

"Yes, I would. Please. I don't care what flavor."

Luke fixed Rakes a beef stroganoff and the same for himself. While the water was boiling, Luke fed Jack.

"That's a nice dog you got there," Rakes said as he watched Jack gobble up his food. "I've never had a dog. We only had barn cats when I was a kid."

"Yep. Jack is a pretty good dog. He's one-quarter Labrador retriever and three-quarters chow hound."

Rakes didn't laugh or even smile. Luke wondered if he ever did.

As they ate, they talked. Rakes told Luke all about the cougar attack and how he'd killed it with one hand, strangling the cat.

"I have pretty strong hands," Rakes said deliberately. "Always have."

Luke was surprised by the slow cadence of Rakes' speech. One might conclude by listening to him that Rakes was not very smart. But as he listened and looked into Rakes' eyes, he knew there was an intelligence concealed by his unhurried way of talking. Rakes spoke proper English. He just did so deliberately. Luke wanted to get into the murders but thought it would be better to wait and learn more about the man while they waited for the deputies.

"So, where'd you grow up?" Luke asked, although he already knew the answer based on the information Captain Davis had sent him.

Rakes told him about his childhood growing up in Havre but left out the details on how the kids called him names.

"Did you play sports?" Luke asked.

"Naw, I pretty much just did stuff by myself. I hunted and fished and trapped. I like being outdoors."

"Me too," Luke said.

"I guess you know about the girl I killed in Spokane," Rakes finally said after finishing the second pouch of dried food.

"Yeah, I heard about it. Did you know her?"

"No, I just picked her up in my delivery truck. She was hitchhiking. I pick up hitchhikers quite often when I'm hauling parts. It helps pass the time to talk to folks."

"You don't worry about someone doing something to you?" Luke asked.

Rakes shook his head. "Look at me. No one's going to do anything to me. They're afraid of me as soon as they see me."

"You kill any other hitchhikers?"

"No, and I didn't intend to kill that girl either, but she was cruel. She threw her Big Gulp on me and called me retarded. I just got so mad, I grabbed her and broke her neck."

"That would make me mad too," Luke said.

"The kids in school called me a retard because I talk slow and move slow. So did their parents behind my back. I learned to hate those people and everyone who is cruel. If you pay attention to folks and watch them around others, you can see who the good ones are and who the bad ones are."

Luke didn't say anything and just waited for Rakes to talk more.

"You know about that woman I killed in Idaho?"

"I heard you were a suspect in a woman's death down around Boise. She had a broken neck."

"Yeah, I watched her be awful mean to a waitress. She was vile, that woman. I figured the world would be better off without her nastiness, so I killed her and dumped her body."

"I think we've all run into people like that," Luke said. "But society takes a dim view of just killing folks you don't like."

"I understand that fully," Rakes said slowly. "And if I get the chair for that one, so be it. I did the world a favor. I have no regrets and haven't felt bad for one minute."

"I don't know what the punishment is for killing a person in Idaho, but you won't get the electric chair in Washington. We did away with capital punishment years ago."

"I hate the thought of sitting in a cell the rest of my life," Rakes said. "I would just as soon die."

"That would be tough for me too," Luke said. "But I'm not sure I'm ready to die. You probably don't know this, but the media is saying you've killed women all around the West, and authorities are wanting to talk to you about several unsolved murders."

"I killed a couple of women in Billings and one in Havre, but that's it," Rakes said. "If they think I killed some others, then they're wrong."

Luke believed him. He got Rakes to talk about the other women he'd killed. And started to get a real picture about who he was and why he did what he did. Luke didn't know if Rakes was a sociopath and a psychopath, but he figured a head doctor would call Rakes one or both of those things. He obviously had no remorse whatsoever about killing the women he did.

"I took some light fishing line and rigged smiles on the faces of the two women I killed in Billings. They were laughing at me and calling me names," Rakes said. "I wanted them to be found with smiles on their faces since that's what caused them to die."

Luke felt a cold chill run down his spine. Yes, the big man was injured, but Luke planned to pay close attention to him at all times. The last thing he needed was to have Rakes get hold of him with his good hand.

After refreshing the towel with icy creek water for Rakes' swollen hand which continued to respond to the cold, Luke sat down next to Jack and asked about the van crash. Rakes told him about the big truck trailer swerving into their lane and running them off the road into the tree.

"What about the other prisoner in the van? They think you killed him."

"That idiot deserved to die," Rakes said slowly. "Jenkins was his name. He told me he killed his wife and her mother for no good reason. When I saw him trying to kill the officer in the passenger seat after the wreck, I decided to step in and stop him."

"That was nice of you," Luke said. "I'm guessing the officer is beholden to you."

"He was passed out, but still alive. He probably doesn't even know he was in danger. Jenkins was going to strangle him with the seat belt."

"I'll be sure to let the investigators know about that," Luke said.

"Not that it will do any good," Rakes said. "Even if he wasn't going to kill the officer, I might have killed Jenkins anyway. He was not a good person. He was a perfect candidate for the hangman's noose. The thought of me having to listen to him out here, well, I would have killed him if I hadn't already killed him."

Luke chuckled. "I know a few people like that."

"Yeah, but I'd actually do it. You seem too nice."

It was nearly dark now, and Luke stoked the fire. He noticed Rakes fighting to keep his eyes open as he lay against the stump.

"You ever kill anyone?" Rakes asked after a bit.

His question startled Luke because he thought the big man had fallen asleep.

"No, but I shot a man after tracking him for a long time. I hollered at him across a canyon to stop, and he shot at me. I was ready and shot him in the hip. Didn't kill him, but he'll never walk the same."

"What did he do to have you on his tail?"

"Killed several women."

Rakes nodded his head. "Like me, eh? I guess it's a good thing you caught me in that shelter. Maybe you would have shot me too."

"You never know," Luke said and left it at that.

"I thought game wardens just caught poachers and wrote tickets for no fishing license and stuff like that."

"Oh, we do plenty of that. I just got done working an undercover sting. Three guys killing deer, elk, and turkeys out of season. They even shot some wolves."

"Did you catch 'em?"

"I did. Took a couple months. I had to work in a lumber mill to get inside their group."

Rakes thought about that for a while.

"That sounds interesting. Maybe I should have become a game warden."

"It has its ups and downs," Luke said. "Lots of meetings and paperwork. It's not all fun and games."

"I do like my delivery job," Rakes said unhurriedly with his eyes still closed. "I get to see quite a lot of our little corner of the world. My boss likes me. Said I was his best driver. Guess I won't be doing that again anytime soon."

"No, probably not."

"I knew you were going to catch me today," Rakes said.

"Oh, how's that? I didn't even know myself."

"I get these weird dreams where people I've killed are alive again, and they are telling me stuff about the future. That idiot Jenkins popped right up off the van floor after I killed him and said you were going to catch me today."

"Did he mention me by name?" Luke asked.

"No, but it wouldn't have surprised me. The first person I ever killed, a scraggly little woman who worked at a gas station in Havre, pops into my dreams now and again."

"Why'd you kill her?"

"She was like the others. Just a rotten person. She treated me like a dog and spit in my burrito. I'd had enough of it. Made the world a better place, and I didn't think twice about it."

"How old were you?"

"Eighteen. Just before I graduated from high school. Made it look like a fall in the bathtub. Far as I know, they still haven't figured out I did it."

Luke knew from the files Davis had sent him that the officials in Havre had reopened the investigation on that death and suspected Rakes, but he decided not to say anything.

"Hopefully, your killing days are over," Luke said.

"I'd like to be around only nice people," Rakes said. "But how likely is that going to be in prison?"

"You can choose to be around nice people and just ignore the rest."

"That's easy for you to say. My guess is someone in prison will do something that will make me want to kill them."

"Well, no need to think about that now," Luke said and changed the subject. "Have you ridden horses before?"

Rakes told Luke he had when he was a kid, on the plains of eastern Montana near Havre.

"Good," Luke said. "We're going to get you on another one and walk you outta here. Do you think you can ride tonight?"

"I think so. I would like to get this hand and arm looked at. They won't quit throbbing. And I still got the fever."

"The deputies will be here soon with the horses, then we'll be on the way to medical attention."

Luke didn't want to remind Rakes he was also headed to prison for the rest of his life.

CHAPTER 32

L uke kicked dirt on the fire and then used Rakes' old bent-up coffee pot to haul water from the creek to pour on the embers. When he was sure the fire was out, he looked at Deputy Hart and asked, "Are we ready?"

"I think so," Hart said.

The deputies had arrived only fifteen minutes earlier. Hart, along with Deputies Dan Reece and Brenda Hale, were happy to finally find Luke, and even though they'd been riding most of the day, were ready to head back to the highway.

"We kind of wandered around looking for your tracks," Reece said. "I think we can take the trail straight back and cut a couple of hours off getting back."

"That would put us back at the highway around seven tomorrow morning," Hart said. "That's counting rest stops."

"Sounds good," Luke said. Then he looked at Rakes and said, "You sure you want to start back now?"

"I gotta get some help for this arm," Rakes said as if it was hard to put the words together.

As they were getting him ready to go, Luke fashioned a sling out of one of the coats Rakes had and placed it over Rakes' head and shoulder so that it would carry his injured arm and swollen hand in front of him. Luke rinsed the towel one more time to try to keep the hand cool.

They helped Rakes up on Reece's horse because it was the biggest, and they all felt it could carry a man of Rakes' size and weight. They didn't give Rakes the reins. Reece walked ahead and led the horse holding the reins. Deputy Hart led the way riding her horse, followed by Reece leading Rakes, then Hale on her horse, and finally, Luke and Jack.

Luke wanted to bring up the rear so he could keep an eye on everything. They were dealing with a man who took human lives and had no regrets. Even though Rakes seemed to only kill people he deemed as cruel or unkind, he was on his way to prison for the rest of his life, and Luke wanted to make sure he didn't do anything to try to get away during the ride out. He certainly didn't want to, but Luke wouldn't hesitate to shoot Rakes if he had to protect the deputies and to keep Rakes from escaping again.

As they rode and walked uphill, Luke looked at Rakes humped over in the saddle, swaying back and forth with the steps of the horse. He didn't think the man had any energy left to try to bolt away on the big pony. He would probably fall off if he tried.

It was a three-quarters moon, so there was some light by which to see. Horses have good night vision and will avoid anything in their path, but on this well-worn trail, there was nothing to avoid. So, they plodded on.

Luke was definitely tired, but he figured he could sleep after he transferred Rakes to Sheriff Chambers. His boss had offered up six weeks paid leave for taking this assignment, and Luke thought he might just use the first week to sleep.

They'd been on the trail for almost two hours and Luke, thinking of sleep, was half asleep when the horses stopped abruptly, head and ears up, and started blowing air out of their noses. Luke took a quick look at Jack, and he, too, had stopped, hackles up, ears forward, sniffing the air.

Luke remembered seeing some dancing horses at the state fair one year act just like this as they walked by a live animal display that included an African lion and a Bengal tiger. The horses had never been around those big cats in their life, but the second they smelled them, they sensed danger and were hard to manage.

He hustled up to Hart. Her horse was nervous, and although the deputy was trying to get him to move on, the chestnut-colored gelding wasn't budging.

Hart clicked her tongue and said, "Let's go, boy."

"They smell something out there," Luke said. "My dog does too. Could be a cougar, or maybe a bear."

"Whatever it is, he doesn't like it," Hart said.

"My horse is acting the same way," Hale said.

"Let's take a break here," Luke said. "It's time for a breather anyway. I was about to fall asleep just walking."

"Let's build a fire and boil up some coffee," Reece said. "A little caffeine will do us all some good. I think Rakes needs to be off the horse for a bit too. I thought he was going to fall off a while back."

"I'm okay," Rakes said, pain in his voice. "But I would drink some coffee."

Luke was not a coffee drinker, so he never carried any in his pack. The deputies all had some in their saddlebags, and they got busy getting the fire going to heat some up. Hale watched Rakes as the others gathered some dry branches and pine needles.

"I'm going to take Jack out and look around," Luke said. "The horses are sure there is something out there, and they're almost always right."

"Want me to come with you?" Hart asked.

"Naw, get some coffee and take a break," Luke said. "We won't be gone long."

Luke kissed his lips to get Jack's attention and patted his hip. Jack came over and followed Luke up the trail. With his rifle at the ready, Luke slowly walked ahead. He tried to see into the trees, but even with the moon, the understory was dark as a bunch of black cats.

Jack walked along with Luke, but he was intent on watching an area off to the left of the trail. So, Luke turned his flashlight on and shined it into the trees in that direction. What he saw scared him immediately. He counted five pairs of eyes shining back at him not eighty yards away.

"Wolves," Luke said to himself.

About that time, Jack took off after them.

"Jack, no!" Luke screamed. "Come!"

But the big yellow dog wasn't coming.

A pack of wolves could tear your garden-variety Labrador into about fifty pieces in short order. Luke was not going to allow that to happen, so he raised his rifle and shot just short of the closest set of eyes. That got things moving.

At the sound of the shot, Jack stopped like he was trained to do, and the wolves took off running.

"Jack, come!" Luke yelled again.

This time the dog obeyed. He came back and looked up at Luke like, "What did you shoot? And what do you want me to retrieve?"

"Heel," Luke said in a stern voice. "Those things would have tore you up."

Jack heeled as Luke turned around and headed back to where the deputies had the fire going. The wolves might have kicked his butt, but Jack sure would've liked to give it a go.

Just before Luke and Jack got back to the deputies, the eerie howls of the wolves broke the silence of the night from off in the dark.

"Is that what you were shooting at?" Hart asked with a shiver after Luke and Jack stepped into the light of the fire.

"Yes, but I was only shooting to scare them off. Jack decided he wanted to take them on."

"Sorry, Jack," Hale said. "That wouldn't have ended well."

✻

Before they'd left the spot where Rakes had been captured, Hart had radioed Sheriff Chambers to let him know they were heading back to the highway and to expect them sometime around seven o'clock.

"Sounds good," Chambers said. "Take it easy. You don't have to be in any hurry to get here."

"Mr. Rakes is in some serious pain, probably from an infection, and he would like to have some medical assistance as soon as possible."

"10-4. We'll have EMTs here waiting for him when you arrive."

"We'll radio in when we are an hour out," Hart said.

"10-4. Be safe," Chambers said and signed off.

✻

The group stopped every two hours. They would build a quick fire, brew up some coffee, eat some energy bars, and just rest. They picked some of the same spots where Rakes had built fires next to creeks as he had headed north on the trail.

"I boiled water because I didn't want that beaver fever," Rakes said. "I had it once as a kid. It wasn't pleasant."

"That guy I shot," Luke said, mostly to Rakes. "The reason I caught up to him so quickly is he was having to stop constantly to deal with diarrhea from drinking from the stream he was following."

"Was that the guy who had killed all those women and dumped their bodies in the mountains near Yakima?" Hart asked.

"Yep."

"We all read about that, and about the kidnappers you ran down up by Lake Chelan. You stay pretty busy, Officer McCain."

"I blame Jack," Luke said, nodding at the yellow dog asleep next to the fire. "He gets me into all kinds of situations."

"Like shooting at wolves in the dark," Reece said.

They all laughed. Except for Rakes. He just groaned in pain.

CHAPTER 33

Around six o'clock the evening before, one of the networks had gone live from the site where officials anticipated Rakes would be coming out of the woods tomorrow morning, escorted by four armed law enforcement officers. The reporter told anxious viewers their network would be carrying the event live, starting at nine in the morning, Eastern time. Other than that, there wasn't much activity around the TV trucks.

Winsor sat in his little nest in the trees and watched, but nothing at all was happening. He had done some scouting and knew where he wanted to be come daylight. Until then, he decided he would go back to his truck and try to get some sleep.

*

Chambers called Bob Davis in Yakima to let him know that Luke had caught up to Rakes and now had the killer in custody. He gave the captain all the details he had. Rakes was suffering from some kind of injury and had given up peacefully. Three deputies were riding in on horses to help Luke bring Rakes out. They should be back to the command post by early morning.

Davis in turn called Sara and relayed the information.

"Geez. When are they going to sleep?" Sara asked after she heard they were coming out of the mountains that night. "Luke is going to be one grumpy Gus when all this is settled."

"You know him," Davis said. "He would do it all over again right now if he had to."

"I know. Still, I'm the one who has to live with him when it's over."

"Just let him catch up on some sleep. He'll be fine."

"I will. I'll just be glad when he and Jack are home. If you believe the news, this Rakes guy is a combination of Charles Manson, Son of Sam, and Ted Bundy."

"Luke can handle himself just fine," Davis said. "Get some rest."

Sara thanked the captain for his call and thought about Luke and Jack up in the mountains with the mass murderer Claude Rakes. Davis was right. Luke could take care of himself. But she would feel a whole lot better when she knew he and Jack were home safe and sound.

＊

The other call Chambers made was to Olympia. This time he did get to speak to the man himself.

"Great news about the capture," the governor said after he picked up the phone.

"Yes, it is," Chambers said. "Our people have decided to bring Rakes out tonight. They should have him to the command center by around seven o'clock tomorrow morning."

"Excellent. I will make arrangements to be there at seven. My public information officer will let the media know."

"Just remember, I have no control on when they get here. That's just their estimate."

"I totally understand. I'll have the helicopter ready in case you hear they're going to be there earlier than seven. I want, no, I have to be there."

"I'll stay in touch," Chambers said. "Have a good evening."

Unlike Luke and the deputies and Chambers, the governor would be enjoying a good night's sleep.

*

Every time the horse string stopped to rest, it took longer for the crew to get back in the saddle and moving down the trail. The deputies were rotating who walked with Rakes' horse, so each got to ride two-thirds of the time. Even though they offered to let Luke ride, he declined. As tired as he was, he still wanted to be watching over things from the back of the string.

Their final stop for a rest was the longest. They had cooked up the last of Luke's dried food pouches, along with some that Hart had brought along. With warm food in their bellies, they just couldn't fight off sleep any longer.

Luke pulled out his phone and set the alarm for one hour.

"I hate to do this to you, Mr. Rakes, but I need to keep you here, not that I believe you are in any shape to run."

"Do what you have to do. I need sleep, but I also need to see the medics. My hand is worse. I'm not going anywhere."

Luke looked at Rakes' hand. It was turning black. He pulled out his handcuffs and put one cuff around Rakes' right wrist and the other around a small tree trunk near where Rakes was sitting.

"It might be a little uncomfortable," Luke said, but as he looked at Rakes who had lain down when Luke was securing the cuffs to the tree, he saw the man was already asleep.

The deputies hobbled the horses so they could feed on some grass nearby and then came back to the fire and stretched out. They, too, fell asleep quickly.

Luke fought to stay awake, but it was impossible. He tried to figure out how many miles he had walked in the past thirty-nine hours. It was more than he had ever walked in that short of time. He knew that, for sure.

✳

Sunlight was just starting to peek through the treetops when Luke's alarm went off.

"That was the fastest hour ever," Reece said as he stood and stretched. "I'll get the horses."

Luke looked around. Rakes was still dead out next to the tree. The two other deputies were stirring.

"Can one of you check Rakes to see if he's still alive?" Luke said as he was putting a heavy coat he had used as a blanket into his pack.

"He's alive, but he doesn't look good," Hart said.

Luke had pulled his GPS out and was waiting on the connection to the satellites.

"It looks like we are only about three miles from the road," Luke said after his screen came up. "We should be down there within an hour."

"I'll radio the sheriff," Hart said as she looked at her watch.

Everyone got busy getting stuff loaded.

"Mr. Rakes?" Luke said as he unlocked the cuffs on his wrist. "We need to get going."

After a minute, Rakes asked, "When will we be there? My hand feels like it is going to fall off, and I'm feeling heat burning all the way to my shoulder."

"We'll be there soon, but we need to get you up on the horse so we can get going."

Luke heard Hart talking to the sheriff.

"Officer McCain says we should be there inside an hour."

"Good to hear. We'll be waiting for you."

"Are the medics going to be there?" Hart asked.

"They're here now, standing by."

"Good. Rakes is in rough shape. He'll need immediate attention."

"10-4. See you soon," Chambers said.

*

As soon as Chambers knew what time the officers would be coming down off the hill with Rakes, he sent word to the governor. He was en route from Olympia in his helicopter and would be there in a half hour.

Again, Chambers sent the word out to the media. The governor would be arriving in a half hour, and the posse, with Rakes, would be arriving a short time after that.

Within ten minutes, there were camera crews moving around the different television trucks, gathering gear and heading to the spot that was now being called "the command center." All it was really was a spot off the highway where Sheriff Chambers had parked his SUV, not far from a flat spot where the governor's helicopter had landed before and presumably would be landing again.

A red, square-backed ambulance was now parked next to the sheriff's rig. The two EMTs stood next to the rig, talking to Chambers.

"Any idea what we'll be dealing with?" one EMT asked.

"They think Rakes has an infection in an arm and hand where a cougar bit him," Chambers said. "Sounds like he has a fever and is a bit delirious at times."

Of course, the EMTs knew who Rakes was and what he was being accused of. You had to be living under a rock the past three days not to know about the mass murderer and the manhunt taking place.

Even though the EMTs wouldn't say it, not even to one another, they were a bit star-struck and anxious to meet and work on America's most wanted man. They felt lucky to get the call and even secretly hoped they might be seen on national news giving aid to the fugitive.

"We'll be ready for him," the other EMT said.

*

All the activity didn't go unnoticed by Adam Winsor. At daybreak, he circled around and was now situated on the same side of the highway as the TV trucks, the sheriff's SUV, and a newly-arrived ambulance. His new nest on the hill was hidden by trees. He was farther away from all the activity, but it gave him a much better view of the other side of the road where the tracker McCain and the fugitive Rakes should be coming down a well-worn trail.

Winsor no longer needed to be down around the reporters and camera people. He could watch everyone from his spot with binoculars. Their activity would tell him what was happening.

He had seen the deputy walk to all the TV trucks, and then people started hurrying around. Winsor was watching the tall reporter chick with the dark hair walking down to the sheriff's rig and ambulance with several other people when he heard the thumping of helicopter rotor blades.

In the next minute, a chopper swooped right over his head, circled around, and landed near the ambulance, kicking up dirt and leaves in a sixty-yard circle. Twenty seconds later, four people ducked out of the helicopter and hustled over to the sheriff who was holding a hand on his cowboy hat so the updraft from the chopper blades didn't blow it into the next county.

Winsor picked up his rifle and looked at the people through the scope. One man was the center of attention, and Winsor figured he might be the governor, although he wouldn't know him from the next guy. Being an Idaho resident, he had never seen a photo of the governor of Washington and frankly, he didn't care. He put the crosshairs of his twelve-power scope on the governor's heart and said, "Bang, you're dead."

Then he watched the helicopter lift off and fly back over his head. It was over the hill and gone in seconds.

*

Chambers and the governor stood together with their backs to the trail the posse would be coming down at some point. The camera crews gathered around in a half circle, and the reporters stuck their microphones out to pick up whatever the two officials were going to say. The governor had three dead aspen leaves stuck in his hair, blown in from the helicopter's departure. None of his three assistants noticed it until he started speaking to the TV cameras.

"As you know, our people have tracked down and captured the fugitive Claude Rakes. It has been a valiant effort, and the people of Washington, and the country, are incredibly proud of these brave men and women who risked their lives to bring this murderer to justice. I was in contact with them and Sheriff Chambers every step of the way to help this come to a quick and successful conclusion. We expect the arrival of the posse members within the next half hour. I will let the sheriff answer any of your questions."

Chambers almost started laughing at the statement about every step of the way, like the governor had been out there in the wilds with McCain and the deputies, but he bit his lip.

He took a few questions from the reporters, mostly regarding the newly arrived ambulance. He told them most of what he knew. Rakes had been injured, and he was going to need medical assistance when they got here.

"Was he shot?" Tiffany Brooks asked.

"No, he wasn't."

"Then how did he get injured?"

"It's not clear. Our deputies say Rakes has an injured hand that seems to be infected and will need immediate attention."

Chambers knew the injury was caused by a cougar attack, but he didn't know enough details about the attack to get into it with the reporters.

After a few more questions and answers, Chambers told the reporters that he was in contact with the posse and would give everyone a heads up when they would be coming down the trail so that their camera people would be ready.

*

Thirty-four minutes after the governor spoke, Chambers' radio crackled.

"Sheriff, we're about to crest the last hill," Deputy Hart said. "We'll be visible on the trail in about five minutes. Please have the medics standing by. Rakes needs attention immediately."

"10-4," Chambers said and turned to talk to the EMTs. "They're coming down the trail now. Can you pull your rig up onto the highway? They want you as close to the trail as possible."

The medics jumped into their rig and pulled it out of the staging area and up onto the highway. Chambers radioed his deputies to hold all traffic on the highway coming from each direction.

The ambulance's movement was notice enough to the TV people. They grabbed up their gear and started moving to the highway too.

*

The last hour had been miserable. Besides just flat being exhausted, Luke had walked alongside Rakes sitting on the horse and kept him from falling off several times. He and Reece had taken turns dealing with Rakes' three hundred pounds of almost dead weight that gravity was desperately trying to pull off the horse. The end of the trail couldn't arrive soon enough.

When they broke out of the trees and could see the highway, with the TV trucks and other people and vehicles below, Luke took a deep breath. This had been a long, trying ordeal. Now it was over.

Almost.

CHAPTER 34

The bullet hit before they heard the shot. Rakes, who was already slumped over, went limp and tipped off the horse right into Luke's arms.

"Get down," Luke yelled, although his brain had already processed what was happening and he believed there would be no more shots. Rakes was the target, and the sniper had hit his mark. No need to shoot any more.

The deputies jumped off their horses and took cover. Luke lay Rakes down next to the trail, pulled his rifle off his shoulder, and focused on the facing hillside where he believed the shot had originated. He scanned the trees through his rifle scope and caught a movement. He looked just in time to see a person, maybe a kid, running through the trees. Luke didn't have time to take a shot, not that he would have anyway. He didn't know if the kid was the shooter or running from the shooter.

Seeing nothing else moving, Luke knelt next to Rakes. The man was still alive, but barely. Blood was oozing out of the wound in his chest.

"I guess I won't be spending the rest of my life in prison," Rakes said to Luke even more slowly. "I'm okay with that."

Luke didn't know what to say, so he went with an old cliché. "Hang in there. Help is on the way."

He wasn't lying. The medics, as well as the rest of the world, had witnessed Rakes being hit by the rifle shot, and the EMTs were running up the hill with their backpacks to give him assistance.

Rakes, now whispering so Luke had to lean in closer, said, "Tell them I have no regrets. Those people I killed were nasty human beings. The world is a better place without them."

Then the big man, the one viewers all over the country were tuning in to see brought to justice, let out a long, slow breath and was gone.

Luke looked down into Rakes' eyes, but they were blank. Unbelievably, the big man had a slight smile on his face. Luke wondered when the last time was that Rakes had smiled.

He probably shouldn't have, but Luke felt sorry for Rakes. He reached down, closed Rakes' eyes, and stood. The deputies and the EMTs were standing there watching, waiting for what they needed to do next. If they had looked closely, they would have seen tears welling up in Luke's eyes.

*

As the old saying goes, the shit hit the fan when the sniper shot Rakes as he was being led down the path to the ambulance.

The governor thought the sniper was shooting at him, so he ducked down behind Chambers and his assistants. The deputies nearby turned and looked toward the place where they thought the shot had been fired from. There was some confusion on that because the rifle shot echoed between the two mountains, some believing the shot had come from behind them, while others thought it had come from the same hillside the horse string carrying Rakes was on. It was the famous grassy knoll conundrum.

The TV crews, in their ongoing effort to bring America the news as it happened, ducked but kept filming. When they heard no more shots, they zoomed in on the now prone Rakes being assisted by a lawman with a rifle on his shoulder.

A second later, the lawman pulled his rifle off his shoulder and started aiming over everyone's head onto the hillside behind them. In unison, the camera people turned and started aiming their cameras at the trees. The cameraman for CNN got lucky and caught a quick shot of a person, maybe a teenager, running through the trees on the hillside.

Chambers, who hadn't tried to hide, got on the radio.

"Tell me what's happening, Jessica."

"Rakes is down," Hart said. "McCain is with him. Looks like he is hit in the chest. We're trying to get a visual on the shooter but no luck. The shot came from straight across the valley. Probably two hundred yards up, in the trees behind you."

"10-4," Chambers said. "I'll get deputies up there immediately."

And it went like that for a while. Deputies and two state patrol officers were running up the hill, then back down. The TV crews were scurrying about, trying to get footage. The governor and his people just stood and watched.

The EMTs, after checking on Rakes and verifying he was, in fact, dead, had walked back down to the ambulance to retrieve a stretcher to carry Rakes' body the rest of the way down the trail.

As soon as he knew Rakes was gone, Luke whistled for Jack, and they went back up the hill. His intention was to find a high spot where he could glass the opposite hillside to try to see the shooter. He called Chambers on the radio to tell him what his plan was and to let him know he had seen a person running through the trees over by where the shot had come from.

"What did the person look like?" Chambers asked.

"I only saw him for a flash," Luke said. "He was a white male, might have been a teenager. He was wearing blue jeans, a camo shirt or hoody, and a black baseball-style cap."

"I'll get the word out," Chambers said. "You think he was the shooter?"

"No idea, but he was in the general vicinity of where the shot came from," Luke said. "You might have your deputies looking for a person who fits that description in any vehicles in the area."

"10-4. I'm going to let the sheriffs in Chelan and Skagit Counties know to be on the lookout too."

"Good idea. I'll call if I see anything."

*

The second he touched the trigger, Winsor knew his shot was true. The recoil of the rifle kept him from seeing the impact of the bullet, but he heard it hit Rakes with a thump. He got right back on the scope and saw his target fall off the horse into the lawman's arms.

There was no time to sit and admire his shot. Winsor took one more look, then he was off and running through the trees headed west. He had a little over a mile to go to get to his truck. His grandaddy would be proud of him, Winsor thought as he ran. The old rifle shot true and straight, and it did what needed to be done. He had ranged the shot with his handheld rangefinder and made the adjustments needed to make an accurate shot.

The reading on the rangefinder was four hundred and seventy-three yards. Winsor had killed deer and bears at longer ranges than that. He knew the ballistics for the rifle and the ammunition he was using. When he aimed at the big man in the saddle, he held five inches above his heart. There was no wind to speak of, so when he had a clear shot, Winsor let all the breath out of his lungs, waited a split second after he felt his heart beat, and squeezed the trigger.

The infamous Claude Rakes would be killing no more people's loved ones.

Winsor hadn't done much thinking about what he would do after shooting Rakes. He figured people would be so happy with what he had done, maybe they'd give him a parade. But when he took a second to look down at where the sheriff's rig was parked, there were law officers running all over the place. Some were running right at him.

He needed to get to his pickup—and fast.

*

Luke worked up the hill as quickly as his overused legs would carry him. He was in good shape, but walking that many miles in the past two and a half days had taken its toll. There was a bald knob he was heading for, but it seemed like it was taking forever getting there. When he did finally reach it and sat down to glass back across the highway, he couldn't focus because he was breathing so hard.

Luke tried to slow his breathing down by taking deep breaths in through his nose and exhaling through his mouth. It helped a little. He put his rifle scope to his left eye and started searching. Mostly what he saw was trees. Lots of trees.

The person he had seen running was headed to the west. Logic told him that was the way he would continue to run if he was the shooter. So, Luke looked to the west and searched in every small opening he could see. It was the same way he hunted deer and elk. Take an area, and move the scope very slowly up and down, and over, and up and down, looking for the slightest movement in any opening.

He had been searching like that for three minutes when he spotted the kid again. It was a long way off, but Luke could see the young man leaning against a tree in a little opening, breathing hard. He had a rifle slung over his shoulder.

"Gotcha," Luke said and picked up the radio.

"Chambers, this is McCain. I have a visual on our shooter. He is due southwest of your position about eight hundred yards. White male, blue jeans, camo jacket, wearing a black cap, with a hunting rifle slung over his shoulder. He's breathing hard from running."

"10-4. I'll get my deputies moving that way."

"My guess is he is heading for a vehicle," Luke said. "Are there any roads over that way?"

"There's a forest service road about a mile from here."

"I'd get someone on it immediately and look for any parked vehicles. The shooter is only a half mile from that road now, and he's off and running again. I just lost him."

"10-4," Chambers said again and was gone.

Luke sat and watched for the running kid, but never saw him again. When he was sure the shooter was out of sight, Luke lay back in the grass and closed his eyes. The warmth of the morning sun hitting him felt so good, in a minute he was sound asleep.

*

It had been a while since Winsor had run so far. He used to run cross-country in high school and was pretty good. He took fourth place in state when he was a junior. But he started smoking his senior year and quit competing in any sports. That had disappointed his mom, but she got over it.

Now Winsor wished he hadn't started smoking at all. It felt like a lung was going to burst. He did okay on the flats, but running uphill was a killer. He had to stop and get his breath several times. If he could just get to his pickup, he thought he could get out of there. He had looked at some maps and saw where the Forest Service road he had parked on would lead to another back road and then deliver him to the highway several miles from the crash site.

When he was nearing the Forest Service road, Winsor slowed his pace. His truck was parked in a little gravel turnout three hundred yards up the road. He was almost there.

He stopped and listened for any vehicles coming. Hearing none, he slipped out onto the road and jogged the rest of the way to his truck. He was just about to open the driver's door when he heard movement behind him.

"Hands in the air. I have a gun on you," Deputy Hart said.

Winsor raised his hands and dropped his head. Maybe he could take her, he thought. He slowly turned around and then thought better of it. The deputy was bigger than he was, and she had a pistol pointed right at his face.

"Don't even think about it," Hart said. "I'm in no mood for it. Now, throw that rifle over there in the brush and turn around with your hands behind your head, fingers interlocked."

It pained him to throw his granddaddy's rifle into the brush, but Winsor did it anyway.

As Hart put the handcuffs on Winsor, he asked, "How'd you know where to find me?"

"Good police work. Did you really think you could get away with shooting that man?"

"Doesn't matter," Winsor said. "I did what I came to do. My mama and granddaddy would be proud."

After Hart had spotted the empty pickup truck, she parked out of sight and sat in the brush and waited. She had only been there five minutes before Winsor showed up. He fit the description McCain had given and he was carrying a rifle.

She took Winsor's wallet out of his back pocket and looked at his driver's license. She smiled and placed the kid in the back seat of Chambers' SUV. The sheriff had told her to take it when Luke had called in about spotting the shooter.

"Hart calling Sheriff Chambers," she said into the radio.

"This is Chambers. Go ahead."

"I have our suspect in custody. His name is Adam Winsor. That name ring any bells?"

"Not that I can think of. Should it?"

"I remember reading that the woman Rakes is suspected of killing down by Boise was named DeeAnn Winsor. That can't be a coincidence. Adam here is twenty-one. He must be her son."

There was a long silence.

"I'll be damned," Chambers finally said. "That's got to be it. Good job!"

*

Luke was dead out asleep in the grass on the hill when Chambers radioed to tell him they had caught Rakes' killer. He was groggy and not totally getting what Chambers was saying.

Something about the son of a woman in Boise.

When his head finally cleared, he understood. The shooter was the son of the woman Rakes had killed in Boise. The kid had shot Rakes as revenge.

As he had been hiking up the hill before he'd spotted the shooter, Luke had tried to figure out who might have wanted Rakes dead, and why. There was a chance that someone just wanted to be famous for killing Rakes. People still remember who Jack Ruby was after he shot Lee Harvey Oswald.

More likely, someone wanted revenge. Luke figured it might be a boyfriend of the girl Rakes killed in Spokane. Or maybe it was a deranged customer who liked watching the girl dance at the club. He hadn't thought about the woman in Idaho.

According to Rakes, that woman was evil. The thought of someone like that having children never crossed Luke's mind.

It felt so good just sitting there in the sun, Luke didn't want to leave. He looked around, and Jack was totally zonked. The dog had also covered many miles in the last few days with very little sleep. Luke reached over and scratched Jack's ears, but he didn't move.

"C'mon, boy. I know this feels good, but we better get going or we'll never get home."

CHAPTER 35

The assassination of Claude Rakes was must-see TV. Unfortunately, the millions of viewers on the East Coast missed it live, as they were already at work or on their way there. Some probably were able to stream one of the live newscasts of Washington State police officers escorting Rakes out of the Cascade Mountains and witnessed the improbable shooting of the suspected mass murderer.

With warnings of the graphic nature of the video, many others watched the shooting of Rakes on their phones, iPads, and computers throughout the day via Facebook, Twitter, and a hundred other streaming services.

The national news stories about the shooting also included some grainy footage of Adam Winsor running through the woods just after Rakes was shot. The footage was compliments of CNN, whose alert camera operator spotted the shooter running through the trees just seconds after Rakes toppled off the horse. No one said it was just blind-ass luck the cameraman got the footage of the shooter.

Winsor, according to the stories, was suspected in killing Rakes as revenge for Rakes killing his mother in Boise, Idaho. The authorities hadn't given that part of the story to the news reporters, but it only took them a few minutes longer than it had Deputy Hart to put two and two together once the name of the suspected shooter was released.

Luke and Jack had stumbled down the hill after Chambers radioed to tell them Rakes' shooter was captured, and Luke hoped his part in all of this would be overlooked by the media in all the excitement. Unfortunately, Tiffany Brooks spotted Luke coming across the highway and quickly got her camera guy to shoot footage of them heading to the command center, which now was just a couple of sheriffs' rigs and the ambulance that was carrying Rakes' body. The governor, his three minions, and Sheriff Chambers stood by one of the SUVs and chatted.

"Officer McCain! Officer McCain!" Brooks yelled as she ran toward Luke. "Can we get an interview?"

Luke groaned under his breath but said, "Sure, if we keep it short. I've only had a couple hours sleep since yesterday morning."

"Fine," Brooks said. "Just a couple questions."

Luke felt like hell and figured he looked like it too. Oh well, nothing he could do about it now.

"We've been told that Claude Rakes was attacked by a cougar while he was on the run out there in the mountains. Can you confirm that?"

"I didn't see it happen, but Mr. Rakes told me about it. Looking at his wounds and his description of how it happened made me believe it did. He said he strangled it to stop it from attacking him. I found the dead cougar as I was tracking Mr. Rakes, so I have no reason to think he was lying."

"Weren't you scared for your wellbeing when you caught him? He's killed so many people."

"No, I wasn't scared. He was injured, fighting a fever, and possibly a bad infection. Plus, he had no beef with me."

"What's that mean? Did he have a problem with the women he killed?"

"It seems he did."

"Can you explain?"

"Not right now," Luke said. "I'm in desperate need of a hot shower and a bed."

Luke turned and walked toward the governor and Chambers standing by the rigs.

"Well done, Officer McCain," the governor said as he walked to Luke and shook his hand. "I had complete faith that you'd find Rakes and bring him in."

"I almost got him here," Luke said.

"Well, yes," the governor said. "You did your job, and I know speak for the people of Washington when I say thank you for you heroism and effort."

Luke's bullshit meter was pegging in the red.

The whole time the governor was talking with Luke, several of the national news stations were filming them. Luke hadn't noticed but the governor sure did. He did his best to smile in several directions as he talked.

"I'm sure you're beat," the governor said. "Let's get you someplace where you can rest and get something to eat."

The three minions heard the governor and jumped into action They hustled over to Luke and escorted him to the sheriff's SUV where a giant white ice chest sat, filled with sandwiches, water, and soft drinks.

One of the reporters hollered over to the governor, "Are you going to be making a statement sometime soon?"

The governor spoke to Chambers, who turned and walked to where the reporters were all gathered.

"Give him ten minutes, then he and I will be happy to talk to you," Chambers said.

Luke sat on the ground with his back up against the back tire of the sheriff's SUV. Jack lay next to him. After downing a bottle of water, Luke grabbed another and poured some for Jack.

When they were done eating sandwiches—Luke devoured a turkey and a ham, and Jack ate the meat out of three roast beefs—Luke watched the governor and Chambers talk to the horde of reporters. He couldn't hear what they were saying, but he knew it must be good. The reporters were hanging on to every word both men said.

Food in his stomach made Luke even more sleepy. But he couldn't sleep yet. Now that he was back to the highway, he turned his phone on. He had two bars. Just enough to call Sara.

"Who do you think you are, Tom Cruise or someone?" Sara said with a laugh when she answered the call. "I've been watching all morning, and the cameras just love you."

"I'm much taller than Tom Cruise," Luke said. "How are you?"

"Better than you by the looks of things. You look like you've been dragged through a knot hole. Jack looks good though."

"Jack always looks good. I feel like I've been through a knot hole."

"I was watching when they shot Rakes right next to you. Were you scared?"

"No, not really. I figured whoever was shooting was trying for Rakes, and he hit him so . . ."

"I guess. Still weird to have the guy die basically in your arms."

"Yeah, it was sad really. I won't admit it to anyone but you, but I kinda liked him. He was only killing people who treated him or others badly. I know that's no justification for killing someone, but he wasn't a threat to the rest of the world. He'd had a rough upbringing and life. I just felt bad for him."

"Well, he won't be killing anyone else. When you coming home?"

"As soon as I'm physically able. Right now, I need some sleep. I'm not sure where I'll do that, but it is going to happen soon."

Luke asked her to call Captain Davis to let him know what had happened. She said she would but thought he, like the rest of the country, had probably watched everything live on TV.

"I'm glad you're safe," Sara said. "By the way, it looks like the governor has a man-crush on you. Let me know when you're on your way."

"I will," Luke said, ignoring the thing about the man-crush. "I love you. Talk to you soon."

He turned his phone off, looked around, spotted some grass in the sunshine over by a fence, and walked that way. Jack followed along. The two of them lay down on the grass and immediately fell asleep.

Chapter 36

It had been three weeks since the manhunt for Claude Rakes took place in the mountains of northcentral Washington. Captain Davis kept his word and gave Luke six weeks of paid leave. It took him a few days to catch up on his sleep and to rest his tired body, but pretty soon Luke was enjoying his time off. He, Sara, and Jack traveled to northern California to see some of Sara's cousins, and they spent some time at one of the Oregon beaches.

By the third week of his leave, Luke was itching to get back to work. He didn't mention it to Sara, but she could tell he was ready just by watching him.

"Call the captain and tell him you're coming back," Sara said one morning as she was getting ready for work. "Get him to give you the extra weeks some other time."

"I guess I could do that," Luke said. "I am ready to get back in the field."

"Do it," Sara said as she kissed him goodbye and headed for the door.

Davis was happy to hear from Luke and said, "Start whenever you want. Hargraves has been sick, so we're short one now."

"I'll be in this morning," Luke said and hung up.

He enjoyed his time off, but what he loved most was being in the mountains, around the lakes and streams, driving the roads, hiking the trails, and talking to the people who also loved those things.

Luke flashed back to the conversation he'd had with Claude Rakes while sitting by the fire the day he and Jack found him in that makeshift shelter. Rakes was right. Game wardens did check a lot of hunting and fishing licenses. But the job was much more than that. Luke believed he was protecting the resources that were for all to enjoy, and when he caught poachers like Buck Thomas, Manny Hernandez, and Ricky Carter, he was saving the animals they were stealing from the citizens of Washington.

He met many good, nice people in his job. He also met some bad ones. As he thought about it, Luke didn't believe Claude Rakes was one of the bad ones.

*

Luke spent the first hour in the Region 3 office, talking to some of the biologists and others who worked there. They all wanted to hear about Claude Rakes. They razzed him about being on national television and asked about being so close to Rakes when he had been shot.

When he got to his desk, it didn't look as bad as he feared. With the time he spent undercover, then in the mountains pursuing Rakes, and then out on leave, he figured his desk would be buried in papers. Someone was looking out for him. He would have to figure out who it was and thank him or her.

He had just sat down at his desk and was logging onto his computer when the receptionist buzzed his desk phone.

"There is a call on line three," the receptionist said. "Something about someone shooting turkeys on private land up in the Yakima Canyon."

The woman on the phone said she and her husband owned orty acres along the Yakima River up near Ellensburg, and some unters had come in and were shooting her turkeys.

"I'm not sure, but I think they have shot several," the woman aid in a shaky, worried voice.

Luke took her name and phone number and said he would ead right out.

He thought about running to get Jack but decided he should et to the woman's place as quickly as possible. It was the last day f turkey season, but hunters could only take one turkey in this egion during the spring hunt. And they certainly couldn't hunt on rivate property without permission.

Just before he arrived at the woman's place, Luke spotted two nen dressed in camo, walking toward the highway. Both had a arkey slung over their shoulders and carried a shotgun in their ands.

He pulled over next to where an empty Toyota pickup sat in a arnout and waited for the men.

"Good morning, fellas," Luke said as the men, one older and ne younger, crossed the fence next to their truck.

"Good morning," the two men said in unison.

"Looks like you had some luck this morning."

"Yes, sir," the older of the two men said with a big smile. Then e looked at Luke and said, "Say, aren't you the officer who caught nat mass murderer up in the North Cascades a while back?"

"Guilty," Luke said. "Do you know you are hunting on private and?"

"Yes, sir," the younger man said. "We have permission though. even have a text that says so."

The man pulled out his phone and showed Luke the text. It vas from a man with the same last name as the woman who he had alked with earlier.

"Okay," Luke said. "There seems to be some miscommunication. his man's wife, or I assume it is his wife, called in a trespassing report. And she believes you, or someone, shot more than one turkey each."

"No, sir," the younger man said. "We each got one, although Steve here had to shoot three times to kill his."

Steve gave a sideways grin and said, "It wasn't my best shooting performance. But we ended up getting him."

Luke checked their licenses and tags. They were properly placed on the turkeys' legs. Then he took their contact information.

"I think we're all good here," Luke said. "I'm going to go talk to the property owners and see where they got their wires crossed. I'll call you if I have any other questions. Congratulations on your birds."

"Thanks," the older man said. "Do you mind me asking? What kind of a guy was that Rakes fella?"

Luke thought about it a minute and said, "He seemed like a decent guy who had been bullied his whole life and just had had enough with some folks who were treating him badly."

"Hmmm," the man hummed. "I guess there's a lesson in there for all of us. Still can't go around killing people though."

"No, you can't," Luke said. "Have a good day."

When he arrived at the woman's house, an older gentleman met Luke in the driveway and apologized for the call. He explained that his wife had dementia, and even though he had told her he had given permission to two men from their church to hunt their land, she had forgotten.

"Those turkeys are kinda like her pets," the man said. "They're getting to be a bit of a nuisance if you ask me, pooping on our patio and raising a ruckus all hours of the day and half the night."

"Well, there are two less nuisances in the flock, thanks to your friends," Luke said. "Sorry about your wife. Have a good day."

It was getting close to lunchtime, so on his way back to Yakima Luke pulled into the little café connected to Red's Fly Shop, sitting on the river in the middle of the canyon.

When he stepped inside, he saw two familiar faces watching

him come through the door.

"Hey, there's the famous Luke McCain," Jim Kingsbury said with a big grin.

Kingsbury was sitting with his buddy, Frank Dugdale, the man with three first names.

"Hey," Luke said. "I run into you guys even when I'm trying to avoid you."

The two men laughed. Luke looked at Kingsbury's t-shirt. It read: I HAVE TOURETTE'S SYNDROME, I SWEAR! There was a rumor going around that the man had a different t-shirt with some funny or clever saying on it for every day of the year. No one had ever seen him in the same shirt twice.

"So, sit down here and tell us all about the hunt for the most wanted man in America," Dugdale said. "We'll buy you lunch."

Luke sat down with the two gentlemen and thought, it sure is good to be home.

ACKNOWLEDGMENTS

Thanks to retired Washington State Fish and Wildlife police officer Gene Beireis for his continued council and advice on all things law enforcement within the Fish and Wildlife Department.

And thanks to Corrections Officer Brandon Jewett for his assistance on the equipment used, and information on how prisoners are transported in Washington State.

ABOUT THE AUTHOR

Rob Phillips is an award-winning outdoor writer and author of the bestselling Luke McCain mystery series featuring a fish & wildlife officer and his yellow Lab, Jack. Rob and his wife, Terri, live in Yakima, Washington with their very spoiled Labrador retriever.